VEIL AND COWL

VEIL
AND
COWL

Writings from the World of
Monks and Nuns

EDITED BY
James B Simpson

PREFACE BY
Theodore M Hesburgh

Ivan R. Dee · Chicago

Library of Congress Cataloging-in-Publication Data:
Veil and cowl : writings from the world of monks and nuns / edited by James B. Simpson ; preface by Theodore M. Hesburgh.
    p.   cm.
Includes bibliographical references and index.
ISBN 1-56663-051-7 (alk. paper)
1. Monastic and religious life.   I. Simpson, James Beasley.
BX2435.V384   1994
255-dc20   93-46074

Drawings by Kathleen Elgin from Nun, copyright © 1964 by Kathleen Elgin, published by Random House Inc.; and by Perry W. Carsley.

Grateful acknowledgment is made to the following for permission to reprint materials included herein: Georges Borchardt Inc, for Hospital: A Meditation, copyright © 1988 by Richard Selzer; Carmelite Monastery, Piedmont, Okla, for This Is My Beloved, copyright © 1955 by Mother Catherine Thomas; Collins Publishers for Naught for Your Comfort, copyright by Ernest Urban Trevor Huddleston, and Something Beautiful for God by Malcolm Muggeridge, copyright by The Mother Theresa Committee; Community of St Mary the Virgin, Wantage, England, for Mother Maribel of Wantage by Sister Janet CSMV, copyright © 1972 by the Community of St Mary the Virgin, and Mother Jane Margaret CSMV by Sister Janet CSMV, copyright © 1974 by the Community of St Mary the Virgin; Curtis Brown Ltd for Black Narcissus, copyright © 1939, 1966 by Rumer Godden, and In This House of Brede, copyright © 1969 by Rumer Godden Productions Ltd; Doubleday, a Division of Bantam Doubleday Dell Publishing Group Inc, for With Love and Laughter by Sister Maryanna, copyright © 1960, and Changing Habits, copyright © 1988 by V V Harrison; Margaret Wyvill Ecclesine for A Touch of Radiance, copyright © 1966 by Margaret Wyvill Ecclesine; Hamish Hamilton Ltd for I Leap Over the Wall, copyright © 1949 by Monica Baldwin; Harcourt Brace Jovanovich for The Seven Storey Mountain by Thomas Merton, copyright © 1949 by Harcourt, Brace, and Nun, copyright © 1983 by Mary Gilligan Wong, and James Gould Cozzens: A Life Apart, copyright © 1982 by Matthew J Bruccoli; Houghton Mifflin Co for Once a Catholic, copyright © 1987 by Peter Occhiogrosso; International Creative Management for Little Moon of Alban, copyright © 1959, 1961 by James Costigan; King Features Syndicate for Black Swans, copyright © 1976 by Jim Bishop; HarperCollins Publishers for Mariette in Ecstasy, copyright © 1991 by Ron Hansen; Little, Brown & Co for The Nun's Story by Kathryn Hulme, copyright © 1956 by Marie L Habbis, and The Courage to Change, copyright © 1975 by Mary Griffin; Macmillan Publishing Co for My First Seventy Years, copyright © 1982 by Sister M Madeleva; Maryknoll Sisters for No Two Alike, copyright © 1965 by Maryknoll Sisters of St Dominic Inc; Joseph E Maston for Jewel Within a Casket, copyright © 1962 by Joseph E Maston; William Morrow & Co for Taking the World in for Repairs, copyright © 1986 by Richard Selzer; Pantheon Books for Migrations in Solitude, copyright © 1992 by Sue Halpern; Penguin Books USA for Black Robe, copyright © 1985 by Brian Moore; St Gregory's Abbey, Three Rivers, Mich, for "Brother Abraham" by Jim Newsom, copyright © 1992 by St Gregory's Abbey; Molly Sullivan, for the Estate of Richard Sullivan, for Jubilee at Baysweep; Charles Turner for The Celebrant, copyright © 1982 by Charles Turner; University of Chicago Press and John Murray Ltd for The Nun, the Infidel, and the Superman, copyright © 1956 by Dame Felicitas Corrigan.

In memory of
Canon Michael Stolpman
and in gratitude to
Mother Virginia of All Saints
who persevered
with strength and love
to hold the line

Contents

VEIL AND COWL

Joy is the flag of the soul
that is flown when the King
is in residence.
    —Fr Herbert Kelly, SSM
        Founder of the Society
        of the Sacred Mission

I have desired to go
Where springs not fail,
To fields where flies no sharp and sided hail
And a few lillies blow.

And I have asked to be
Where no storms come,
Where the green swell is in the havens dumb
And out of the swing of the sea.
                —Gerard Manley Hopkins, SJ
            "Haven Heaven: A Nun Takes the Veil"

Introduction

Many people have experienced at least a fleeting interest in seemingly mysterious, little understood monks and nuns—"religious," as members of Religious Orders are called—glimpsed in passing on streets or in crowded terminals, in schools or hospitals, or encountered in biography or history, a novel, a play or film, even opera. For me it was an interest that caught fire: it lingered, it dwelt! From it stems a book that celebrates good writing about religious by scores of authors whom I have read and reread over more than four decades.

The cowled monks and veiled nuns who emerge in these pages are eloquent witnesses to the love of God in a triune, almost mystical milieu of solemn vows—poverty, chastity, and obedience—which have both confounded and fascinated the world.

Thirty-three Roman Catholic orders and nine Anglican/Episcopal communities are represented here: Benedictines, Carmelites, Cistercians, Dominicans, Franciscans, Jesuits, Passionists, and others less known.

Since the Vatican Council of 1962–1965 vastly changed and almost emptied some convents and monasteries, most people under thirty have never seen the high, starched headdress of a Daughter of Charity of St Vincent de Paul, the black-and-white crackling crispness of a Sister of Mercy, or a monk in rough serge and sandals. They have had little or no personal acquaintance with the light humor or glowing spirituality of a true religious.

Looking backward as it does, this book was very nearly subtitled "Monks and Nuns *as They Used to Be.*" If that suggests a

3

time warp, it is transcended by a few of the authors here, notably Mary Griffin and Joan Chittister, who reflect on their earlier lives as seen in the light of the Council reforms.

A few pockets of traditionalism have bravely survived despite the onslaught of more change in the last thirty years than in the previous three hundred. Best known to me are the All Saints Sisters of the Poor, an Episcopalian order which came to the Baltimore area from England in the 1870s. I expect there will always be a few conservative communities that still embrace the old ways; in time they may find they are the only ones who continue to attract and sustain aspirants to the Religious Life, lived and cherished in all its fullness.

Imbued with nostalgia, courage, and shining faith, the pieces in this book may inspire a new respect and appreciation for the distinctive demands made on religious and of sacrifices almost taken for granted. Even the most casual reader may gain a new understanding of exemplary lives of the past, of a quiet allegiance in our own times, and of future vocations yet to be realized and shaped.

"One of the greatest needs of contemporary Christianity is an understanding of the way in which God works through lives in which prayer is not so much a mere accessory to effort but the very mainspring of all zeal and dedication," said a recent Bishop of Oxford.

In the pages to follow, we see the entire cycle of religious life, the span of years embracing postulancy, novitiate, profession, retirement, and that final reward of glory so well earned and richly deserved. Only yesterday an aged monk, professed perhaps for sixty years, died a good death, surrounded by his brothers, upheld by the prayers of the wider community. Early tomorrow, or maybe a bit longer nowadays, a pimply youth and one or two mature individuals who have already had successful careers will arrive at the monastery gate. The life goes on.

In compiling this book I have consulted with many religious. Among laity, Ruth and Dan Boorstin were initial readers, careful, objective, and enthusiastic. I also thank Lura Young of the Cosmos

Club library, the Rev Edward M Story who frequently discussed the project with me, and three other early readers—Dorothy Mills Parker of *The Living Church*, the Rev John Owens, Chaplain General of the All Saints Sisters, and the Rt Rev James W Montgomery, twelfth Bishop of Chicago. I am especially grateful to Jane Garvey of Templegate Press, Springfield, Illinois, who remembered *They Are People*, an anthology edited fifty years ago by Sister Mariella Gable, OSB. Lastly, I express deep appreciation for the cordial, unusually helpful responsiveness of the public library system of Washington, DC, especially the Georgetown branch as well as Alexander W Geyger of Language and Literature, and Marian Holt and Mineta Rozen of Biography.

While the writer and critic Cyril Connolly once introduced a collection of excerpts from great English novels with the hope that "those who read this anthology will find all long books rather absurd," I like to imagine that these samplings may send people looking for the entire book of which they have read just a portion. Whatever the case, I believe readers will find that a persistent probing—who *are* they, *what* is behind such deep devotion—pervades this book. These are questions asked by religious of themselves and their communities and, most certainly, by the world at large. They are central to all my reading, research, interviews, and thought, and to them this book replies.

J B S✝

Washington, DC
Lent 1994

Preface

This is a nostalgic collection of biographies and articles by or about Anglican and Roman Catholic religious. The word nostalgic leaps out with the implication that these religious men and women are a phenomenon of the past, long gone, and remembered wistfully. This is both a true and a false impression.

First of all, there are many fewer religious men and women in the world today. For Roman Catholics, Vatican Council II (1962–1965) was a kind of religious watershed. All the old religious realities were looked at, critiqued, and many of them dropped. One thinks of the disappearance of religious habits (hence the title of this book, Veil and Cowl), except on very special occasions. One thinks of those boot-camp-like novitiates where silence, solitude, total rejection of the world and worldliness, even family, and the practice of severe corporal penance became the order of the day once one entered the gate. Then there were all those young people lying prostrate on the floor of the chapel before taking final vows of poverty, chastity, and obedience before some high churchman, followed by orders to go to some godforsaken place like the Congo, Huehuecastinanga, or Pago Pago, often never to see one's family or country again. These extremely stern practices are largely gone, and gone with them over the last twenty-nine years since Vatican Council II are thousands of men and women religious who perhaps in some cases were leaning on the walls for support and could not stand on their own when the walls came down and the ancient rules began to change. Other thousands left for a variety of other reasons so that one can truly be nostalgic for all of those who were religious of the old type and are no more. This book's look at the largely old-type religious will bring back some bittersweet memories.

But this is only half the story. The substance of the religious life has in many ways been enriched by the changes. There are smaller numbers taking the vows today, but they take them for the same reason that the men and women chronicled here did: to live in a community vowed to Christian perfection and the service of God's people—which means all people. Their style of living may be different, in many ways more difficult without the old props, but their life's purpose is the same as those who wore veil and cowl everywhere, every day.

I know this for certain because I have lived more than fifty years in a religious community with vows. I pronounced the perpetual vows in a mountaintop monastery in Italy on August 16, 1939.

My religious community, the Congregation of Holy Cross (CSC), has certainly changed in all of the ways mentioned above. I still have a habit but have not worn it in many years. I hope to be buried in it. Half my religious life was under the old regime, half in the new. I would not say that the latter half was better; in fact, I am rather glad that my formative years were in the first half. Yet I like the second half better, despite the fact that many of the external props are gone and I probably need more daily grace to develop interior props, more personal, no less spiritual. Prayer is even more important now because I must more often make time to do it on my own without a surrounding community doing it with me several times a day. The community is still there, always present when needed, but I have to work harder at contributing to it rather than passively accepting its benefits. We are still given assignments—which were then called obediences—and these still take many to difficult apostolic tasks in far-off places. Money is more available, but not for foolish or worldly superfluous purposes if one is working on detachment from material things, as a religious should. Chastity is more difficult because of temptations being more available in today's wild world, but Chastity remains the commitment to belong totally to God and to serve all His people.

Veil and Cowl tells how it was done in another age. It seems to me that we could well have another companion volume on how it is done today. Nostalgia would then give way to new visions, new challenges, new apostolic and religious enterprises, but the same human and divine impulse to serve God and His people in a religious community under vows. It is still an unusually good and fulfilling life for those few who are called to serve God and His people in a special way. May their tribe increase.

(THE REV) THEODORE M HESBURGH, CSC
President Emeritus, University of Notre Dame

VOCATION

• Born in 1915 of American parents living in France, Thomas Merton grew up on Long Island, graduated from Columbia University, and, after failing to realize a vocation with the Franciscans, joined the Order of Cistercians of the Strict Observance (OCSO), better known as the Trappists, and was professed as Father Louis. The appearance of his biography in 1948 brought the world to a new awareness of monasticism and was responsible for many vocations to the religious life. Many other books flowed from his hermitage in Kentucky, and after the relaxation of enclosure following Vatican II he began to lecture widely. He was electrocuted by a faulty electric fan while visiting Bangkok in 1967.

THOMAS MERTON

The Seven Storey Mountain

The thought of those monasteries, those remote choirs, those cells, those hermitages, those cloisters, those men in their cowls, the poor monks, the men who had become nothing, shattered my heart.

In an instant the desire of those solitudes was wide open within me like a wound.

No, it was useless: I did not have a vocation, and I was not for the cloister or the priesthood. Had I not been told that definitely enough? Did I have to have that beaten into my head all over again before I could believe it?

"I am going to a Trappist monastery to make a retreat for Holy Week," I told a friend. The thing that jumped into his eyes gave him the sort of expression you would expect if I had said, "I am going to go and buy a submarine and live on the bottom of the sea."

"Don't let them change you!" he said, with a sort of a lame smile.

"It would be a good thing if they did change me," I replied.

I traveled from upstate New York to Cincinnati and to Louisville and after nightfall got a train out to Gethsemani [the Abbey of Our Lady of Gethsemani], on the line to Atlanta.

It was a slow train. The coach was dimly lighted, and full of people whose accents I could hardly understand, and you knew you were in the South because all the Negroes were huddled in a separate car. The train got out of the city into the country that was abysmally dark, even under the moon. You wondered if there were any houses out there. Pressing my face to the window, and shading it with my hands, I saw the outline of a bare, stony landscape with sparse trees. The little towns we came to looked poor and forlorn and somewhat fierce in the darkness.

And the train went its slow way through the spring night, branching off at Bardstown junction. And I knew my station was coming.

I stepped down out of the car into the empty night. The station was dark. There was a car standing there, but no man in sight. There was a road, and the shadow of a sort of a factory a little distance away, and a few houses under some trees. In one of them was a light. The train had hardly stopped to let me off, and immediately gathered its ponderous momentum once again and was gone around the bend with the flash of a red tail light, leaving me in the middle of the silence and solitude of the Kentucky hills.

I put my bag down in the gravel, wondering what to do next. Had they forgotten to make arrangements for me to get to the monastery? Presently the door of one of the houses opened, and a man came out in no hurry.

We got in the car together, and started up the road, and in a minute we were in the midst of moonlit fields.

"Are the monks in bed?" I asked the driver. It was only a few minutes past eight.

"Oh, yes, they go to bed at seven o'clock."

"Is the monastery far?"

"Mile and a half."

I looked at the rolling country, and at the pale ribbon of road in front of us, stretching out as grey as lead in the light of the moon. Then suddenly I saw a steeple that shone like silver in the moonlight, growing into sight from behind a rounded knoll. The tires sang on the empty road, and, breathless, I looked at the monastery that was revealed before me as we came over the rise. At the end of an avenue of trees was a big rectangular block of buildings, all dark, with a church crowned by a tower and a steeple and a cross: and the steeple was as bright as platinum and the whole place was as quiet as midnight and lost in the all-absorbing silence and solitude of the fields. Behind the monastery was a dark curtain of woods, and over to the west was a wooded valley, and beyond that a rampart of wooded hills, a barrier and a defense against the world.

And over all the valley smiled the mild, gentle Eastern moon, the full moon in her kindness, loving this silent place.

At the end of the avenue, in the shadow under the trees, I could make out the lowering arch of the gate, and the words: "*Pax Intrantibus.*"

The driver of the car did not go to the bell rope by the heavy wooden door. Instead he went over and scratched on one of the windows and called in a low voice:

"Brother! Brother!"

I could hear someone stirring inside.

Presently the key turned in the door. I passed inside. The door closed quietly behind me. I was out of the world.

The effect of that big, moonlit court, the heavy stone building with all those dark and silent windows, was overpowering. I could hardly answer the Brother's whispered questions.

I looked at his clear eyes, his greying, pointed beard.

We crossed the court, climbed some steps, entered a high, dark hall. I hesitated on the brink of a polished, slippery floor, while the Brother groped for the light switch. Then, above another heavy door, I saw the words: "God alone."

"Have you come to stay?" asked the Brother.

The question terrified me. It sounded too much like the voice of my own conscience.

"Oh, no!" I said. "Oh, no!" And I heard my whisper echoing around the hall and vanishing up the indefinite, mysterious heights of a dark and empty stairwell above our heads. The place smelled frighteningly clean: old and clean, an ancient house, polished and swept and repainted and repainted over and over, year after year.

"What's the matter, why can't you stay? Are you married or something?" asked the Brother.

"No," I said lamely, "I have a job..."

We began to climb the wide stairs. Our steps echoed in the empty darkness. One flight and then another and a third and a fourth. There was an immense distance between floors; it was a building with great high ceilings. Finally we came to the top floor, and the Brother opened the door into a wide room, and put down my bag, and left me.

I heard his steps crossing the yard below, to the gate house.

And I felt the deep, deep silence of the night, and of peace, and of holiness enfold me like love, like safety.

The embrace of it, the silence! I had entered into a solitude that was an impregnable fortress. And the silence that enfolded me, spoke to me, and spoke louder and more eloquently than any voice, and in the middle of that quiet, clean-smelling room, with the moon pouring its peacefulness in through the open window, with the warm night air, I realized truly whose house that was, O glorious Mother of God!

How shall I explain or communicate to those who have not seen these holy houses, consecrated churches and Cistercian cloisters, the might of the truths that overpowered me all the days of that week?

Yet no one will find it hard to conceive the impression made on a man thrown suddenly into a Trappist monastery at four o'clock in the morning, after the night office, as I was the following day.

Bells were flying out of the tower in the high, astounding darkness as I groped half blind with sleep for my clothing and hastened into the hall and down the dark stairs. I did not know where to go, and there was no one to show me, but I saw two men in secular clothes, at the bottom of the stairs, going through a door. One of them was a priest with a great head of white hair, the other was a young man with black hair, in a pair of dungarees. We were in a hallway, completely black, except I could see their shadows moving towards a big window at the end. They knew where they were going, and they had found a door which opened and let some light into the hall.

I came after them to the door. It led into the cloister. The cloister was cold, and dimly lit, and the smell of damp wool astounded me by its unearthliness. And I saw the monks. There was one, right there, by the door; he had knelt, or rather thrown himself down before a *pieta* in the cloister corner, and had buried his head in the huge sleeves of his cowl there at the feet of the dead Christ, the Christ Who lay in the arms of Mary, letting fall one arm and a pierced hand in the limpness of death. It was a picture so fierce that it scared me: the abjection, the dereliction of this seemingly shattered monk at the feet of the broken Christ. I stepped into the cloister as if into an abyss.

The silence with people moving in it was ten times more gripping than it had been in my own empty room.

And now I was in the church. The two other seculars were kneeling there beside an altar at which the candles were burning. A priest was already at the altar, spreading out the corporal and opening the book. In that great dark church, in little chapels, all around the ambulatory behind the high altar, chapels that were caves of dim candlelight, Mass was simultaneously beginning at many altars.

The silence, the solemnity, the dignity of these Masses and of the church, and the overpowering atmosphere of prayers so fervent that they were almost tangible choked me with the love and reverence that robbed me of the power to breathe.

Almost simultaneously all around the church, at all the various altars, the bells began to ring. Christ was on the Cross, lifted up, drawing all things to Himself. Faint gold fire flashed from the shadowy flanks of the upraised chalice at our altar.

After Communion I thought my heart was going to explode.

When the church had practically emptied after the second round of Masses, I left and went to my room. When I next came back to church it was to kneel in the high balcony in the far end of the nave, for Tierce and Sext and then None and the Conventual Mass.

And now the church was full of light, and the monks stood in their stalls and bowed like white seas at the ends of the psalms.

As the week went on I discovered that the young man with black hair, in dungarees, was a postulant. He was entering the monastery that day. That evening, at Compline, we who were standing up in the tribune at the back of the church could see him down there, in the choir, in his dark secular clothes, which made him easy to pick out, in the shadows, among the uniform white of the novices and monks.

For a couple of days it was that way. Practically the first thing you noticed, when you looked at the choir, was this young man in secular clothes, among all the monks.

Then suddenly we saw him no more. He was in white. They had given him an oblate's habit, and you could not pick him out from the rest.

The waters had closed over his head, and he was submerged in the community. He was lost. The world would hear of him no more. He had drowned to our society and had become a Cistercian.

After the long Good Friday liturgy the monastery was silent, inert. I could not pray. I could not read any more.

I got Brother Matthew to let me out the front gate on the pretext that I wanted to take a picture of the monastery, and then I went for a walk along the enclosure wall, down the road past the hill, and around the back of the buildings, across a creek and down a narrow valley, with a barn and some woods on one side, and the monastery on a bluff on the other.

The sun was warm, the air quiet. Somewhere a bird sang. The atmosphere of intense prayer had pervaded those buildings for the last two days. The pressure was too heavy for me. My mind was too full.

Now my feet took me slowly along a rocky road, under the stunted cedar trees, with violets growing up everywhere between the cracks in the rock.

Out here I could think: and yet I could not get to any conclusions. But there was one thought running around and around my mind: "To be a monk . . . to be a monk . . ."

I gazed at the brick building which I took to be the novitiate. It stood on top of a high rampart of a retaining wall that made it look like a prison or a citadel. I saw the enclosure wall, the locked gates. I thought of the hundreds of pounds of spiritual pressure compressed and concentrated within those buildings and weighing down on the heads of the monks, and I thought, "It would kill me."

Back in the monastery the Retreat Master, in one of his conferences, told us a long story of a man who had once come to Gethsemani, and who had not been able to make up his mind to become a monk, and had fought and prayed about it for days. Finally, went the story, he had made the Stations of the Cross, and at the final station he prayed fervently to be allowed the grace of dying in the Order.

"You know," said the Retreat Master, "they say that no petition you ask at the fourteenth station is ever refused."

In any case, this man finished his prayer, and went back to his room and in an hour or so he collapsed, and they just had time to receive his request for admission to the Order when he died.

He lies buried in the monks' cemetery, in the oblate's habit.

And so, about the last thing I did before leaving Gethsemani was to do the Stations of the Cross, and to ask, with my heart in my throat, at the fourteenth station, for the grace of a vocation to the Trappists, if it were pleasing to God.

• Born in 1903, Malcolm Muggeridge studied
at Selwyn College, Cambridge, and was a
lecturer at the University of Cairo before
becoming a journalist. For four years in the
1950s he was editor of Punch and then
turned to radio and television documentaries
for the BBC. He died November 14, 1990.

MALCOLM MUGGERIDGE

Something Beautiful for God

It is, of course, true that the wholly dedicated like Mother Teresa do not have biographies. Biographically speaking, nothing happens to them. To live for, and in, others, as she and the Sisters of the Missionaries of Charity do, is to eliminate happenings, which are a factor of the ego and the will. "Yet not I, but Christ liveth in me," is one of her favorite sayings. I once put a few desultory questions to her about herself, her childhood, her parents, her home, when she first decided to become a nun. She responded with one of her characteristic smiles, at once quizzical and enchanting; a kind of half smile that she summons up whenever something specifically human is at issue, expressive of her own incorrigible humanity. Her home, she said, had been an exceptionally happy one. So, when her vocation came to her as a schoolgirl, the only impediment was precisely this loving, happy home which she did not wish to leave. Of course the vocation won, and forever. She gave herself to Christ, and through him to her neighbor. This was the end of her biography and the beginning of her life; in abolishing herself she found herself, by virtue of that unique Christian transformation, manifested in the Crucifixion and the Resurrection, whereby we die in order to live.

• A native of New York State, Mother
Catherine Thomas was superior of the
strictly cloistered Order of Discalced
Carmelites at the Carmelite monastery
originally located in Oklahoma City and
now at Piedmont, Oklahoma.

MOTHER CATHERINE THOMAS

This Is My Beloved

My vocation came to me in a slaughterhouse.

It was a dilapidated barn in the village of Monticello, NY, and whenever a truck filled with livestock would come by, the boys and a few curious girls, like myself, would run to witness the slaughter.

One day the butcher came down the road with some lambs in his wagon. Rabbi Betowsky, a dignified, silent, patriarchal-looking gentleman with a long white beard and small blue eyes, walked alongside, reminding me of Michelangelo's magnificent Moses.

The lambs were roughly taken from the cart and lined up without the slightest suspicion of what was in store for them. Their innocence always made me cry, and I was wishing we might buy them all and put them with our own little flock.

As I stared through misty eyes at the scene before me, the picture of the spear-pierced lamb on the classroom wall and the story of the Lamb of God began to run through my mind. In class, Sister Geraldine, the Dominican nun whose name I took at Confirmation, had explained the whole symbolism to us. How St John the Baptist had greeted Christ, "Behold the Lamb of God . . ." How the prophet foretold about Our Lord's death, "He opened not His mouth: He shall be led as a sheep to the slaughter, and shall be dumb as a lamb before his shearer, and He shall not open His mouth..." And the story Sister told us about St Agnes—whose name means "lamb"—also ran through my excited mind—how she was martyred for the Faith.

But my musings were cut short.

It was time for the first lamb to be slaughtered. Rabbi Betowsky readied his knife, and the butcher reached for the animal. I expected to see the usual tussle between victim and butcher that the oxen always gave, but to my amazement the poor silent lamb, with merely a suggestion from the butcher and with absolute trust and meek obedience, confidently got down on its knees and actually raised its head for execution. I turned. It was impossible to look. Weeping, I ran home and hid myself in the attic.

Lamb of God. The true Lamb that was stricken for our transgressions. In a vague imperfect way the idea of sacrifice began to dawn on my childish mind. Our Lord showed His love for His Heavenly Father and for us, by laying down His life; then *I* should be a lamb also and do likewise. . . . The "I should *like* to be a nun" had taken a definitive advance. From that time on the thought was "I *ought* to be a nun."

• A native of Wisconsin, Sister M Madeleva attended St Mary's College administered by the Sisters of the Holy Cross at Notre Dame, Indiana; she returned to join the Order, later served as president of the college, and was well known as a poet.

SISTER M MADELEVA

My First Seventy Years

Always, always there was that unanswered question, "For what has God made me?" I had long since resolved that if I could only find out what, I would do it with all my might as long as I lived.

In desperation [at St Mary's College, South Bend, Indiana], I used to steal down to Sister Rita's classroom evenings to ask for help. At the door I would turn and go back to my room and my confusion. I knew that I would do whatever Sister told me to. Suppose I did what she wanted rather than what God wanted! No, I would take no chances even for her.

On Memorial Day I went up to the classroom of one of my teachers for a little visit. From her north windows I looked out at the novices and postulants at recreation. They were walking and talking together; a lively team was playing baseball. Again my old restlessness. "I wonder what I will be doing ten years from now," I said, half questioning Sister.

"I suppose if you thought that you might be a Sister you would be furious," was her astonishing reply. "Why, I would be the happiest girl in the world," I burst out with conviction, "but I know that I could never be a nun," with equal certainty.

One afternoon Sister and I walked on the river bank and

talked of the religious life. No one had ever spoken of it to me before. I listened breathlessly, reverently. "I will do anything that God wants me to," I said, "if I can only find out what it is."

"That is all that one needs for a religious vocation," was Sister's easy, simple answer. How it comforted me! She gave me an equally simple, easy booklet on vocation which was apocalyptic to me.

When I went to tell Sister Rita goodbye she gave me an inscribed copy of *The Story of Fifty Years*, her own history of the Sisters of the Holy Cross. All the way on the train to Madison I read it like a starved person. Afterward, Mother told me that when I got off the train, despite my huge Merry Widow hat and smart clothes, she knew that I no longer belonged to them.

I went up to the lake to our cottage with our inseparable crowd of girls. I waited breathlessly for a letter from Sister Augustine. Finally it came. In substance, her instructions read that if I still thought as I did when talking to her, I should write to Mother Barbara, the mistress of novices. This I did, telling her that I should like to enter the novitiate if and when she wished. These alternatives I volunteered: I might return to finish college. I might stay home for the year with my parents. I might come at once. Or I might do none of these things. My absolute wish was to become a Sister of the Holy Cross. The decision she would make for me.

She wrote me to come at once, on September 14, specifically, and sent me a list of questions to answer. I mailed my reply on the feast of St Augustine, August 30, 1908. I had two weeks in which to get ready.

Such a wardrobe for a girl who had lived for clothes! And such subterfuges in buying black cashmere shawls and petticoats! Finally, the humorous little trousseau was in order. Not so my family! My father, not a Catholic, was sick with dismay. What had he done to me that I should want to leave him! Mother had too much of the fear of the Lord in her conscience to permit even a question.

My friends knew nothing of my plans. I thought that I would

go, ostensibly back to school. I was almost sure that although I had been accepted in the novitiate I would probably be sent home. It might be better for my pride if dismissal came from the college rather than from the convent. I had refused ultrasocial invitations to house parties and the like; solicitous boy friends were more than curious as to my reasons. I would give them only half-answers. Late in the summer I put on my prettiest dress for the senior ball at Wisconsin. All blue voile and taffeta, I went to my last dance with Vern. Only he and I knew that it was a valedictory.

The day I was to leave was bleak. Neither my deep nor my superficial joy could buoy them up. Traintime came and I was off. I cried in the Pullman most of the night at my father's grief. Arrived at the Northwestern station in Chicago, I ran over to the desk and wrote hurriedly: "Dear Papa, If you want me to, I will come home. Sis."

Before the letter could have reached him I was the happiest of postulants, having really come home.

Chicago almost undid me. The St Mary's girls were getting back to school. In my own great preoccupation I had forgotten that this was opening day. Half of my crowd were at the LaSalle Street station. We went down to South Bend together on the New York Central. But the questions! How much food was I bringing back? From whom had I heard? How had I spent the summer? Evasion characterized my answers to these and like queries.

In South Bend I had to buy two pairs of high black-laced shoes—I whose heart was in my regiment of assorted pumps and low shoes! How could I explain my new footwear to the crowd? Somehow I got a taxi to myself and drove to the shoe store and from there to the novitiate. Mother Barbara received me graciously. God had begun to answer my question. This was the fourteenth of September, the Feast of the Holy Cross. I was going to be a Sister of the Holy Cross!

BEGINNINGS

CARSLEY

• A housewife and mother of eight, Margaret
Wyvill Ecclesine was living in Rye, NY,
when she wrote her first book, a biography
of her aunt, Sister Honorat of the Bon
Secours Sisters. Mrs Ecclesine grew up in
Upper Marlboro, Maryland, attended St
Joseph's College in Emmitsburg, Maryland,
graduated from George Washington
University, and worked as a senior staff
writer for the National Broadcasting
Company. The Ecclesines now live in San
Diego.

MARGARET WYVILL ECCLESINE

A Touch of Radiance

The life of a religious might be compared to the building of a
cathedral. Day by day the stones are laid, in the beginning one
hardly distinguishable from another. Some stones are made up of
prayers and sacrifices and efforts to conquer human frailties. Others
represent virtues such as patience and charity and willingness to
take direction. They are important only in view of the gaping
holes that would result if they were not there.

Once a firm foundation has been laid, the building rises
slowly. There are arches when the spirit soars, and dark days
when the pieces do not fit, so that the windows are boarded
up temporarily and the beautiful hoped-for light does not shine
through. There are stones laid joyously, in the glory of morning,
and those added mechanically at the end of a weary day.

But through it all there is order and symmetry, and a vision of what the completed edifice will be; a vision of a perfect structure, dedicated wholly to the honor and glory of a great, good, and loving God.

The postulant who gives herself joyfully to the program planned for her arrives at an attractiveness of manner, a charm of soul, and an exaltation of spirit she probably did not dream could exist within herself. The days multiply this revelation.

The life of a religious is not too different from that of any dedicated woman. But she builds by a surer blueprint, guided by centuries of architects who have mastered the intricacies and called them by name.

• Jim Newsom writes of his initial six months
in a Benedictine community of Episcopal
priests and brothers at Three Rivers,
Michigan.

JIM NEWSOM

Postulancy

My usual day at St Gregory's begins with the buzz of my alarm
clock at 3:35 a.m. My first reaction is to tell myself that Jesus
doesn't really want me in a place where I must get up so early.
Then I think about the possibility of a large fish swallowing me if I
ever were to move away, and decide to get up. Without embarrassment, I could even say that excitement builds as I get ready for
Matins. I am ready to praise God, complain to God, and ask God
to fill my needs. I feel it a great privilege to be an intercessor for
the many people who send prayer requests to the Abbey. Often I
just sit in the church and enjoy God's company, like sitting on a
couch with a good friend when words are unnecessary.

One of the jobs I have been given is cooking. The work can
be tense, but is not nearly so tense as teaching fifth-graders how to
play musical instruments, as I did before coming to the Abbey.
The daily round of prayer, work, and reading is interrupted by
meals and recreation. During warmer weather I often took walks in
the woods, swam in the lake, or rode a bike. Now that I have
experienced my first real winter, I have ridden a toboggan, been
skating on the lake, and tried cross-country skiing. I have also
looked out the window and wished for spring to arrive. Sundays
and holidays are special, and wouldn't seem right without joining
two of the brothers for an afternoon of fun. It was on one such

occasion that we learned what happens when a high-velocity toboggan meets a high-density tree. The tree won.

I have not yet experienced a great deal of bodily mortification, but I have experienced moderation, which might pass for mortification in some circles. Now if I eat a couple of extra cookies, it seems like a great treat, while in my former life I pigged out on ice cream and chips. Even sleep has not been a big issue. I don't get the nine or ten hours of uninterrupted sleep every night that I was used to, but I do manage eight hours of sleep a day, which is more than a lot of people "out in the world" are used to.

Since I arrived at the Abbey in August, things have gone much better than I had expected. I was bracing myself for long, sleepless nights of soul searching and painful battles to tame my pride. Neither of these trials has happened—yet. Of course at times I have been sad and lonely, but I was sad and lonely sometimes before I came here. I have been tired and depressed sometimes but I was tired and depressed at times before coming here. I was told by friends that by moving to a monastery I was running away from the world, but I have found that by moving here I have stopped running.

I have been truly blessed by God's pushing me here. It is great to live in such a dangerously creaky old house on a farm with a forest for a back yard. The community life ensures that every day will be different and boredom doesn't creep in. Sometimes life here is real good, sometimes it's real fun, others times it's real hard, but usually it is just real.

• John Tettemer, born in St Louis in 1876,
writes of his youthful profession in the
Passionist Order. After secularization he
came to the United States, married, fathered
three children, and acted in films, including
the role of a priest in Lost Horizons. He
died in Victorville, California, in 1949.

JOHN TETTEMER

I Was a Monk

In the late 1890s, at the beginning of the novitiate, the novice
was given a new name, further emphasizing his separation from his
old life and his entering upon an entirely new one. On this
morning when Father Master announced that we five postulants
were to be clothed with the Passionist habit, he also said that he
had selected five names for us, writing them on separate pieces of
paper, which we were to draw by lots. On the way from the choir
to the chapter room, where the drawing was to take place, I prayed
earnestly to Our Lady that I should draw the name of the saint
who in his life had been most devoted to her.

As we filed into the chapter room and arranged ourselves
around the long table down the center, Father George placed the
five bits of folded paper in his biretta. Then, after a short prayer on
our knees, each of us went to the head of the table and drew his
name.

The names turned out to be Walter, Ethelbert, Pancratius,
Ildephonsus, and Eustace. Not much to choose from for euphony. I
fell on my knees and, with a fervent prayer, drew the last but one
of the remaining slips of paper. Ildephonsus, Archbishop of Toledo

in Spain in the ninth century, noted for his devotion to Mary. Mathematicians might speak of odds, but to me there was no doubt that Our Lady had christened me with the name of one of her special servants.

In the ceremony of clothing we postulants lay on our faces on the floor of the sanctuary, prostrate before the Blessed Sacrament. We then knelt before the Master of Novices. Our upper garments were removed and the hair cut from our heads in the form of a cross to symbolize the putting away of the materials and vanities of this world. "For ye are dead, and your life is hid with Christ in God."

The long, heavy, black woolen habit was slipped over our heads. The leathern girdle having been fastened about our waists, a mantle of the woolen material, reaching to the knees, was thrown over our shoulders. On our heads a crown of thorns was placed, and a large wooden cross was laid upon our right shoulder with the admonishment that we were taking upon ourselves the livery of Christ crucified. "If any man will come after me, let him deny himself, and take up his cross, and follow me."

In the sacristy the moment came for completing the full monastic dress—sandals and our "regimentals," the loose canvas-like drawers, reaching to a little below the knee and threaded through with a cord drawing them together like a great bag around the waist. A heavy, woolen, loose-fitting shirt was put on over the head to fall over the drawers nearly to the knees. Lastly we were given large blue bandanas which we rolled up and carried in the wide sleeves of the habit for a handkerchief.

We wore our robes night and day. They were too hot in summer and not warm enough in winter. The comfort of pajamas was unknown to the monastery, and on retiring we took off only our sandals and belts, rolling onto our beds with a mighty swing, hoping to avoid serious entanglement in the yards of our habits. But with this minimum of undressing we were ready at the signal for Matins and able to rise quickly in the middle of the night and get to the choir in the allotted five minutes.

I loved my habit, the badge of my vocation, the symbol of all my incentive and aspiration.

"You can be speaking all around," said the Novice Master, hurrying us along to recreation. "Speaking all around" was the term applied to an interval of being permitted to talk with everyone instead of only the novice regularly assigned by the Master as our companion during the regular hours of recreation and walking. These were changed every few weeks to give opportunity to become acquainted with everyone. "Speaking all around" was a real treat.

We enjoyed the day, chanted and prayed in the choir, and retired. Clumsily I composed myself for sleep on my hard bed and the unruly folds of my habit. My soul was filled with contentment and a great peace.

• A member of the Sisters of Charity of the
Blessed Virgin Mary (motherhouse:
Dubuque, Iowa), Sister Mary Griffin taught
at Mundelein College in Chicago and more
recently in Mississippi. She has written
widely on ecumenism and the changing
status of women.

SISTER MARY GRIFFIN

The Courage to Choose

The night I entered the novitiate of the Sisters of Charity of the
Blessed Virgin Mary I felt that I was moving backward in time to
some magic country where nothing would ever change. In a
certain sense I felt that my life was ending. I knew there would be
work. I knew there would be prayer. I'd been told there would be
austerity and discipline and an inevitable loneliness as one sought
to unite oneself perfectly to the will of God.

Yet the dispatch with which we postulants were channeled
through entrance formalities and whisked into the nuns' refectory
for a marvelous cold supper suggested not the chilly remoteness
of cloister but opening day of the new term in boarding school.
What I remember vividly are the healthy appetites with which we
demolished stacks of homemade bread and piles of thinly sliced
ham. Afterwards the forty-seven of us crowded up the narrow
pine stairs for Benediction. Hurriedly we whispered names and origins ("Terrific—another Californian!"), laughing the bright hectic
laughter of the young who must not cry, aware of a rising sense of
excitement and adventure. Perhaps this was not the end at all, but
the beginning of something strange and new and wonderful.

The BVM Motherhouse was pure Victoriana from its red plush bishop's parlor to its high drafty corridors lined with portraits of ancient mothers general and punctuated here and there with clumps of fern, a life-sized bronze crucifix, a Virgin wrapped in marble. But the chapel was a surprise: a bright spacious expanse arched over by a deep blue ceiling. It was refreshingly unencumbered, marred only by three white wooden altars with gingerbready spires and conventional statues. Its silence struck a hush into the postulants and we tried vainly to soften the clatter of high heels down the long polished aisles. A waning September sun filtered bluely through an old-fashioned stained-glass Madonna, incense rose in a bright cloud, and a sinuous Gregorian melody sprang toward the gold monstrance now in place. "A-do-re-mus in aeternum." It floated away to the merest whisper, then rolled back over the bowed heads of the professed nuns in a tremulous legato. And in that moment, which hangs still in my memory like some long-remembered luminous jewel, the new life began.

Later, during choir practice, I discovered the unsuspected nuts and bolts that riveted together that enchanting bridge of song. "Arcisthesis, Sisters, Arcis-thesis. Linkers and breathers, remember. We must sustain the tone without a seam." Plump little Sister Roselle rocked back and forth on her shiny-toed shoes in what we laughingly termed her "liturgical movement."

Aching from dormitory scrubbing, sweating in long-sleeved poplin habits, the postulants stifled their boredom and for the nth time undertook the sweet-somber Ambrosian Gloria they would sing at Reception the following March when, the initial six months of candidacy past, they would themselves receive at the hands of the archbishop the "holy habit of religion."

The night before, I knew, they would cut our hair in preparation for the close-fitting veil. Then at last we would be novices, with serge skirts and twelve-inch-wide sleeves, and lily-seed rosaries hanging from the narrow leather cintures at our waist. At the moment we were curiously in-between, rather like girl acolytes in ankle-skimming skirts and short capes that swung open to reveal young high bosoms still encased in worldly Maidenforms. Our shoulder-length hair bounced and shone as we climbed rickety ladders to high-dust the spotless postulate. Our fingers reddened and cracked, peeling their way through a thousand bushels of green apples, new potatoes, and carrots. Our tender knees sprouted protective scabs as they shifted from scrubbing pad to wooden kneeler in an already boring rhythm.

We rose at five in the chilly November mornings, splashed in the icy water that had stood all night on our bedside commodes, fought back sleep during pre-Mass meditation, fitting into the ancient novitiate routine of work and study and prayer aimed at perfection. This was our boot training. We were learning how to become nuns, how to strip away the last remnants of our vain, worldly selves. "Ora et labora" announced an ornate little motto in the postulate. And I began to realize that for me at least the two were indistinguishable.

Contrary to all the holy cards I had garnered through a Catholic girlhood in a parochial school—cards depicting a nightgowned child knocking insistently at a little gold tabernacle door, the Apostles and Our Lady gazing ecstatically heavenward as tiny tongues of flame leaped above their heads, or the Little Flower fondling her crucifix through a coverlet of roses—prayer, I discovered, was tedious. Prayer was hard. Prayer was, to be honest, a one-sided bore. And, I found to my horror, nuns were expected not only to pray for interminably long hours (meditation at 6, Mass at 7, examen at noon, a visit to the Blessed Sacrament at 2, spiritual reading at 8, and night prayers at 8:30), they were expected to live always in the presence of God.

They fell asleep in Solemn Silence with God on their minds and woke up with God on their lips. The rising prayer, said aloud in company with the other novices in your dormitory, made certain that the day's first spoken word was in praise of God. I recall that first morning when I woke at dawn to the chilling clank of metal rings being swept along curtain rods as the novices emerged from their alcoves, their high-pitched sleep-filled voices announcing, "In the name of our Lord Jesus Christ crucified, I rise from this bed of sleep. On the last day may I rise to everlasting happiness."

Months later I would one morning electrify the inmates of Holy
Angels dormitory with my own inaccurate but anguished version of
the rising prayer. "In the name of our Lord Jesus Christ crucified, I
rise from this bed of happiness. On the last day may I rise to
everlasting sleep!" The heinous crime of provoking hilarity during
Solemn Silence brought me to the Postulant Mistress. And she
brought me to my knees.

Back in the 1930s, when entrance groups of 65 and 70 were
not unheard of, a very shrewd Mother General had named Sister
Mary Angelice as Postulant Mistress. Fortyish, with liquid brown
eyes that could be alarmingly stern or wickedly funny, she was a
natural for her job. After fifteen years as prefect in a boarding
school, she played on us like an organist on his keyboard. In a
joyless world of starch and silence, she was an oasis of delight.
Long before we had arrived on the scene, she had painstakingly
done her homework on each new postulant. So when the storm
broke—as break it must during those first harrowing weeks of
incarceration—she was ready for us. Her knowing gaze fixed on
the red-eyed postulant worrying a convent handkerchief across the
desk from her, Sister Angelice ran through her roles in a stunning
repertoire.

Now, long years later, piecing together a thousand fragmen-
tary conversations, I begin to perceive the scope of her art. She
could be confessor ("Well, why not tell me about John? It might
make it easier"), spiritual guide ("You don't *have* to feel that God is
listening; you just have to will yourself to pray. You must *want* to
want to"), fellow conspirator ("Here, don't ask me where I got it;
just thank your stars it's Bristol Cream sherry"), friend ("I
screamed when I read this last night. Just don't laugh out loud in
the dormitory. God knows you get enough of spiritual reading").

So tears melted into rueful smiles, anger exploded, fears
vanished, and kisses brushed one's cheek. All that was demanded
was silence in the conspiracy. Utterly true, we told no one—not
even each other. We knew only that these moments of humanity,
like touches of gentleness in a night of terror, made possible the
terrible austerity of conventual life. The endless round of Spartan

days with their spiritless tasks—malodorous toilet bowls to be scrubbed to sweetness, infirmary sheets to be washed and re-washed, spotless corridors to be scrupulously dusted morning after morning, silence to be kept for longer and longer hours—these seemed somehow bearable because at some unforeseen moment of each day, there would be a surreptitious interim of laughter and affection with Sister Angelice. If she could bend her will to live a life she had never wanted either, then certainly we could. For reasons beyond our ken, God in His eternal wisdom had hand selected each one of the forty-seven of us to do for Him a work that no other person could do. He wanted us to live a life devoted exclusively to His concerns, to strive for detachment from self, to form an attachment to Christ that would, after two more years of novitiate, make it possible for us to vow ourselves totally to Him in poverty, chastity, and obedience. At first for a year, then for five, then forever.

The finality of that "forever" sent premonitory chills through our hearts. Of course we'd be tempted to leave, to think that we didn't *really* have the call to this demanding life. But that would just be the voice of Satan. The very fact that we were *there* testified to the authenticity of God's call. Certainly we could all remember the moment—at a senior prom, in the back seat of a convertible, on the verge of a promised trip to Europe—when something made it all crumble to ashes and we seemed to sense some finer thing we were called to. It didn't matter that you despised this gloomy motherhouse with its miles of gleaming corridors. It didn't matter if in that bleakness of your starving youth you smothered sobs at night in the thin narrow pillow. In the morning you would again take your place with the others in the big airy postulate, folding your long cotton skirt about your knees and awaiting the swish of Sister Angelice's serge habit as she swept into the room to mesmerize you one step further into the desert of religious life.

You must *will* to follow Christ. (Her serious brown eyes held us.) When, some day in the future, you had succeeded in filling your heart with Him alone, then the happiness that would flood you would compensate for everything you had left for His sake.

God would not be outdone in generosity. He would repay us a hundredfold. And His grace, as St Augustine reminded us, would work its way in us, "in hard material and against the grain."

Meanwhile, you found yourself with the best companions you could want—bright, wholesome, generous American girls as alike as a row of cookies from the same cutter, all of them looking toward fields white with the harvest, eager to bear to a parched world the refreshing good news of the Gospel. These girls would be closer to you than your own blood sisters. Two years later on Profession day you would part from them with a wrench more agonizing than that dreadful tearing which had initially separated you from your home and family. So Sister Angelice promised her postulants as she schooled them in the Rule morning after morning, preparing them to receive the habit. On that fateful day they would be transformed into novices. The shining caps of hair would at last be veiled. The little military capes would be replaced by long closed serge ones topped by high, stiff Roman collars, capes beneath which hands could be folded away and only serious young faces left to confront the dread Mistress of Novices who would replace Sister Angelice. And as always, she was right. The night they cut our hair the desolation of the postulants was complete— in part, over the mutilation involved; in part, over our leaving Sister Angelice.

At 7 o'clock in the evening we entered the darkened chapel two by two. The privacy was total. Only those on ceremony could be present: the Postulant Mistress, her face unexpectedly grave; the expressionless Novice Mistress; old Sister Mary Realmo, representing the Community Council; and to assist each, a novice with eyes studiously averted. In the dim light of flickering vigil lamps at Our Lady's shrine, I could make out the gleam of scissors, the large willow baskets lined with sheeting, the bent heads of the postulants as they buried their faces in cupped hands. If your hair was long enough, it hung in two thick braids to make the cutting easier. If short, it was pursued in a series of artless forays that left the victim skinned and somehow shamed looking. After the first few cuttings, I couldn't watch any more. The sound of snipping shears, the strangled sobs of a few less Spartan postulants seemed to signal the end of youth and laughter, the end of beauty, the yawning of the dungeon. Thus did one separate oneself from the love of things seen and give oneself utterly to the love of things unseen. I fingered my own cropped head and felt that there should have been a death bell tolling.

But bell or no, in the days that followed we began to die to our old selves and to put on the new. The initial cleavage from the past deepened as we entered the novitiate. It was now that the door really swung closed on the world. In the ensuing year we would be canonically sealed off. There would be no visitors, no "secular studies," no leaving the cloister. This is the year of spiritual testing. And only the staunch survive it.

One by one we had lost our distinguishing characteristics: first our possessions (listed and stored against possible defection), then our privacy. We were issued institutional clothing, assigned numbers, told when to bathe, distributed to dormitories, instructed in regulations, and finally, on Reception morning, given new names. In many ways, this was the hardest deprivation. I could stand the heavy cotton stockings, the ugly underthings, the torturing headdress. But my whole being resented being stripped of my name when the archbishop announced publicly, "Agnes Griffin, your name in religion will be Sister Mary Ignatia." Ig-na-tia! My outraged ear fastened on that hideous initial syllable and my soul wept for the ugliness of the sound. In a burst of detachment I had left the choice of name to the inspiration of the Holy Spirit. He was omniscient. He had to know how I hated the name Agnes. He knew I despised all hard g's. Yet here He had scattered the lovely "Mauras" and "Joans" and "Carols" to each side of me, and saddled me with a corrupted form of Ignatius Loyola, the military founder of the Jesuits. In my mouth was the acrid taste of betrayal at a very high level.

The loss of one's name was enormously effective in eradicating from the postulants any last remnant of "singularity." Absolutely forbidden from the moment of our arrival was the mention of anything which might set us apart from our companions. We were not to discuss nationality, the social position of our families, our family incomes, levels of education, opportunities for travel, and the like. Entering the congregation was like undergoing a corporate rebirth from which everyone emerged really equal at a level of deadly sameness. No one went so far as to suggest that we think of ourselves as fragments of a universal mind. But we were constantly reminded that we shared one life in God. Together with millions of baptized Christians, we formed the corporate mystical Body of Christ. We were temples of the indwelling of the Holy Spirit. Distinctions among us, therefore, would be incongruous, unthinkable. The eye did not think itself better than the foot. The possessor of a doctorate was certainly no more precious to the community than was the housekeeper. (There was a funny story going the rounds, nevertheless, about the superior who shouted to the lifeguard attempting to rescue two nuns spilled out of their canoe, "Save *that* one. She just got her Ph.D.!") While, in the sight of God, the analogy was certainly valid, its long-range earthly effect was to encourage among novices a regrettable anti-intellectuality.

Unremittingly they were reminded that it was better to practice than to be able to define compassion. That it was possible (and preferable) to do both, and that the acts might reinforce each other, was as far from the minds of our Novice Mistress as from that of St Thomas à Kempis. If, during novice instructions, you felt inclined to remark that Plato had spoken of connatural knowledge, you swallowed the observation as prideful and turned out for the rest of the hour. This too would pass. And once beyond the novitiate, one could begin thinking again.

As I look back now, I observe in myself and in my companions a noticeable regression during the postulancy. Day after day we were urged to work for humility, dependence, the simplicity of a child, to try to be to our superiors as "limpid water in a crystal vase." The result was often a kind of infantilism and a resurgence of childhood needs of reassurance, security, affection—rewards for being good children, striving for self-abnegation, discipline, self-surrender to God.

In the novitiate, however, like Victorian children thrust from the warmth of a tender family into the bleakness of a state orphanage, we grew up in a hurry. We put on the habit and stepped unawares into a life that was to prove radically alien to each of us. Whatever our feelings about the first six months, we found the transition from the honeymoon of the postulancy to the icy asceticism of the novitiate, to say the least, bracing.

With Sister Majella there were to be no moments of humanity. With Sister Majella there would be unswerving obedience, continual denial of self, a ceaseless routing out of one's faults, and an incessant training in the submission of the will. There would, in short, be the putting on of Christ with a vengeance.

Our Novice Mistress gave herself no quarter. She expected to give us none. She marched before her novices like a goose-stepping Prussian general. I had always the feeling that I ought to click heels, drop my broom, and salute smartly whenever she appeared. And appear she did, frequently, and always unexpectedly. From the start there was between us an unspoken contest of wills. She had, months earlier, forfeited my respect by tongue-lashing a novice in public over some trivial infraction. She had not missed the shock and contempt in my face. And I entered the novitiate with a score to be settled.

Sister Majella was convinced that, no matter how perfect the novice, there was at her core a fatal flaw of character. She saw it as her task to evoke this demon—to set the stage, if need be, for the inevitable exorcism of our hubris. However polymorphous its form, she could discern it at a glance. A contraband apple bulging out a pocket; a whispered conversation at the door of the chapel, a sympathetic arm twined about a disconsolate novice shoulder— these were moments of epiphany which in a flash revealed a hapless novice to Sister Majella as the weak, self-deceiving, luxury-loving Sybarite she had all along known her to be. Saddened by our depravity, Sister Majella yet remained sternly hopeful. She might not have been able to define faculty psychology even to herself, but she was a fierce believer. One must *will*. One must *pray*. And all would be well. Indeed, all manner of things would be well.

To the last moment of my two years as her novice, I paid for the effrontery of my unvoiced criticism. When duties were assigned, I drew the antiquated bathrooms used by the professed nuns. When classes were posted, I found myself with an additional corridor to clean ("After all, she *has* her degree"). On innumerable occasions I was privately castigated for pride of demeanor and attachment to my Postulant Mistress. I would be publicly corrected for vanity in dress, lateness to prayers, and a "particular friendship" with my partner. So we fenced our way from month to month. In the end it was a draw. I could be humiliated, but I could not be leveled. In a way, I had Sister Majella to thank for my perseverance. I would not be *pushed* out—and certainly not by her! We parted finally, without regret on either side, and without a truce. Deep inside my independent soul, I knew that it didn't augur well. That was my fatal flaw. And I could only hope to hang on till Profession day would spring me.

Profession day, the day of my vows, the day I put aside the white veil of the novice and felt the black one being slipped onto my head while the archbishop waited to receive our vows. It was both a beginning and an end. The novitiate was over at last. Dragonish Sister Majella was behind me. The world was all before me. But a different world from the one I had left thirty months before. In December of 1941 Pearl Harbor had catapulted the United States into the war. There was, of course, no television, none of us had radios of our own, even newspapers rarely found their way into the convent recreation room. As a result, World War II was a strange distance from the nuns at the academy where I was missioned. We prayed a lot longer, adding a Holy Hour every afternoon during which we said Pius XII's prayer for peace. We ate a lot less and tried to master the intricacies of rationing. We sold war bonds. We shared letters from home with their accounts of fighting in the Aleutians and the Solomon Islands and their guarded references to boys we'd known ("4-F, thank God!" or safely home or missing in action). My freshmen worked at the USO in town, took over for mothers on the late shift at the defense factory, sang unremittingly of "the wild blue yonder." I knew very little more than they of the grim realities of it all.

Writing this as Vietnam is winding down, a war that, like many another nun, I have actively tried to impede, I find that earlier isolation from life almost unbelievable. It was an astonishing self-exile, a spiritual focusing of one's energies and sights as total in its way as the withdrawal of the Carmelite or the Trappist. *In* the world, we were effectively not *of* it. The system worked. There can be no doubt about it. And except for Selma, for Vatican II, for the handful of Franciscan nuns who mounted a picket line outside Loyola University in Chicago the summer of 1964, for me it might be working still. Instead, along with innumerable other American nuns, I have been almost totally assimilated into the contemporary world.

I look at my Mexican work skirt, and I think of the total lack of ceremony with which four years ago I took off the habit in which I had once been solemnly clothed. I find myself jammed into a film-showing with some two hundred black students down here at the bottom of the map in the Mississippi land-grant college where I teach. I think that I am here of my own choice, not under orders from a religious superior; that when I refuse to pay taxes to support a war I consider morally wrong, it is I who will tangle with the Internal Revenue Service. And if the path of my dissent leads to criminal proceedings, I'll have to take my chances, run my own risks. I have chosen to reinvolve myself in the world I once thought I had to leave in order to save.

The commitment endures, the essence of the life remains. Not without a nostalgic backward glance, my congregation has resolutely moved into the modern world. The bright clouds of incense, the soaring Gregorian chant, the dark-veiled nuns in their medieval robes—with the rush into the future these have become the remembrance of things past. Their charm remains, their curiously evocative power of symbol, but they seem at once anachronistic and anomalous.

I have a new set of memories now, all of the recent past. There is the night we "kicked" the habit, the day we emerged upon an open-mouthed world in what we confidently termed modern dress. What had gone on behind the scenes was not to be believed. A score of nuns invaded the recreation room and eyed the ready-mades Sister Emily had had sent home for us.

"Let's see. I wore a 12 when I entered. But that was twenty years and fifty pounds ago!"

"God help us, Claire. You can't sit like that in a short skirt. They'll have the vice squad out."

"Well, that may be the way you wore your hair in 1942. But it makes you look like an elderly Shirley Temple now!"

Someone gave us a shipment of bank uniforms—severely tailored bright blue gabardine. And for weeks we looked like a seedy branch of the First National. There were nuns determined to wear out any still serviceable convent item and who gave their smart double-knit suits the unexpected fillip of policeman's shoes. There were the reluctant Sisters who clung to the veil, topping off a brown turtleneck sweater with a wisp of chiffon for a kind of Foreign Legion look which convulsed their students. Parochial school kids no longer had to guess whether or not Sister had hair. ("I saw a nun in the hospital once, I tell you. It looked like there was an empty Sister hanging on the door and an old man in bed!") The new question was, "Is it a wig or isn't it?" As Sister moved from coif to coiffure only her superior knew. And, being in a similar situation, she was unlikely to talk.

There are, to be sure, moments of nostalgia: one searches for an earring and finds it tangled in a broken rosary. A snapshot forgotten in a book lent to a friend turns up on one's desk with a penciled "Wow!" on the back. Mother Teresa, the Yugoslavian missionary to the thrown-away poor of India, looks with luminous eyes out of a TV screen and one wishes for an instant for the veil which once symbolically bonded nuns. But that instant is fleeting. One knows that American nuns will never go back to an outworn symbol. Long ago, Christ suggested the essential sign that one was Christian—it had to do with loving one another. When we've managed that, it will be sign enough.

VOWED

MONICA BALDWIN

I Leap Over the Wall

Built originally round a small open courtyard, my Belgian convent had grown with the centuries till it lay like a long, grey, sleeping lizard, clutching two other courtyards and a cloister garth between its claws. In winter, the cold cut into you like a knife. The pale light crept in through deep-silled, leaded windows and was frozen immediately into the same wan blue as the whitewashed walls. You might have been standing in the heart of an iceberg, so strange it was, so silent, so austere.

Out of the cloister, heavy oak doors led into the rabbit-warren of the kitchen quarters; the Infirmary; to the Refectory; and to the great damp vaults below.

The Refectory was the oldest part of the building. I never entered it without an instinctive feeling of reverence. The wide, open space in the middle was paved, like the cloister, with grey and white flagstones, worn irregular by daily contact with generations of heavily shod feet. The massive, beamed ceiling was ornamented with sacred monograms in low relief, and delicate moldings whose sharp outlines had been blurred by the repeated whitewashings of centuries. The unglazed paintings on the walls were such as one sees in Continental churches: a Nativity, a Flemish *grisaille* of the Adoration of the Magi, a Marriage of St Catherine, and, behind the Prioress's table, a great, tragic canvas of the Crucifixion, with weeping child-angels who held chalices beneath the wounds of the tortured Christ. Under the pictures, a dado of plaited rushes hung behind the narrow benches. Long, massive, polished tables, dark with age, stood, like the benches, on a platform of boards raised a couple of inches or so above the level of the floor.

Nothing here had been changed since it was built three hundred years ago. The same thick-paned latticed windows over-looked the same high-walled garden; the same bare, oak tables were set with the same plates of dinted pewter and brown earthen mugs at each one's place. Above all, the same quite indescribable atmosphere of silence, aloofness, and a kind of spiritual intensity hung in the air like some delicate, distilled fragrance from another world.

Further along the cloister, important-looking double doors opened into the Community Room. This, though more homely than the Refectory, had none the less a severe and simple dignity of its own. The light from its long row of windows poured in upon what was practically the livingroom of the nuns. Whitewashed walls; a bare-boarded floor, scrubbed to an unbelievable degree of spotlessness (the Mother Subprioress could be thoroughly unpleasant to people—especially novices—who came in from the muddy garden without wiping their feet); an ugly, carved Renaissance altar with twisted barley-sugar columns and a display of aspidistras, and a series of narrow oak tables set close together in a long line just under the windows, where sixty nuns or more could have sat comfortably side by side.

Against the walls, a row of heavy rush-bottomed chairs alternated with plain oak cupboards and massive chests, in whose deep, coffin-like drawers the nuns might keep their books and work. Above, the score or so of Prioresses who had ruled the convent looked down—stern, ascetic faces, pale, tight-lipped, tranquil, under the medieval coifs of fine starched linen and shadowy veils.

Here the nuns sat sewing from 9 to 11 in the morning and from half-past one till 3; and again from 4 to 5 in the afternoon. It was always "out of recreation," which meant that nothing that was not absolutely unavoidable might be said. No wonder that the walls seemed saturated with the silent aspirations, the unspoken joys and sorrows—sometimes agonies—of so many human hearts. For nuns, after all, are only human; and until a kind of mystical death has taken place in the earthly nature, resulting in the triumph of what is spiritual over what is merely natural, suffering cannot be avoided. It has been truly said that suffering is the price of sanctity.

Here, too, the community assembled for recreation. This took place in the evening, after supper. The Prioress sat at the top of the long row of tables with the nuns down either side. The rule of silence no longer held; the walls echoed with laughter and conversation. The Community Room was indeed a kind of sanctuary of the Common Life. A grave room, so large that even when the entire community were assembled it never seemed crowded. Order and decorum produced an impression of space.

Quite at the end of the cloister was the Library. This was the largest room in the convent. What an enchanted kingdom for anyone in need of an escape. From the floor of dangerously polished parquet to the ancient ceiling-beams, were stacked tier upon tier of books—each in its way a magic casement opening on the foam of—sometimes—perilous seas. Here were Didon's lovely romantic *Life of Christ* and the more modern and realistic study by Francois Mauriac; Fouard and Le Camus, besides the many-volumed masterpieces of Le Breton, Lagrange and de Grand-maison. The Library contained, in fact, everything that could possibly be needed for instruction or enlightenment upon every possible aspect of the spiritual life.

Besides the Great Cloister, there were two others, wide, lofty, cool, with their chill atmosphere of perpetual silence; the stern, somber Chapter House leading through the Lay Sisters' Chapel to the domed Renaissance church with its altar of apricot-colored marble and the stained-glass windows, where the light poured through two not oversuccessful compositions—one a symphony of grey and indigo, the other rust-red and copper-gold.

High up, at the back of the church and over the Lay Sisters' Chapel, was the long, beautifully proportioned Choir. It had a fine, wrought-iron grille before it, and the double row of dark carved stalls on either side was reflected in a parquet floor, so highly polished as to suggest the sea of glass in the Apocalypse.

Throughout the convent—except in the nuns' cells, which were as small as possible—one was met by the same atmosphere of cold, clean spaciousness. The place breathed silence and consecration. In fact, living there was rather like being perpetually in church.

• Dame Felicia Corrigan, a Benedictine of
Stanbrook Abbey in Worcestershire, writes of
the abbey's most famous member, Dame
Laurentia McLachlan, and her longtime
friendship and correspondence with George
Bernard Shaw. "An enclosed nun with an
unenclosed mind," wrote GBS.

DAME FELICIA CORRIGAN

The Nun, the Superman, and the Infidel

At the close of Vespers on the afternoon of 5 September 1884, an
18-year-old girl clad in rich bridal attire knelt on the altar steps in
the sanctuary of the church at Stanbrook before the Right Reverend William Clifford, Bishop of Clifton, and the following dialogue took place:

"What do you ask?"

"The mercy of God and the grace of the holy habit."

"Do you ask it with your whole heart?"

"Yes, my Lord, I do."

"May God grant you perseverance, my daughter."

The Bishop then proceeded to shear off her long fair hair. A
few minutes later, divested of silks and ornaments and habited in a
plain wide-sleeved tunic of rough serge, she once more knelt
before him to be formally clothed with a girdle, scapular, and
white veil symbolizing her official reception into the thirteen-
century-old Order of St Benedict. The great enclosure door swung
open in answer to the novice's importunate knocking, and presently closed slowly again behind her, shutting out the world and its
vanities forever.

On the evening of that same day, an earnest group of high-minded socialists met together in the London home of E R Pease, and duly enrolled the name George Bernard Shaw in the eight-months-old Fabian Society.

Greater contrast can scarcely be imagined than between the girl who withdrew into the fastness of the cloister to live a life of subjection and poverty according to the counsels of the gospel of Christ, and the man who went forth into the world to proclaim a doctrine of justice, brotherhood, and equality according to the gospel of Karl Marx. That their paths should ever cross seemed inconceivable.

"My dissipations have begun again," wrote Sydney Cockerell, a friend of the nuns, to the woman, Dame Laurentia, who had entered the convent over two decades earlier.

"Yesterday at the Bodleian from about 10 till 4," he said. "Then to town and supper with Lady D and with her and her husband to a lecture by Bernard Shaw on 'Socialism and the Middle Classes'—and very good it was. I wonder whether GBS's fame has got as far as Stanbrook, and whether he is there regarded as an imp of the devil—I have known him for many years and regard him not only as one of the cleverest (that is nothing) but as one of the best and honestest of living Englishmen."

Apparently, however, acquaintance with even the name of Bernard Shaw was an exception to that seeming universality of knowledge of Dame Laurentia which had so struck Sydney Cockerell at their first meeting. "I have never heard of Mr Bernard Shaw," she replied, "but perhaps others in the house have. I don't like to think that a person whom you regard with respect should be to us as a limb of the evil one!"

Sydney Cockerell was one of Bernard Shaw's oldest friends and one of his greatest. He first made his acquaintance in 1889 and during the early years of the twentieth century he watched Shaw's growing fame as a dramatist whose brilliant and argumentative dialogue, besides reflecting current problems of science, religion, and economics, was also recreating and revolutionizing the English theater.

Feeling by instinct that spirit would answer spirit, it was this man whom he hoped one day to bring into contact with Dame Laurentia. But how to get one whom all London was lionizing to a tiny parlor in a strictly enclosed convent in the remote village of Callow End?

Callow End is no more than an overgrown hamlet. Yet one notable landmark Callow End does possess—the pile of Victorian Gothic buildings known as Stanbrook Abbey. It stands on a slight eminence beyond a sloping green meadow at the very entrance of the village, somewhat aloof but clearly visible from the main road which sweeps round in a wide curve below.

When Joan of Arc was canonized in 1920 and became the subject of Shaw's famous play *St Joan*, Cockerell disciplined himself not to mention it to Dame Laurentia but waited for her to make the first move. All unsuspectingly she fell into the trap and Cockerell sent her the play.

A fortnight later she returned the book and innocently gave him the opportunity for which he had longed ever since he had known her. The play had pleased her enormously: possibly its author would do likewise.

On 24 April 1924 Dame Laurentia received a letter from Mrs Shaw with visiting cards and saying that "our friend Sydney Cockerell has urged us very strongly to call upon you. We feel a little diffident about doing so, and hope you will not think us intrusive. But it would be a great pleasure to see you."

Without awaiting a reply, they arrived in the afternoon of the same day. It is apparent that both parties enjoyed the visit but when Cockerell asked Shaw when he was going again, Shaw replied, "Never." Then on reflection he asked, "How long has she been there? Nearly fifty years? Oh, that alters the case. I'll go whenever I can."

Of that decision, Dame Laurentia later wrote that Shaw had "thought I had come in ready-made from the world, but when he found that whatever I am is the result of my life here he was impressed. This gives me confidence to hope that God may use me for this soul's salvation. If it were only a matter of his liking me, I should think little of it, but it seems that the life here, and therefore the Church, does attract him. God give grace to help this poor wanderer so richly gifted. . . ."

GBS wrote Dame Laurentia some days later that "we are just off for a trip to Scotland (how I wish I were enclosed, and never had to pack or not know at what hotel to lay my head!) and we may return south by way of Worcester, in which case we shall certainly blow in—if that is a proper way to visit an Abbey."

"I am in possession of my own St Joan," she wrote Sydney Cockerell, "adorned with the inscription 'to Sister Laurentia from Brother Bernard'! Mr Shaw is becoming quite monastic!"

She found that she was able to tell him of the mass devised for St Joan's feast day and, in an aside to Cockerell, she remarked that "I shall not bother Br B again, but when he next shakes my bars I shall make some further remarks."

With her letter, Dame Laurentia was able to send Shaw a book on Thomas More from the Abbey press. His reply began a regular correspondence that was to extend over a period of twenty-five years until his death in 1950.

GBS showed himself surprisingly alive to the implications of the contemplative life and to the freedom paradoxically symbolized by the double iron grille. The coolness and effrontery originating from his extreme shyness, the love of shocking lion-hunters with outrageous remarks, and—most Irish of all his traits—the levity with which he disguised his deepest feelings, found no place before Dame Laurentia. Brilliant, disconcerting, and dynamic he could not help being, yet his fundamental humility, tact, and quick understanding became more and more apparent in his relations with her as the years passed.

In 1929 Cockerell accompanied Shaw on one of his visits to Stanbrook, later confessing that he saw a GBS almost unknown to him. "He was on his good behavior," Cockerell told one of the nuns, "and seemed to admit that he was in the presence of a being superior to himself."

The following year, when Shaw paid an unexpected visit and Dame Laurentia could not receive him, he fancied "that some meddlesome saint or other has made you ill to make your friends feel how much your friendship means to them."

When he visited the Holy Land he sent Dame Laurentia a special report of thirteen pages. One marvels, to take but one instance, at the ease with which he sums up the very essence of a religious vocation and tosses off in a single neat phrase the age-long contention between protagonists of the active and contemplative life, Martha versus Mary—"girls whom you might enlist for Stanbrook without expecting them to excel in doing as well as being."

A short time later Dame Laurentia was elected Abbess, and in 1934 she celebrated her golden jubilee as a member of the community. Shaw took the announcement to be a notification of her death and immediately sent a letter of sympathy to the nuns. The mix-up served to heal a breach in their friendship caused by the Abbess's shock at GBS's book, *The Adventures of an African Girl*. Their friendship was resumed with all the old esteem and an ever-deepening veneration.

In 1944, Shaw sent a letter hoping it "will not arrive late for your Diamond Jubilee. It is too late for mine by twenty years. I was 88 last month but one. The saint who called me to the religious life when I was 18 was Shelley. But you have lived the religious life: I have only talked and written about it."

In reply Dame Laurentia wrote that her "years of enclosed life leaves me happier than ever for having chosen this path—though, as Tagore sang: 'We cannot *choose* the best. The best chooses us.' If people only knew the freedom of an enclosed nun! I believe you can understand it better than most people and I only wish we shared the faith that is its foundation."

Prayer had invariably loomed large in his correspondence with Dame Laurentia. Never did he make such a simple and open profession of faith in its efficacy, however, as in a long letter typewritten by himself, at age 92, on 17 August 1948.

"Do not forget me [in your prayers]," he wrote. "I cannot explain how or why I am the better for them; but I like them and am certainly not the worse."

At 93 he expressed belief that "God must be tired of all these prayers for this fellow Shaw whom He doesn't half like. He has promised His servant Laurentia that He will do His best for him, and we had better leave it at that. The thought of Stanbrook is a delight to me. It is one of my holy places."

Shaw died a few months later at dawn on the morning of All Saints Day, 1950.

Within three years Dame Laurentia herself was dying. For nearly seventy years she had sung, prayed, meditated, worked, and joyfully lived in the seclusion of her monastic cloister. During the few days preceding her death, each nun saw her alone, without any formality, rank, or dramatic leave-taking. She made one exception in the case of a young nun on the eve of her solemn profession whom she bade a simple *au revoir* in characteristic monosyllables: "Child, I am going to God. That is what I came for—what we all came for—to go to God. I am sorry I shall not be alive for your profession, but, Child, I *shall be there*. Give yourself wholly to God, to be entirely consecrated, sanctified, glorified."

At a quarter past five on Sunday the 23 August 1953, as her nuns stole down in the grey morning light to chant God's praises, signed with the sign of the Cross, she drew a great, deep breath and slept in peace.

• A native of Pittsburgh, Sister Maria del
Rey worked on the Pittsburgh Press before
joining the Maryknoll Sisters in 1932. After
teaching in the Philippines (she was interned
by the Japanese from 1941 to 1945) she
wrote several books on the Maryknoll
missions and, as the Order's public relations
officer, arranged for the Mother General to
appear on the cover of Time. She is again
teaching in the Philippines.

SISTER MARIA DEL REY

No Two Alike

Joy moves over the face of Sister Anne Cecilia like sunshine
sweeping a landscape, as she freely gives you, with wide gesture,
whatever she has—a crisp cookie just tossed off the hot baking tin,
an extra stint of work, or hours of her free time to listen to your
troubles. She learned the formula from her mother back in the
Depression days of the 1930s in the shoe factory town of Brockton,
Massachusetts.

When she was at the Motherhouse I liked to sit out in the
cloister court with Sister Anne Cecilia. In summer it was a cool
spot, a good break from the bakery where Sister spent most of her
twenty-four hours, extracting bread, cakes, pies, and cookies from
the hot abysses of our five-story ovens. Her strong arms lifted pans
lightly and quickly and slid them on the marble-slab tabletop so
they would not jar or fall. She was all over the bakery at once,
seeing that the inexperienced novices did things right.

"Sister, turn down that mixer; you're going too fast."

"Now just a little more milk in that. Too dry."

"Never mind rolling out the pie dough right now; get on with the cookies. We'll need them tonight."

And, to welcome a gift-giver, "Nuts! Aren't you good to think of us. Put them right here in this corner. We'll use them for fancy bread on Easter. Here, take this"—stuffing bags with rolls and cinnamon buns—"and this. (Dear me, I was hoping to get nuts from someplace!) Don't go without an apple pie, too."

But out in the court, her hands stayed quiet in her lap. Her sweat-soaked cotton habit flapped around her spare figure. The large green-brown eyes followed a robin hopping on the grass as she threw him bits of the bread and jelly she ate with mid-afternoon coffee.

She was Lithuanian through and through. She should have worn boots and blouses thick with embroidery. She loved wild music and rich cakes and bright colors and singing in the choir. She worked in a frenzy, producing an endless stream of superb baked goods for the 350 of us. We at the Motherhouse never had such before and don't expect ever to have it again. Sisters on mission around the world speak of her, one of many helping hands who gave joy to the days of training and made it possible for others to go out.

Now and then she would sit out under the trees and, with head thrown back, exalt in sunshine and shadow. She closed her eyes, the strong features relaxed and one knew she was saying, "I love you, God," in a thousand ways.

She said aloud, "I never wanted to be anything but a Sister. My mother insisted that I finish high school, and I did, but I came right after."

"Why did you want to?" I asked.

"To give. To give and give and give to God. He has been so good to me!"

I watched her that evening as we sang Compline. Her woolen habit was nicely pressed, her collar and cuffs immaculate. She stood in the ranks of Sisters massed in the choir stalls, all of them decorously looking at their books. But Sister Anne Cecilia's head was thrown back and the eyes closed, for she knew the words by heart. Her voice—strong and true—I could distinguish from the others in choir although I was on the opposite side of the chapel.

Her face was wreathed in happiness, like a child's as he stands out to let the rain fall on his face and roll down his neck and chest. Sister Anne Cecilia was drinking deep of the fountains of the Lord.

She who gives and gives and gives, also gets and gets and gets.

• Born into a physician's family, Richard
Selzer also became a doctor and taught at
Yale Medical School. Based on a long stay
with Benedictine monks on the island of San
Gregorio, in Venice, this essay, "Diary of
an Infidel," is from a collection entitled
Taking the World in for Repairs.

RICHARD SELZER

Taking the World in for Repairs

"San Giorgio!" calls the boatman who has brought me across the
bay from Venice. *"Permesso, permesso, signore, prego!"* and he pulls
back the bar. I cross the great stone terrace and rap on the door.

"I am a wayfarer seeking shelter," I say to the monk. "I would
like to stay in your guest house, *il foresteria*," I tell him.

"I am Dom Pietro, the guestmaster," he says in English,
without the least surprise. He does not ask my name or whether I am
expected. "I will show you to your room." He pivots momentously
and leads the way into the abbey. He does not offer to carry one of
my bags. Perhaps the idea does not occur to him. Perhaps it is his
unworldliness. Perhaps he is rude. The staircase is narrow and
winding. Ahead, he is all grace and figure, while, clumsy with
baggage, I bump and scrape to keep up with him. At the door to
what I see is to be my room, he pauses.

"Enter, Christ," he says.

"Well, not exactly," I say.

"Four hundred years ago the abbot himself would come to
bathe your feet."

"How long have you been here?" I ask.

64

"We have been here one thousand years."

The room is not a cell but good-sized with a high beamed ceiling. A large casement window opens out to reveal the Byzantine domes of San Marco directly across the water. The furniture is heavy, Renaissance. The floor, marble; there is no rug.

"You have arrived very late in the day," says Pietro. "It is just now time for Vespers. Come." I deposit the suitcase and typewriter and follow him down a long corridor, descend a curved flight of stairs, cross a foyer, and step into what proves to be the side door of a great church. Inside it is black. Never, never has there been darkness like this. It is the first darkness, undiluted from the beginning. I can see nothing. Ahead of me the monk's black habit has become part of the immense blackness of the church.

"Come," he whispers. "We shall be late." I take one blind cautious step and pause again. A hand slips into mine and exerts firm pressure. We walk for what seems a great distance, then stop. The hand is disengaged and with a sweep of pale palm I am invited to sit. In a moment he is gone. Slowly my eyes accommodate and I understand that I am entirely alone in a huge vaulted building. Far away, two small candles, like stars. And like stars, they shine but give no light. I sit for a long time in the absolute silence. Slowly the church forms itself about me. I establish the site of the nave, the great altar. High above, an angel hovers in full finial display.

All at once, there is a barely perceptible noise, a soft rumble as of thunder. The sound dies without discovery of its nature or source. It returns, seeming to come from all directions at once, like ventriloquy. One moment it is subterranean; the next, it gathers from on high. Is it the wind? Tricking among the roofs and towers? A construction of the water? A vagrant noise from the Piazza San Marco? At last it emerges from its mystery, grows into a tremulous hum, and solidifies into chanting. The music has no tempo. There is no breathing audible in it. No one voice stands out; it is the fusion of all that produces the effect. Long-held notes which at last modulate again and again the calm rhythm of the heart. *Systole, diastole.* Something, I think, that must be performed in tranquility, a kind of respiratory yoga. I am suspended in the sound. And charged. My fatigue lifts and is replaced by a drowsiness. The headache which has plagued me for three days is a distant muted pulse at my temple.

The chanting dies away as gently as it began. Once again there is the unanimous voice of silence. In a moment Dom Pietro is back. I have no idea how long the service has lasted. Time, it seems, as well as space is immeasurable here.

"It is the hour for the evening meal," the guestmaster says as we leave the church. "When you enter the refectory the monks will be standing, each behind his place. You will be seated at the head of the U-shaped table next to the abbot. Stand in front of the table and wait. Soon Padre Abate will arrive. He will come up to you at once and hold out his hand. You must take his hand in yours, bow, and kiss his ring. He will then conduct you to your seat. The meal is taken in silence."

"Kiss his ring?"

The abbot is bulky but he is not obese. Rather, his body is conscious and suave. It has the gracefulness of power. His smile is warm, papal. Behind those hooded eyes burns a superb intelligence. When he holds out his ring I bob to it. Against my lips it has the unyielding smoothness of a ram's horn. I sit next to the abbot on the right at what amounts to a high table. The others are seated at the two long tables of which we are the connecting link. Scanning the tables I see that all but one of the monks are big, fleshy men; that one is candle thin. The monk serving the meal places a large tureen of soup on the table from which the abbot serves first me, then himself. The tureen is borne away and placed in front of the monk nearest me. This man takes from it and passes it to his neighbor. Now the abbot tinkles a small silver bell. One tink. And a young monk seats himself at a lectern. He begins to read aloud, in Latin first, then Italian. His voice, though monotonous, is devoid of weariness or boredom. I do not get much of it. The lives of the saints, I think. Or the Rule of St Benedict.

A cruet of red wine is at each place along with a small loaf of bread, fat in the middle, and tapering at the end, thus repeating the bodily configuration of its devourer. The abbot takes my glass and, holding the cruet of wine high above it, pours so that the red stream appears to have a solid permanence. Not a drop is spilled or runs from the lip of the vessel. The meal, other than the soup of rice and noodles, consists of hard grey meat encased in a jelly. I think of toads and half expect one to poke its nose up for air. I can eat nothing but the bread, wine, and apple. The eating of such food could never be thought sinful. I think of the thousand marvelous restaurants in Venice.

The monks, even the thin one, pile their plates high. Looking neither to the right nor to the left, they eat. I spend the time worrying my food into insignificance on the plate. Another tink! and the silenced reader takes his place at the table. It is the time for talk.

"You are most welcome to our abbey and our table." The abbot's voice is smooth and practiced, furry. "But you have eaten nothing." A smile shows concern.

"Please pay it no mind. I am famous for it."

"It is the rule here that you must finish everything on your plate."

"Then permit me to serve myself."

"It is my pleasure to serve my guests."

"But you all eat so much. One is not accustomed."

"St Benedict has said that he who works shall eat."

"Then I must have some work to do here. You must give me a job. I am not comfortable when I am idle and all about me are fully engaged."

"There is no work for you here."

"Then I am to be an ornament? Please, I am a doctor, I can give the monks each a physical examination. Or, if you prefer, I would be happy to help in the kitchen or laundry. The garden. Whatever."

"No," he smiles. "You are not to work here."

"But I have always worked. Upon my tombstone shall be carved, 'He kept busy.' "

"No."

"Then why am I here?"

"The reason has not yet been revealed to me." The hands part briefly, then rejoin, and I understand that the subject is closed. Well, then, I shall develop my unrealized genius for elaborate repose. If I can do no work here, so much the better. Like the poet. I'll loaf and invite my soul.

"Tell me," says the abbot, "is there an English word—*tempiternal*? I read it the other day. How does it differ from *sepiternal*?"

"I think it was a misprint," I tell him. He laughs. Just that, and we are to be friends. He fingers the bell, and we rise. One of the monks with his cowl at full mast and his arms hidden in his surplice recites a prayer of thanks. The others listen very carefully. The departure from the refectory is made in silence, and then there is a procession that is very far from the kind of academic slouch which I am used to at Yale commencements. They go *en file*. Moments later they are cowled silhouettes merging with the night.

At the door of the refectory I am retrieved by the guestmaster. So far as I can tell, none of the other monks has so much as glanced in my direction. Once again in my room, Dom Pietro becomes the perfect chamberlain.

"The bathroom is just outside your door. No one else is permitted to use it during your stay. The armoire is fifteenth-century Florentine. The bed, too. Only the desk is Venetian. All of the icons are of the same period save for the amethyst crucifix on the desk which is thirteenth century. The bed is firm and comfortable. The pope slept in it on his last visit."

"I am to sleep in the pope's bed?"

"It was before his election."

"Oh, well then."

Pietro lifts one eyebrow.

"By the way, Dom Pietro, what are the rules? I must tell you that I am incompletely housebroken and do not want to disgrace myself. Tell me what I must do?"

"The only rule here is that of St Benedict and that, of course, does not apply to you. But there are three things. Turn out the lights when you leave the room. If you smoke, collect the ashes and butts and give them to me to discard. Do not put them in the wastebasket."

"Where, then?"

He points to an inkwell made of horn on the desk. "That will do fine. Above all, close the window when you leave the room."

"That's all?"

"And oh, yes, one other. You must eat everything on your plate."

"It was hardly Belshazzar's feast."

"Nevertheless, you must. It is the rule here."

"*Per la penitenza,*" I murmur. Pietro is not amused.

The temperature is frigid in this place. I am shivering and my nose has begun to run. In the morning I shall have to chip myself out of bed with a little pickaxe. I fit the stopper in the huge claw-footed tub and turn on the faucets. From one, there is nothing at all; from the other, a pathetic twine of cold water. While waiting for the tub to fill I go to the windows and push them outward. Venice snaps open like a fan. Directly across is the Piazza San Marco and the Palace of the Doges. My room is on the second story at the front of the abbey adjacent to the façade of the church. I shall be able to pick out this window from the vaporetto. I lean on the ledge until a huge black shape erases Venice. Silent as a monk the freighter noses toward Yugoslavia beyond the sea. The wind of its passage blows the smell of cuttlefish into the room. The spell is broken and I go to my bath. After half an hour, the vast bathtub holds three inches of cold water. For my sins. I strip and tiptoe in. There I crouch, not daring to sit, and with the help of a soapy rag, rearrange the dirt on my body. It seems that my suffering soul is forcing my body to keep it company. No sooner have I re-dressed than there is a knock at the door. Pietro. Am I to have constant attendance?

"Ah, I see that you have bathed."

"In a way. Might you have a bath towel?" He goes to inspect the bathroom.

"But you have washed the tub. I am to do that for you."

"The monk does not live who washes my tub. My rule." He

disappears briefly and returns with an ancient frayed towel that I could conceal entirely in one of my ears.

"Also fifteenth century?" I ask.

"Will you be smoking tonight?"

"Yes. Do you mind?" I light up. "I don't suppose you..." Pietro smiles and reaches out to accept. I light it for him. He drags profoundly and exhales slowly. I see that he has not had a cigarette in recent memory.

"Will you have a brandy?"

"You have brought brandy here?"

"One does not set out to explore a savage country without bringing something to appease the natives," I tell him. And pour two large hookers. He sips with pleasure.

"Padre Abate and I are the only ones who speak English. The others are not permitted to speak with you unless necessary."

"Do you have many visitors such as I?"

"Guests are rare here. The occasional priest on his way to Rome, a visiting abbot come to concelebrate mass with Padre Abate, and of course, once, the pope."

We smoke three cigarettes each and drink another brandy.

"It is strange," I tell him, "the austerity amidst these gorgeous surroundings, all this vast treasure."

"Not austere enough," he says. "We are too fat." And he taps his belly with two fingers. "I myself should have preferred a thornier path. But it was not given me."

"Whatever for?"

"The conquest of self is the more complete in a severe monastery."

I am extremely tired. Pietro does not notice and makes no effort to leave. All at once, I am set rattling by the sound of a loud bell. It is exactly like the bell used to mark the end of a period in Public School No. 5 in Troy, New York, and, five minutes later, the beginning of another. It is a harsh, prisonlike jangle, meant, I think, to startle rather than remind. In a country full of beautiful bells it is the cruelest noise that calls these monks to prayer. At the sound Pietro stands.

"Compline," he says. "Come and you will hear me sing."

"Another time," I say. "I am through for the day."

He urges me to relent and come to the noonday meal.

"It is the best one," he says. "Very good pasta, fish."

"No, I cannot eat so much."

"It is you who are the monk, a Carthusian. On a single loaf of bread a week."

He laughs at his joke.

At last I am established in my room, the noise of the tiny far-off world on one side of the window, and on the other side, the limitless silence of the monastery.

Morning, after the very soundest sleep. The bed, though narrow, is deep. It molds itself to fit the body so that one is not so much in it as of it. All night long there were the lapping of waves and the dark shapes of freighters gliding past. I have begun writing an essay on surgery. My plan is to work on it a few hours each day. I have just taken a seat at the desk when Pietro arrives.

"Padre Abate wishes to give you a tour of the monastery."

I follow him to the foyer just inside the front door where the abbot and four other monks are waiting. With the abbot presiding, I am led from one spectacle to the next: the refectory with its great ornamental lavabi, the twelfth-century cloister of the cypresses, a monumental staircase, a long pristine white dormitory with, on either side, the black doors of the cells, each with its little wicker. For spying, I suppose.

The church, designed by Palladio, is in the form of a cross with a cupola above and an adjacent campanile affording, I am told, the best view of Venice. The façade, facing San Marco square, is of the finest Istrian marble.

From the outside, the dome of the basilica is one big tonsured scalp. Inside, it is wallpapered with scenes from the Bible: the Annunciation. There is the archangel impregnating Mary with words. Mary, herself, looking up from her book with that "who? me?" expression on her face. There the Last Supper. The Israelites collecting manna. At the head of the nave is the choir where the great altar is situated and which, in turn, is three feet higher than the main portion of the church. The whole is a great prismatic box where light and tone interact to produce something greater by far than either one—a conspiracy.

There is no stained glass, for which I am grateful. I have always resented stained glass, its way of getting between me and the sky, always demanding attention. Whenever I see it I imagine the wickedest sins being committed behind it. The building is made entirely of stone and has the coldness of stone. What little there is of wood is in the furnishings, the ornately carved choir, the crucifixes. The altar is decorated with a large round copper ball placed over four figures of the Evangelists. It is this that serves as the tabernacle for the Holy Sacrament. All this is explained to me by Padre Abate. To me this church is a vaulting paradise where voices ascend, multiply, and are gathered beneath the dome, where pillars and arches stretch away and away in every direction into far distant darkness. Here is a building that is never still, but alters its angles and curves to fit each new position of the body, pressing against one until it occupies the heart. I am struck by the great number of angels placed strategically upon every ledge and mantel, a whole host *tenentes silentium*. It is too beautiful, too perfect, the columns too straight and soaring. Humility alone dictates that one wall be defaced, one pillar be pulled askew by ropes.

Several hours later we pass through a pair of immense carved doors into a great hall or throne room. It is a huge square space about the periphery of which have been set three semicircles of thrones in tiers, twenty-four in each, as in an amphitheater. In one corner of the room, a small black pot-bellied stove with a chimney. On the wall in back of the altar, a large painting depicting St George having just impaled the dragon on his lance.

"Carpaccio," says Pietro.

"This is the Conclave Room," says the abbot. "In the history of the church only one pope was elected outside of Rome. It was here that the election took place. The year was 1700. The College of Cardinals gathered to this place. These are their thrones, preserved just as they were. The name of each priest is carved at the back. "There," he points, "the little stove where the ballots were burned while across the lagoon all Venice watched for the puffs of smoke. We are very proud of this room." Dom Pietro touches the abbot's arm and they speak together in Italian. The abbot turns to me.

"Dom Pietro has reminded me that you are still tired from your journey. We shall rest here. Please," he motions, "be seated."

Gratefully, I climb the first step to the middle row of thrones, walk in one, two, three, and sit in the fourth. All at once the four monks turn to each other and begin to jabber, using their hands wildly. I know at once that I have committed a gaffe. Something Pietro neglected to warn me against. I spring to my feet.

"What is it?" I ask. "I have done something wrong."

Padre Abate explains. "You have chosen to sit in the place of the man who was elected pope in this room. You must forgive our agitation."

My relief is as vast as their excitement.

"A coincidence," I say. The abbot shakes his head firmly.

"Providence," he says. And that's that.

O twice elected! I sleep in one pope's bed; I sit in the throne of another. From that moment I have free rein to go anywhere in the monastery. Only the dormitory of cells is forbidden me. About them I am immensely curious. To think that within such grandeur there are those little pockets of modesty.

It is only with Pietro that I can speak freely, converse. His visits to my room, made in the role of guestmaster, are frequent and prolonged. While, in the beginning, the unpredictability and duration of his presence were annoying, I find myself less than exasperated. I tell myself that it is because he speaks English, but I suspect I have grown fond. Honesty forces me to admit that I look forward to that soft rapping at the door, the inch of opening through which looms that huge mound of black.

What a great powerful woman of a man he is. A diva bursting with temperament. Well over six feet tall, and hefty, with skimpy blond hair combed straight forward to conceal frontal baldness. Much the tallest of the monks, he holds himself ramrod straight, which accentuates his height above them. His voice is baritone with just the hint of brogue. He is, after all, Irish from Dublin. The eyes are Anglo-Saxon blue; the nose fleshy with mobile nostrils. When he turns to speak, it is with his whole body rather than his head only, as though he were on a stage and playing to an audience. It is a flattering gesture in that it lends the impression that his entire attention is given to you alone. Turning, he lightly fingers the material of the habit which he does not so much wear as model. Whereas the others seem unaware of their costume, Pietro makes every use of it to express himself. By carriage and mien he is apart from the community. In file across the cloister the heads of the others are downcast and forward. Pietro's head is down too, yes, but with the chin turned slightly to the side as though he were listening. The others are merely monks. Dom Pietro is pure figure. He seems to have come to understand this abbey with his body the way an old sailor does his boat—the shadows made by the archway, the exact step in the marble staircase where his voice echoes most thrillingly from the domed ceiling. And in these places he lingers to submit, encouraging the building to express itself through his body. In his company, I feel all the more an old clothes-bag.

"Everything we do is in the interest of unity and uniformity," he says. "Our identical habits, the way we walk in line, heads bent, hands hidden in the surplice. Such an unchanging rhythm sets the stage for the appearance of God."

It is the chain reaction of monastic life. They have but to look at each other moving toward glory with submarine grace and their zeal is fired.

"But your walk is different," I tell him. "I would know you at once in a crowd."

He does not hide his pleasure at this.

Pietro has been appointed to look after my needs. Whatever I am to see and hear will be filtered through him. To see more I shall have to stand tiptoe and peer over that massive shoulder. Each time he leaves my room I turn the crucifix on my desk 30 degrees so that, sitting there, I am out of the line of fire. Each

time he comes his first act is to turn it back until once again I am
a bull's-eye.

"When are you going to stop being so childish?" he asks.

"Never," I tell him.

Here at the Abbey of San Giorgio each room and corridor is
aware of every other room and corridor. Perfect in itself, yet in
perfect resonance. It is forbidding. And the whole of the island
enveloped in solitude, cut off. What could have possessed the early
founders to plant their abbey here? Were they fishermen, sailors by
nature that must never be parted from the water? This glowing
house, these walls and columns and cloisters that divide up the
way of life of the Benedictines—no road winds toward it from afar.
It reigns over no fields, only sparkles like a chip of bright stone in
the lagoon. And all this doting upon permanence, antiquity,
which to gaze upon is just as disheartening as it is to peer into the
future. Permanence gives a feeling of oppressiveness to a building.
Here is a fifteenth-century table. There hangs an icon from the
twelfth, and beneath this little glass bell you can see a few strands
of St Lucy's hair. So instructs Pietro, dropping centuries the way
others drop names.

And what a sobersided business it all is. This routine of
Vigils, Primes, Tierces, Sexts, Nones, Vespers, Complines, and
those meals which are only variants of the holy offices rendered in
gastrointestinal terms. Then at dusk two dozen doors close; two
dozen bolts are shot. And we are enclosed.

One day into its night, and again a day with all the hours
jumbled. I watch the monks cruise from the refectory after the
evening meal like widows on some melancholy errand, and I
continue my patrol of the premises. Prowling through corridors
and staircases, I come upon a pair of great doors most emphatically
shut. I open one and find myself in the Conclave Room, the scene
of my earlier triumph. It is windowless and therefore dark save for
the light given by four candles burning upon the altar. I sink into
one of the thrones in the first tier, close my eyes, and drift toward

sleep. Something keeps me from it. It is whole minutes before I know that I am not alone here. A monk is kneeling on the stones directly before the altar. Why has he come here? It is not the time of a holy office. It is the time for rest and recreation. I am curious but wish not to be indiscreet. I lean forward thinking myself to have been unobserved. We are not more than a dozen feet apart. And a world.

Although I cannot be sure, I think it is Vittorio, the novice master. "A very holy man," Pietro had said. In the candlelight the face of the monk is made of wire in glass and wax. He retains only the smallest suggestion of human nature. From his mouth comes a continuous whisper, now and then punctuated by a sigh. It is as though I am watching through a keyhole the upward flight of a soul. I can make no sense of the words. They are whispered conspiratorially, the syllables like pebbles worn smooth by rubbing. He seems in a painful state, a delirium. I am moved by a desire to relieve him of it, to jostle him out of his nightmare. But even were I to shake him, shout in his ear, he would not budge.

His passion rises. *Aves* come foaming from his agile mouth. Next to his lips my own lips are cripples. There is something epileptiform about it—the trembling, the shaking. Has he eaten some marvelous drug? Hashish? Mushrooms? When at last he raises his head, I know the difference between a face and a countenance.

There is no speck of egotism in his love, while the love I have known has been full of nothing else. This kind of love would vanish at the first attempt to analyze it. Its existence depends upon participation in the mystery. I watch him exploring all the limits of his longings and feel in myself for the first time the painful absence of God. For him these visions are privileged moments. He has learned how to summon them forth. My own dreams come of their own volition, without the fanfare of prayer. What is it that he sees each time, all in ochre, burnt sienna, carmine, and flesh? Does he hear the shouts of Roman soldiers, the footsteps of women on the *via dolorosa*, the hammering of spikes. What must it be like to feel trailing at one's feet the whole of the gorgeous Christian epic—

immaculate, murderous, risen? It is a triumph of the imagination. My own fails me at this point. I have no visions. Only, now and then, strange noises in my blood. There are tears on his cheeks! In each drop, a tiny candle flame reflected.

At last, he crosses himself one last time, rises, and still murmuring, comes to sit beside me. He is totally relaxed, unself-conscious. He smiles, his face still moist. His teeth are white as peeled almonds.

"But you were crying," I say. Vittorio raises his eyebrows as though I had just given him news.

"It was not grief," he says.

"What then?"

"It was the hard labor of prayer."

Laboring, then, toward that moment when abbey will stop being abbey and become heaven.

Directly behind and beneath my room is the cloister, punctuated at the center by two ancient cypresses, and at one end by a white stone lavabo. It is the stillest spot that ever was. A cloister, unlike a park or an orchard, is not the place to sit and have a long chat. First of all, there are no benches and one can hardly think of sprawling on ancient sacred grass. Nor, somehow, are the carved hedges and colonnades hospitable to the chasing to and fro of conversation unless, I suppose, it be muttered in Latin. One walks in a cloister. Up and down and all around, slowly, steadily, letting the thoughts turn inward until the mind becomes the very cloister in which one walks.

Though sparsely populated, the abbey is crowded with presences, full of its own story, self-involved, and presenting a profound indifference to the world across the lagoon. Except for the two cypresses in the cloister it is so treeless a place—just bare buildings exposed to the eye of Heaven. Oh, for a bit of dim leafage to sin behind. And someone considerate to do it with. The inhabitants of this place have amputated the past, torn themselves free of their childhood. What fills that place in the mind where memory rules? They are unstirred by the nostalgia and sentiment with which the rest of us alternately console and torment ourselves.

There is the time of work and the time of prayer; the time of rest and the time of eating. It is an immutable order which prevails, a childlike rhythm. They are children but without the child's lovely ignorance of loss and decay. If they yearn for the farmhouses and boulevards of long ago, one can detect no sign of it. Nor do they miss the faces that were once dear and utterly familiar—parents, brothers, and sisters. For them there is only the long, long present lived out in the company of each other.

Every day the coast of Venice seems farther away, receding. It is a perception that now elates, now terrifies me. The abbey is more and more a labyrinth into which I have stumbled and from which I either shall or shall not emerge. What was at first a troubled silence has become a sheltering hush. Having no habit, I wear what amounts to a coat of many colors—red polo shirt, blue jeans, green sweater, and horn-rimmed glasses. In my present state of dishevelment, I should be unrecognizable to the mother who bore me. Yet I am spared the sight for there are no mirrors. Except in the rare puddle, I have not seen my reflection, nor have I heard my name. I have asked Pietro and later the abbot to call me by name, but they do not. I am always addressed directly but never by name. Soon I shall have forgotten it and be forced, like each of the novices, to adopt a new one. It is as though I were disappearing, receding into the insubstantiality. Now and then I light a cigarette and let the smoke curl slowly from my pursed lips, studying the jet for evidence that I still exist.

Again and again I read *The Rule of St Benedict*. It makes no mention of the likes of me in the abbey. Hospitality alone explains my presence, setting aside the possibility of my being Christ. Or perhaps my coming is an opportunity to test their faith against worldly contamination?

The trick to being celibate is to forget that you are a man. Easier said than done as St Jerome discovered in a desert. St Benedict too had his problems. On the back of each choir stall is carved a scene from the life of the saint. In one he is shown building a monastery; in another, he converts the heathen soldiers; still another has him being assumed to glory. My favorite shows the horny old saint fighting off a serious attack of lust by throwing himself into a clump of thorn bushes. Best not to talk. In a week or so I shall be sporting a full rack of antlers. All you have to do is drive out your nature with a pitchfork, make a desert of your heart, and call it peace. Yet I am struck by the evidence of happiness on the faces of the novices. I cannot fathom it. It is a gladness that can come from no human source. I mention this to the abbot.

"It is the gladness of heaven," he says.

Along with human love, what is missing here is reproduction. Nothing, no one is born here. There are no new eyes, new breaths. There are no natives; everyone has come from somewhere else. All the fecundity is in the long ago. It stopped at the womb of Mary. Sixteen men, then, full of unspent sperm, dry as chalk. By what magic do their faces remain unscored, their hair full and black, their hands youthful and soft? With what is their flesh nourished that each one looks twenty years younger than he is? As though he were being returned to the condition of Adam before the Fall. While I, pouched and sacculate, am at the height of my beshrivelment. It is the refrigerated condition of their lives, I think, that holds back decay. Thousand-year-old insects trapped in amber share the same incorruptibility. I watch their shadows fall across each other in the cloister, one monk darkening another who in turn darkens the next. It is their only manner of touching. As for myself, I shall, in the matter of chastity, proceed day by day, secure in the folk wisdom that one does not go blind in the absence of sex.

At San Giorgio instead of irony there is humility; instead of satire, sermon. Irony is the human glance. I am used to it. Eternity is the cool perspective of God. And this God is not ironic; he is earnest and high. This evening I return to the church, trying to feel what it is that is expressed there seven times a day and what lingers in the intervals. Faced by the passionate striving of the last rays of the sun and lingering wisps of scent, I have to remind myself of the inanimacy of stone. At such moments, I would greatly appreciate a reassuring sign from heaven. Whichever way I look I see carved in endless variety of sunlit patches—spaces, angles, arcs. In contrast to the dark half shadows below, the upper galleries deliver an atrium of light that transforms that well of shadows into a luminous cave. I spy on the monks as they chant, drawing as close to the choir as I can without disturbing them. Here, even the faces of the old have the tenderness of youth. They seem to listen as they sing, abandoning themselves, while translating the universe.

It is sunset. The community gathers on the terrace. Only the abbot is missing. No one speaks, as though we had vowed. Paolo holds my suitcase which he does not set down; Sebastiano, the typewriter; Lorenzo, the briefcase. The vaporetto, famous for its punctuality, is late. Why doesn't it come? I implore it to come. The waiting is too hard, too hard. At last, it thumps against the pier. "San Giorgio!" calls out the boatman. The suitcase is handed aboard, then the rest. "*Arrivederci.* Good-bye, good-bye. *Ciago. Ci verdiamo.*" Fifteen hands are clasped.

I do not look back until the boat is well into the lagoon. At last, I must. I turn to see them on the terrace gazing after me, swaying on the stems of their bodies as though their souls were stirring. They are grouped together, all except for Pietro who stands a little apart, erect, his habit billowing, stealing the last scene. Of them all it is he for whom my departure is hardest. Even so, I have to smile. If Isola di San Giorgio were to sink into the lagoon and the command came to evacuate, it would be Pietro and Pietro alone who would remain to die with his beloved abbey, black and erect upon the steps of the church, an exclamation point dissolving into the flood.

All at once, the sun sinks behind Venice and, as it does, for one precise moment the final rays strike the façade of the monastery, turning it red. Every window is filled with flames. The whole of the abbey is a crucible. Every window burning. Except one. Mine! And that one is black as night. It is the window which the abbot flung open in his dramatic act of ventilation and which I had forgotten to close. *I had broken a rule.*

Months later I shall wonder, and try to remember, what it was I felt then. Relief that I had made my escape through that black hole, or regret that I had gone from that holy house, every detail of which lies buried forever at the back of my eyes.

• Among several published authors in the
Community of St Mary the Virgin, Sister
Janet is distinguished as the biographer of
recent Mother Generals. The order was
founded in Wantage, England, in 1848.

SISTER JANET

Mother Jane Margaret, CSMV

In July of 1961, the eighth year of her dozen years as Mother
General, Mother Jane Margaret held a conference with the Superiors of all the branch houses, in which her opening talk gathered
up the rich fruits of her own motherhood.

"Those of you with long experience as Superiors must forgive
me if I say all that you already know," she began with characteristic, gentle humility. "When I first thought of having a Superiors'
Conference I hesitated as to whether I should just talk to the
younger ones, but this did not seem right. We are all one. And I
can at least share my own experiences as Mother with those of you
who are older even if I cannot teach you anything. In a big
Community such as ours the Mother must work very largely
through the Superiors. Therefore the closer the link between her
and them the better. Every Superior is, as it were, a Mother in
miniature. All in the Rule about the Mother applies to her
equally.

"In our Rule the principles for *all* authority are laid down, and
we are left in no doubt as to what they are. We are to place
ourselves beneath the feet of all. To be gentle with the trouble-
some. Loving with the weak. Patient to all. Faithful in keeping the
Rule ourselves. And we are to seek rather to be loved than feared.

Humility, gentleness, love, patience, fidelity—and again, love.

"Leadership is a gift which one may or may not have. It is nothing to do with goodness. Like any other gift it can be used rightly or wrongly, and it can also be trained and developed. It has its own peculiar dangers, and perhaps the greatest is the danger which is attached to any kind of power. Power fosters pride. 'All power corrupts, absolute power corrupts absolutely.' In dealing with individuals, Religious Superiors have more power perhaps than anyone else, and that lays a very great responsibility on us. We have such power to hurt, just as we have such power to help. There is only one possible attitude for those of us who are in authority and that is our Lord's attitude, *I am among you as He that serveth.* St Gregory the Great in his Pastoral Rule says, 'The very height of all ruling is the very height of humility.' That is why the Rule tells us that we must be beneath the feet of all.

"When we are in authority we naturally feel responsible for making things go smoothly and putting wrong things right. But I am learning more and more that one can't do this. One can't make turbulent people tranquil. One can't force the unreasonable to be reasonable. One can't remove difficulties and make all the rough places smooth. One seems to be able to do less and less. It is only God who can still the tempest and subdue the storm. Our part is to bear, and surely in the scale of eternal values our patience and our courage and endurance must carry more weight than a perfectly organized household. I think one of the most fruitful functions of a Superior is to bear, with love and patience and compassion.

"We shall never have perfectly organized and ideally staffed houses. I don't believe it would be good if we could. Our life has got to be one of faith, lived in complete dependence on God. But we have to make the best of such material as we have. We can't choose our Sisters. We have to use those God sends us. We have no others, for they are *all* sent to us by God. We must look for the best *in* them and make the best *of* them, and make each one feel wanted, needed, and used. It makes the whole difference to anyone if they feel they are really needed. We must trust them however fallible they may be and share all we can with them. Our Sisters ought to be able to feel sure of us, sure that they are always going to find us the same. Peace, poise, a bedrock certainty are great attributes to true motherhood.

"No matter how busy we may be, we must never give the impression that we can't be bothered. To be interrupted is part of a Superior's work. We must be approachable. Patient listening is a great part of our work. We *must* listen to what others have to say. They ought to be allowed to express their point of view even if we think it a mistaken one. We ought to be ready at least to consider their suggestions. It is in this sort of way that we can 'use' our Sisters as individuals and not just as workers.

"There are Sisters who have had many ups and downs in their Community life and are quite definitely awkward. They need our special sympathy and love. We must go on and on, burying the past and blotting it out, no matter how many times we may be disappointed by them. We must go on trying to trust, just as if the bad thing had never been. We must go on giving them encouragement after failure, hope in their depression, and go on loving them through it all.

"And there are a few who won't *be* helpful. It sometimes comes to the point where it seems we can do and say no more. We just have to leave them to go their own way—leave them to their own conscience and to God. But we must never despair of them as hopeless. Wonderful things do happen.

"We must always err on the side of gentleness and patience or we might become hard. But we must not confuse gentleness with weakness and indecision. St Francis de Sales said, 'Nothing is so strong as gentleness, nothing so loving and gentle as real strength.' The Sisters need firmness. It makes them feel safe. They need to know where they are with us. We can't supply for ourselves the right mixture of gentleness and severity found perfectly in our Lord. It is supernatural. There is no rule by which we can know just what to say and how to say it. But it will be given us, if we try to keep close to Him in our hearts all the time.

"If we err on the side of gentleness, then, if we have to

rebuke, our rebukes will have more force. They can bear fruit only if they are the outcome of love. In my own experience, the moment I am exasperated with anyone, even in my heart, I know I am useless.

"As regards our work—I have a slogan for Superiors: 'Take care of the Sisters and the work will take care of itself.' This may not be wholly true but there is truth in it. It is God's work first, and after that it is the Community's work for which we, at this particular time, happen to be responsible. We must always try to see the work as part of the whole of the Community's work. Always remember the Sisters are living a life, not doing a job.

"Sometimes it has been said to me that we should attract aspirants if we did this, that, or the other—put out a brochure, reconstruct our buildings. Perhaps we might. I don't know.

"But I *do* know this: The only true attractive power which draws to God is the power of love. In so far as each house is a place where Sisters truly love one another, it is a magnet. It is drawing to God that matters. Drawing to ourselves is quite secondary. *By this shall all men know that ye are My disciples, if ye have love one to another.* And in no other way.

"A house inevitably takes its tone from the Superior. And now, here we are, all gathered together. May it not be a real opportunity given us by God to renew our common aim to have *fervent charity* among ourselves? It means beginning within ourselves, first and foremost. If we *really* love our Sisters, the loveable and the unloveable, it will radiate through them to the whole house, and out beyond it. If the Sisters feel themselves loved they are happy. And there is nothing so winning as happiness.

"Only those who do not know, think of authority as promotion. It is a call to further sacrifice, and for this reason it is a privilege. Though you would agree with me that it brings great joy, does it not inevitably bring real suffering too? Yet, paradoxically, it has been said that graceful retirement from office is more difficult than all ruling. We must prepare ourselves for that. For unless we happen to die in harness we shall all come out of office one day. When the Warden took the Mothers' retreat he talked a lot about that. He said that God would give Superiors at the end a blessed chance to go back again to be ordinary religious, and that this epilogue would be the opportunity for the perfecting of ourselves. So when our time comes we must try to remember that.

"Don't think I attain to all I have tried to put before you. I do not. But I know it is what God is asking of me, just as I know it is what He is asking of each one of you."

RETROSPECT

• Celebrating the hundredth anniversary of its
work in the United States in 1974, the English-
founded Community of St John Baptist
asked two priests, James B Simpson and
Edward M Story, to write a brief history to
mark the centennial. The book was
expanded to trace the Order from its
founding in Clewer in 1852 to the
establishment of its present motherhouse at
Mendham, New Jersey, in 1916, all of it
chronicled in the context of the development
of the religious life in the Episcopal Church.

JAMES B SIMPSON and EDWARD M STORY

Stars in His Crown

The Mother Foundress of the Anglican Community of St John
Baptist at Clewer near Windsor was unwell. All through a "winter
of discontent" and for six years afterwards, the trials of her
daughters at home and overseas were offered up to God in her
petitions. In the evening of her life, her prayers were all that she
could give those near at hand or across the waters—and perhaps it
was her best gift of all.

The doctor's verdict in 1875 that she could no longer continue in active work was laid down while Mother Harriet was
resting at Whitby, that hilly town on the Yorkshire coast where
gulls scream constantly over the streets in contrast to the peaceful
ruins nearby of Whitby Abbey, built by another Mother Foundress,
St Hilda, more than a thousand years ago.

Continuing to live at Clewer would be too exhilarating, Mother Harriet feared, and might compromise her successor. The wisest solution seemed to be a move to a small house, the Hermitage, at Folkestone, on the Kentish coast not far from Dover and Canterbury. There were two CSJB houses in the vicinity; a Sister could always be spared to stay with her, and better still, she would be able to combine the quiet with some degree of participation in community life.

The move to the Hermitage was accomplished in the summer of 1876, and on August 7, then the Feast of the Holy Name of Jesus, the Archbishop of Canterbury came to bless it as "a place of retreat for prayer, praise, thanksgiving, intercession, and adoration." It was more than an official act for the archbishop, Archibald Campbell Tait, was an old friend of the husband of Mother Harriet's cousin. Mass was celebrated for Mother and her companion Sister and permission was given for it to be offered regularly.

Then, in the autumn, the companion and others noticed that the Mother Foundress's characteristic temperament and overflowing energy no longer seemed a frustration. It was a coming true of what she had once said in a letter to a friend that "the shadow of sickness and sorrow falls blessedly often in God's own work, doing more for His glory in the chastened conformity of man's will to God's will than could be accomplished by the most brilliant active service."

She had acknowledged that "hard lessons to learn are hid in God's teaching but the whole body is being perfected by the siftings and the fire that tries each soul, some more, some less, on their journey onward."

Even more profound words still are found on a worn slip of paper, frayed at the edges, on which is set forth in her own distinctive handwriting a personal intention that she made at her little altar on November 15, 1876, "In the Name of Jesus, pray that the active life of our Community may be strengthened and upheld, and the spiritual life deepened, by the prayers of those who in a life of retreat are withdrawn of God into deeper silence and solitude with Himself, that He may speak with them, as He has ever spoken with His chosen ones face to face as with a friend."

To these words she added a favorite saying about CSJB, "A little fountain became a river," and then a cherished text, "Whatsoever ye shall ask in My Name, that will I do, that the Father may be glorified in the Son." (John 14:13)

For the first three years after her retirement, Mother Harriet was able to attend the Eucharist at the parish church nearest the Hermitage. In the last four years she was completely helpless, unable to move from her chair or even to turn in bed without help.

In such a state she still kept up with events in the newspapers, and by dictating her letters she maintained a lively correspondence with many in the Community and beyond it.

All through those final years, and long since as a treasured legacy, the Sisters have kept a few lines that she wrote the year she gave up her duties as the Reverend Mother Superior of Clewer:

My Ideal of a Religious

The one great Aim of her life is the Glory of God.
The one great Example of her life is the Incarnate God.
The one great Devotion of her life is the Will of God.
The one great Longing of her life is Union with God.
The one great Reward of her life is the Vision of God.

• *Trevor Huddleston was born in 1913,
educated at Christ Church, Oxford, and
professed in Anglicanism's largest men's
order, the Community of the Resurrection,
in 1937. Missioned to South Africa and
Northern Rhodesia, he was consecrated Lord
Bishop of Masasi in 1960. Expelled for his
fight against apartheid, he later became a
suffragan in the Diocese of London as
Bishop of Stepney.*

TREVOR HUDDLESTON

Naught for Your Comfort

When fifteen years ago I stood before the High Altar in our great
and beautiful conventual church at Mirfield to make my vows, I
knew what I was doing. I knew amongst other things that the vow
of obedience, willingly and freely taken, would inevitably involve
not the surrender of freedom (as is so often supposed) but the
surrender of self-will. I knew that it would involve, someday,
somewhere, the taking up or the laying down of a task entrusted to
me by the Community, a task to be done not of myself alone, and
therefore not dependent upon my own desires or wishes. I knew
what I was doing. I was glad to do it. I am still glad, and thankful,
to have done it. For it is that vow of obedience which alone gives a
man the strength, when he most needs it, to die by parting from
what he loves. Nothing else could have torn me away from Africa
at this moment. And no other motive than a supernatural one
could be sufficient or strong enough to make sense of such a
parting. Indeed, I should feel I had failed lamentably in all that I

have tried to do if the parting were without tears. For it would mean that the work had been without love. So I have no complaints, no regrets (except for my failures and my sins), only a great thankfulness for the twelve years that are over and for the marvelous enrichment they have meant in my life.

—*On being recalled from South Africa*

• Educated and professed at the Dominican convent in Columbus, Ohio, Sister Maryanna was later a teacher at the Dominican Academy on New York's East Side.

SISTER MARYANNA

With Love and Laughter

Looking back gratefully over the past thirty years, I remember with a smile some of my fears on that August day so long ago when I said goodbye to family and friends and pretty clothes and Broadway musicals.

"You'll be buried alive," said my worldly self, echoing the warnings of relatives and friends.

"Oh, I don't know," countered my sense of humor. "After all, they stopped walling them up in the Middle Ages."

"You'll be terribly circumscribed in your actions. Listen, bounded by four walls, you'll simply die of monotony. Imagine doing the same thing every day year after year. And, for that matter, what *do* nuns do all day long?" my worldly self wanted to know.

"Wait and find out," I told myself.

I did.

Now it is August again as I sit here in a midtown convent in Manhattan, writing this chapter. . . .

Since it is the time of Profound Silence, I cannot use my typewriter, lest I disturb the recollection or the slumber of my Sisters or study for their final examinations tomorrow in science and mathematics at a nearby university.

I turn to papers on my desk where there is a letter from a Dominican colleague, holder of a research fellowship at the Marine Biological Laboratories in Woods Hole, Massachusetts. Beside her letter is one from an Ursuline Sister who tells me that she is teaching Scared Scripture in a college in the South but this, I think, must be a typographical error.

Featured in the church and secular press this week are a Franciscan Sister who is piloting a jet plane, a Benedictine who has written a weighty volume on the Indians of Argentina and Chile for the Smithsonian Institution, and a Maryknoll Sister who has been conducting a weekly television program with puppets of her own invention. None of these Sisters apparently is buried alive. Nor am I, though I have come uncomfortably close to it this summer.

Each morning the academy where I am staying has been invaded by a platoon of plasterers accompanied by a bevy of bricklayers. The building commission, bless them, has decided that certain fire precautions must be taken, so stairwells are being enclosed, archways bricked in, and sixty-three carved walnut and oak doors have been chopped out, to be replaced by fireproof ones. The red velvet is being removed from the walls of the chapel and the gold-leaf Renaissance ceiling in the foyer, designed and executed by an Italian artist, is being pierced by sprinklers. There are piles of Pyrobars in every hallway, bags of cement on each of the six floors, and a film of plaster over everything, including the Sisters. The once-beautiful school is beginning to resemble the bombed areas I saw in Britain. Mr Michael Friedsam, who built this mansion originally to house his famous art collection, is probably spinning like a pinwheel in his grave.

Yesterday one of the young bricklayers, watching me carry my typewriter from one temporary refuge to another, asked, "What are you writing, Sister?"

"A book on convent life," I told him, "but, believe me, it was never like this."

"Lady, you ain't seen nothin' yet!" one of his buddies shouted above the pounding. "It's gonna get a hundred times woise." Although I believe this, it is difficult to visualize.

I have no difficulty in transporting myself in imagination, however, to other and pleasanter scenes of the past thirty years. I remember another August when I stood on the snowy slopes of Mount Rainier in the Cascade Range and saw the mountain flowers pushing through the snow.

I can see again in memory the lacy, wrought-iron balconies of Lafayette Square in New Orleans, the steel-blue waters of the Great Lakes, the golden adobe churches strung like a rosary across New Mexico.

Here in the midnight stillness of my New York convent I can almost smell the clean emerald lawns of Christ Church College in Oxford, or the fresh water of the Stour at Canterbury, where the House of the Greyfriars is built like a bridge across the river whose rowboats glide beneath its arches.

I am back, in still another August, in St Dominic's Church on a hill in Fiesole where a Dutch priest, after hearing my confession, murmured humbly, "Please pardon my pure English."

The books piled high in my cell remind me of a far more beautiful Book, that of Kells, before which I stood entranced in Trinity College, Dublin.

Life in the convent has been far from monotonous or confining. I have prayed my Office on the Super Chief and the subway, in cathedrals and mission chapels, on mountaintops and islands. I have lived in mill towns, slums, and suburbs. Behind my convent walls I have spun stories for children at home and across the sea and written verses, some of which have been translated into Chinese. From convent gardens and roof gardens I have minted the gold of sunset into songs as a testament of beauty for the world.

If I have given the impression that the religious life is all sweetness and light, let me hasten here to rectify it. Into each life, as the poet said, some rain must fall, and the religious life is no exception. There are trials and heartaches, sufferings and disappointments here, as there are everywhere on earth, but somehow they tend to pale into insignificance beside the tremendous joy of living as the spouse of Christ under the same roof with the Blessed

Sacrament. Many times in the past three decades I have meditated upon the great trials and sufferings endured by people in the world, their struggle to make a living and to educate their children. Mothers, and sometimes fathers too, pour out their stories to us, asking for prayers or for guidance—and very sad stories some of them are. I have been especially touched by the plight of the aged and the ill who have no one to care for or shelter them. It is one of the earthly blessings of community life, part of the hundredfold promises by Christ, that the ill and the aged are cared for with lovingkindness. We do not have to worry about food or shelter or money, although our Superiors often must. Since we sought first the kingdom of God, all these things have indeed been added to us. All nuns are, I am sure, at times embarrassed by the honor paid them by good people for having given up so much, when actually they have received so much for their initial sacrifice.

As a student coming home on weekends from boarding school I was struck by the troubled expression of so many commuters whose faces in repose betrayed anxiety or suffering. Today a greater worry or even fear is evident on the faces of many of the people with whom we travel in the subway, although few go to the lengths of the wild-eyed man who yesterday leaned forward, touched the shoulder of the young nun who was my companion, blessed himself, and bolted out of the car. A magazine recently carried a poem by a nun about subway people with dreary, weary faces, riding around with the ground on their heads, all quite dead. The idea of the subway as a long coffin with its corpses sitting up, feigning life, may be a novel one, but it is scarcely true or kindly. These work-worn people who ride the "dark, dank tunnels" are, it seems to me, very much aware of the fact that there are other levels, both literal and symbolic, with light and air and laughter which they would be only too happy to attain.

Often the pressure of their daily lives is such that people in the world have neither the time nor the opportunity to avail themselves of such spiritual refreshment as, for example, the long retreat, mandatory in many religious communities. This is a period of great mental, physical, and spiritual relaxation, in the better sense of the word. In our community, for instance, the annual retreat is eight full days of silence, prayer, meditation, and rest, a time for auditing the soul's books, for talking things over with Christ, for planning ahead for the days to come. How greatly would the tired, frustrated man or woman, caught in the vortex of business and social obligations, benefit from a comparable stock-taking or spiritual oasis. While it is true that retreats for the laity are becoming more widely patronized, there are still many weary souls to whom they remain impossible or even unknown.

Thinking back to my youthful desires to study, to travel, to write, to act, I smile to think that even my dramatic ambitions have been fulfilled in the opportunity to write lyrics for and to act in the summer entertainments that are a pleasant part of community recreation. These productions, though they do not rival Broadway's, are sometimes historical, sometimes humorous, but always "smash hits" with their captive audience.

Yet it is primarily for these benefits, which I might have enjoyed in the world to an even greater extent, that I am glad to be a Sister. These activities, graciously permitted by God and my Superiors are, after all, "empty things of earth," and it is rather for the "things that are above" that I look up with a daily *"Deo gratias"*; the vowed life, the graces that I could have found nowhere else, the guidance, and the fellowship that has been mine as a Dominican Sister.

Looking back over my life in religion, I am forced to admit that they tell a very simple story. There are no great deeds, no heroic acts. Yet it is with deep gratitude that I survey my years that have given me so much more than I ever deemed possible. I am, after all, only one of thousands of women lovingly called "Sister" by those whom they serve. I would not guarantee the same experiences or reactions for everyone, since all our lives, even within the framework of the vows, have their individual differences. I could only promise that Sisters receive far more than they can ever give; I can only pray that after twenty, thirty, fifty years in the religious life, that others, too, can look back with love and laughter.

• *Formerly a chaplain to strictly enclosed Carmelite nuns, Father Joseph E Manton is the author of several books and now lives in retirement at the Redemptorist Monastery at Roxbury, Massachusetts.*

JOSEPH E MANTON

Jewel Within a Casket

I suppose there were the usual number of funerals that sunny May morning last year in Boston. But I am sure there was none like hers. Even the undertaker's men leaned forward with staring eyes and parted lips. Even the clergy, most of us anyway, had never seen anything quite like it.

The corpse was a Carmelite nun, and as she had lived for almost fifty years within those dark brick walls of the old Roxbury monastery, she would not leave them even now in death, but would be buried in body where for half a century she had been buried in spirit.

Though in the course of more than twenty years I had given her Holy Communion hundreds of times, her veil draped down to the lips, I found out her name only now, when no one would ever see her again. In religion that name was Sister Teresita, or little Teresa, a name of double glory in Carmelite history. In the world it had been Helen Dwight. Her father had been Dr Thomas Dwight, Parkman Professor of Anatomy at Harvard Medical School where the Catholic Club was called the Dwight Society in his honor.

But we didn't know this then. All we knew was that lying here in death was an obscure nun, her fingers like little white sticks that once flashed skillful needle and thimble as she stitched

99

some of the most gorgeous vestments that ever glowed against the marble altars of our majestic basilica.

This morning in the Carmelite private chapel the celebrant of the solemn funeral mass was wearing one such flowing cope of velvety black for the obsequies, as we priests formed a mournful circle round the casket. It lay on a kind of simple couch in the center of a tan linoleum floor. Incidentally, when you walked on the thin-worn pattern, every step squeaked poverty; not picturesque, romantic, idealistic poverty, but just plain need.

But yes, the casket—and did I say casket? Think rather of the manger of Bethlehem and you will come closer to the fact. We all knew that the Carmelite nuns, doing penance for a pleasure-loving world, never touched a morsel of meat and slept not on a Beautyform mattress but on hard penitential planks. But we had never dreamed that they carried austerity even into the grave.

But there it was, the casket. It looked as though some carpenter had hastily hammered together a plain narrow box, maybe twice as thick as a soapbox, but made from the same white wood, streaked with the same grain, and spotted with the same rough brown knots. This particular homemade coffin started out a bit wider at the head and tapered in toward the feet.

The Carpenter of Nazareth would have appreciated the workmanlike skill that went into Sister Teresita's box. There also went into it, till it was half filled, clean bristly straw, so that you could not help thinking of a Christmas crib. On either side hung two loops of clean white rope as handles for the pallbearers.

So there she lay on the fresh straw in the plain narrow box, garbed in the brown and white Carmelite habit of coarse wool, but on her head a frail wreath of tiny white roses and in her lifeless fingers a small wooden cross. Fingers and cross both fascinated, each in its own way. Carmelites forswear cosmetics even in death, so those fingers looked like shriveled white wax, and the cross was strange because it was only a cross and not a crucifix. In the Carmelite's cell there hangs a similar large cross, with no Christ hanging on it.

It is the awesome vocation of a Carmelite, by her fasts and

vigils and thorny mortifications and endless self-denial, to take the place of the Christ on the cross to suffer with Him, in penance for a pleasure-mad world.

While the requiem was being sung, the community of some eighteen or twenty nuns were kneeling on the flat floor (they do not even have kneeling benches), their black veils drooping completely over their faces and candles flickering in their hands.

Now the chanting stopped, and one of the Carmelites, I presume Mother Superior, flung back her veil, quietly rose, and approached the deceased. Out of the stiffly curved fingers she gently withdrew the cross and placed in its stead a simple and eloquent white flower, as if to say, "Your penance is over, your reward has begun." Then she took a simple white cloth and reverently laid it over the upturned, unseeing face. I thought she lingered then for the fraction of a second, a Carmelite's farewell.

After that the burial procession slowly moved out of the chapel. As the chanting line wound through the convent corridor and past the open windows, I looked out and saw a glimpse of what the world never sees. It was the lovely convent garden, bright with all the beauty of a golden day in spring. Your eye left the gorgeous blossoms for the stone pillars of the cloister walk and the red-tiled Spanish roof that stood out so bravely amid all the greenery. I thought how the nuns had dug and planted and pruned this stained-glass window of growing things.

But I also saw in this bright hidden garden a symbol. When I had met Carmelite nuns as patients in the hospital, they were the merriest people you could meet. Generally another nun, who is also a nurse, goes along as a companion, and their room always seems the happiest in the hospital. At the grille, too, when you could not see them but heard only bell-like voices, they seemed bubbling with joy.

That garden somehow explained how austerity, gilded with the grace of God, not only lights the tapers of happiness in the convent but throws the beams even into a wicked world.

Now we were marching down the stone stairs to the burial crypt. The great cellar felt cold and shadowy. It was whitewashed all around like a tomb in the New Testament. One wall stretched out as a long burial vault where perhaps fifty nuns had been laid away. On each square marble slab you could read the inscription of Sister Somebody, then her name as a young lady in the world, and finally the date of death. Nothing else, except that on one slab it said, "Foundress of the Carmel in Iceland." There were three or four empty oblong shelves, lined with red brick, still available, and our coffin came to a halt before one of them now.

Solemnly this "grave" was blessed, the holy water sprinkled into the long narrow opening, the fragrant incense swung, the last prayer sung, and the echoes hovered mournfully amid the candles. Then the undertaker's men carefully fitted a plain white board over the coffin box, lifted it silently into its waiting niche, and stood aside for a mason to seal the marble slab. It read, "Sister Teresita, alias Helen Dwight, May 31, 1962."

• Born in Erie, Pennsylvania, Joan Chittister
studied at Erie's Mount St Benedict Abbey,
joined the order, and eventually became
Prioress. She travels widely as a retreat
conductor.

SISTER JOAN CHITTISTER

Sister Says

I always say, it was a case of I came, I saw, they conquered.

I had been waiting to enter religious life from the time I was
three. So I waited patiently, and then I made my freshman-year
retreat, and they told me religious life was a good thing to do, and
then I made my sophomore-year retreat and they were just as
affirming. The retreat usually came around March, and my birth-
day is April 26. Our high school was in the motherhouse, same
building, under one roof. So when all the Sisters have disappeared,
because I don't want the Sisters to know, I go to what is commonly
called the bell system, and I look up the Prioress's number—which
does not take an awful lot of intelligence. The Prioress's number is
always one, and it never occurs to me that nobody ever rings the
Prioress's bell. I ring one, and the door opens across the hall, and
this little Mother Superior comes out, with a certain amount of
chagrin, trying to find out who rang her bell. And I whisper,
"Mother, I rang your bell." She looks over her glasses and says,
"You, my dear? Well, what can I do for you, child?" And I say,
"Mother, I'd like to enter. I'd like to enter the convent." And she
says, "Oh." And she looks at me long and hard, and she says,
"How old are you, dear?" And I say, "I'm 15, Mother." And she
says, "Well, that's very nice but nobody can enter the convent

until they are 16, so dear, you just come back at that time," and disappears.

So I wait, one year goes by, it's April 26, 1952. I go to the bell, I ring one, she comes out of her office—same look—and starts down the hall. I say, "Mother, I rang your bell," and she says, with a slight frown over her glasses, "And what would you like, dear?" And I say, "Mother, I'm 16." She says, "Pardon me?" "I said I'm 16." And she says, "Wonderful," and I say, "Mother, you told me to come back when I'm 16," and she says, "What for, dear?" and I say, "To enter." She says, "Oh yes, I remember you." So I say, "When can I come?" And she says, "I think we better go over here and talk." So she takes me in a little room and she talks to me a minute, and she says, "My dear, you are the only child your mother has and I really do not believe that we can take you. Your mother will need you someday." And I say, "But my mother is perfectly happy to let me go." And she says, "Well, dear, you don't know that." And I say, "I'll bring my mother tomorrow." So the next day, I show up with my mother who tells her that she has never known me in all these years not to do *exactly* what I said I was going to do. So they might as well take me, or at least do us all the favor of saying they weren't going to take me, because otherwise they had trouble on their hands, forever.

So at the age of 16, I entered. And that was it, it was just that simple. On September 8 I showed up at the convent door and, I think with a certain amount of consternation, they took me. The normal minimum age would have been 18. We had just about no one else who came at 16. Someplace along the line I must have picked up the gem of canonical wisdom that when you're 16 years old you can enter religious life. I was a sophomore in high school, and I thought I'd dated everybody in town. I entered the novitiate on September 8, and on October 16, I think it was, I got polio. And after that, it was kind of tough. The whole question was, Would they keep me? I didn't walk for four years. I was in a wheelchair and a long leg brace and an iron lung, and when I think back, the Community must have had just a terrible time trying to determine whether or not in conscience they could keep this kid that they weren't sure could ever really live the life and who would always be, at best, an exception. And they kept me. And I'll tell you people may look now and say, "What has happened to the Erie Pennsylvania Benedictines, have they gone crazy?" And I would say that if you had looked back at 1952 and seen how they dealt with the poor and disenfranchised then, in the person of Joan Chittister, you should have had fair warning about who this group was.

But what initially attracted me to them was that they were such loving people. And furthermore they were extremely prayerful people. When I went home at night, I used to walk out through the schoolyard and be able to hear the Divine Office being chanted and to this night the choral prayer of the Church has never ceased in this Community. There were two things in this Community that were never questioned during renewal, never came up in a *discussion*, although everything else was open for some kind of debate or a review. One was choral prayer and the other was the role of the Prioress.

Before Vatican II, there is no doubt that the spirituality espoused was the spirituality of selflessness that led to self-obliteration. Spirituality after Vatican II was also a spirituality of selflessness, whether the current Church realizes it or not, but it is a selflessness that stems from self-development. The spirituality before Vatican II was a spirituality of interchangeable parts—the Singer Sewing Machine Company could have done as well. Everybody in the Community was a potential fourth-grade teacher, everybody in the Community was a potential high school English teacher. What you did was send in warm bodies. After Vatican II, you began to ask, Who is this person, really? What gifts has she been given for the upbuilding of the Church? How can this Community affirm those gifts, and how can this person promote the charism of this Community? It's a different theological world view. Before Vatican II the emphasis was on a kind of conflict between the spirit and the flesh: duels, struggles with the flesh, that there are two separate things, that one is capable of sanctity and the other is not. After Vatican II you have a much more integrated world view, a much more incarnational world view. You're saying Jesus came enfleshed, and therefore all flesh is holy. Now all flesh has been redeemed and so *everything* speaks of the glory of God again, just as it did in the Garden, and *everything* must work for the coming of the reign of God, and everything does if you let it. Prior to Vatican II you had a religious life that was working *against* the flesh, to put it mildly, and after Vatican II you have a consciousness that the flesh is part of the Kingdom of God.

PORTRAITS

CARSLEY

• *When Monica Baldwin put pen to paper,*
she did so with consummate exactness and
humor, whether describing the treasures
of a sacristy, the characteristics of
other Sisters, or the gentle drama of a mouse's
brief life.

MONICA BALDWIN

Convent Scenes

CUSTRY COLORS

Linens and vestments were kept in a small, ancient room called the Custry. Here were long chests with deep drawers full of cottas and albs, each one folded according to custom, in the tiniest possible accordion pleats and then bound tightly—like a della Robbia bambino—with strappings of linen or tape. The snowy gossamer lawn out of which most of them were fashioned was lace-edged—priceless, historic lace, inducing sharp intakes of breath and wide eye-openings when shown to connoisseurs. And what masses of it. Cream, foam-color, ivory, linen-white, ghost-grey, or palest oyster—all the faint, indescribable quarter-tones between white and white that exist only in lace. Each piece had its pedigree. Most of it was well over a yard in depth.

On wide, sliding shelves, inside deep cupboards, vestments were laid full-length between dust-sheets and damp-proof paper to prevent the gold and silver embroidery from tarnishing. There was a set—complete with cope, chasuble, and dalmatics—of stiff, sprigged Jacobean silk. The enchanting colors—old rose, pale green, and pinkish lilac—made a delicate background to embroidery worked in skill to which the embroiderer's needle can attain. They might have been dipped in the heart of an opal. The whole thing was like a keyhole glimpse of heaven's glory, seen through a veil or iridescent mist.

Finally, there were the splendid copes worn for Vespers at Easter and Pentecost. Cloth-of-silver with a stupendous hood and jeweled orphreys; and one of embossed brocade whose magnificent lining suggested firelight glowing dimly behind claret-colored glass.

CONVENT WINDOWS

In convents, windows are such a subject of contention that it is practically impossible to touch one without getting your fingers burned.

Two parties exist in every religious community: the Fresh Air Fiends, who want the windows open, and the Fug Fiends, who want them shut. The odd thing is that, though the first are nearly always in the majority, it is the second who get their way.

It puzzled me when I came up from the Noviceship to the community. Why, since the lovers of fresh air were so numerous, didn't one of them just rise up and fling the windows wide?

The answer is that, in convents, things simply don't happen that way.

I remember one of the older nuns explaining this to me after I had suggested that certain measures should be taken in connection with window-opening. They were excellent measures, inspired by the most elementary rules of hygiene. And I was much surprised by the lack of enthusiasm with which they were always met. It was then that a certain nun, wise, elderly, and enormously kind-hearted, threw up her eyes to heaven at the crude inexperience revealed by my remarks, and said to me, "Ah, *mon enfant, croyez-moi:* if it were 'umanlee posseeble for those windows to be flung orpen, flung orpen they would be. *Mais—ca ne vaut pas la peine.*"

The old nun, in her long years of community life, made the most of many opportunities. A window-shutting fixation on the part of a certain "difficult member" had deprived her for years of the fresh air that she not only loved, but which was essential to her health. It also, now and again, made virtue arduous among the weaker members of the community.

One day the old nun said to me, "Ah, *chère petite*, you do not onnerstan'. "You t'ink *cette personne-là* a gret orbstacle to *la perfection de la communauté*. An' eet ees not so. She ees a cross, yes—*mais*, what is a cross? *C'est une petite gaterie de Notre-Seigneur.*"

As for '*cette personne-là*,' she insisted that, far from thinking her the curse of the community, she had come to look upon her as its greatest asset. For—*voyez-vous*—did she not provide her religious sisters with almost hourly opportunities of practicing virtue, with the excellent result that most of them were rapidly attaining to a standard of holiness which they might never otherwise have reached? *Enfin*, if *le bon Dieu* had not presented such a person to the community, it would be their duty—*mais oui*, absolutely their duty!—to "go out into the 'ighwez an' 'edges an' *chercher, chercher, chercher*, onteel won wass found!"

All of which only goes to show that, in convents, your success or failure in the matter of acquiring virtue depends entirely upon your point of view.

THE MOUSE AND THE CARDINAL

One day, when a Cardinal was paying a visit to the convent, the nuns, with the Prioress at their head, were just about to enter the choir after saying Grace. At that precise moment, a mother mouse, followed by a family of almost microscopic mouselings, appeared suddenly from nowhere and proceeded to trot, with an air of almost indescribable pomposity, into the choir. The spectacle of these minute creatures bustling along in single file was so comic and unexpected that the nuns paused until the absurd procession had gone by. When, however, I knelt down in my stall, I found that one of the mouselings had taken refuge there. It made no effort to move, so I picked it up and took it with me when I went to my cell. I fancy it must have been the runt of that particular litter, for it was quite the thinnest mouse I'd ever seen. It lay perfectly still in the palm of my hand and showed not the slightest desire to escape. I was just wondering what possible substitute I could find for mouse-milk on which to nourish it when, to my horror, I heard the "tings" sounding for me in the cloister below.

Mouse in hand, I went forth to be told that the Cardinal had sent for me. He had, it appeared, just met or was about to meet my uncle, who had recently become Prime Minister. And he wanted some detail about him corroborated.

As I couldn't think what on earth to do with the mouse, I took it with me. And I still remember the quiet interest with which the Cardinal examined it when I shepherded it very carefully through the grille into his hand. When it washed its minute whiskers with an infinitesimal paw, we both sat spellbound.

The Cardinal, as he returned it to me, said, "And to think that there are people who refuse to believe in the existence of God! How could anything so miraculously small and perfect have come into being unless it were the concept of an infinite Mind!"

I'm afraid that the excitement of that interview was too much for the mouse, because it died that same afternoon, still curled up in the palm of my hand.

Anyhow, it is nice to think that its last hours were spent in the exalted company of a Cardinal!

• Two American laymen have chronicled the
story of Dom Marie de Floris, Abbot of
En-Calcat in southwestern France, who
sheltered hundreds of hunted men and
women during World War II and in 1952
led twenty of his monks in establishing the
first Christian monastery in Moslem North
Africa.

PETER BEACH and WILLIAM DUNPHY

Benedictine and Moor

Dom Marie was perfect for the part of hiding refugees during World War II. It demanded the courage of a martyr and the skill of an actor, and he had both in abundance. An immensely self-possessed person, he never questioned his ability to outthink the Germans. The pose he assumed when he talked to his inquisitors was that of the monk too absorbed in monastic affairs to trouble himself with the unpleasantness going on outside. His native calm was interpreted as the cultivated otherworldliness of the monk. And quite aside from the tonsure and black Benedictine habit, his whole presence was that of one not even belonging to the twentieth century. His face seemed lifted from a tapestry. It was marvelously homely and medieval and mobile. His black eyes were deep set and his nose was short and blunt and had no dip in the bridge. Even his voice did not have a contemporary ring. It was deep and richly modulated, and he carried himself as if he came from another age, walking like a prince sure that every foot of ground he touched either belonged to him or should belong to him.

• A woman of many talents and towering spirituality, both an artist and a skilled administrator, Mother Maribel was the Superior General of the Community of St Mary the Virgin. Sister Janet writes from the Order's motherhouse in Wantage, England.

SISTER JANET

Mother Maribel of Wantage

Lying in the Vale of the White Horse, below the ancient Ridgeway which spans the northern edge of the Berkshire downs, the small market town of Wantage, birthplace of King Alfred, is the site of the motherhouse of the Church of England's largest sisterhood, the Community of St Mary the Virgin. Its old name, "the Home," is true in a very real sense. For here each Sister was "born," from here she was sent out to work in one or other of the Community's houses in England, India, or South Africa. She might be teaching in a school, working in a parish, caring for the aged or for the casualties of life of one kind or another, delinquent girls, un-married mothers, drink and drug addicts, or the mentally defec-tive, all in their different ways in need of understanding and love. Here too, she returned from her annual Retreat, for furlough if working abroad, or, in sickness or old age, to be cared for in the East Infirmary Wing.

"Must be one of them there Treats on up at the 'Ome," a neighbor once confided to another. "Them Sisters are pouring into the town like ink!"

It was in one of the outlying buildings that the artist-nun

Sister Maribel worked long hours in the years between the two world wars.

Tearfully, she had knocked on Mother Sophia's door to confess herself a failure as an art teacher. The Sister Superior of St Katharine's School had said she could do with her no longer as a member of the faculty and that she really must have someone who could "teach properly." Whether the ultimatum was in fact couched in quite such blunt terms, that was how, with a wry smile, its poor recipient always recounted it afterwards, but in any case, there was no doubt about Mother Sophia's prompt response.

"That is just as well, my dear," she said, patting her hand, "because I am not sending you back anyway. Your Christmas Bambino needs its mother and St Joseph, and I want you to make them."

And so, phoenix like, from the ashes of the rejected, dejected erstwhile teacher of art, rose a new and exciting hope.

Ever since the appearance of the first little Babe in the Convent Christmas Crib two years before, requests for Christmas figures had been coming in. Obviously if these orders were to be accepted, it would not be possible to model each separately. Molds would have to be made of one set, from which plaster casts could then be taken. But this would require a considerable outlay for which Sister Maribel, always diffident where she herself was concerned, was hesitant to ask.

Precisely at this juncture, providence stepped in in the unlikely guise of the Allied Insurance Company, which wrote to ask if Sister Maribel might be allowed to paint a portrait of Lord Rothschild for their Board Room, to replace one which nobody liked. She might, and she did; earning thereby not only the entire approval of the Board, but also a check for two hundred and fifty pounds for the Community. This must have been more than acceptable in those hard-up days, but Mother Sophia handed her fifty pounds of it, saying, "Now go and start on the Crib figures and get the materials you need."

So, beginning with the Baby, the Studio was born, and after that, as she remarked later, "like Topsy, 'guess it grow'd.' "

She set up her workshop in a small room, known as the annex, next door to the Church Embroidery room, where Sister Celia, her contemporary from Novitiate days, was one of its highly skilled workers.

Here, during the next few years, there came into being, first the Christmas figures, our Lady, and St Joseph kneeling by the low manger, with the great flank and head of the ox resting protectingly close to the sleeping Babe, the ass on the other side, and the three Shepherds, a small boy squatting reverently on his haunches, a strong young man bringing his lamb and kid, and another, old and blind, raising his hands and sightless eyes to heaven in thanksgiving. The Epiphany group followed, with the three splendid Kings, their attendants, and their camel, offering their gifts to the Child sitting shyly and a little overawed on his mother's lap, while St Joseph, called from his carpenter's bench, stands gravely watching.

There is a springlike, pristine quality about these figures which, though her later work grew in depth and power, Sister Maribel never surpassed. They reflect a spiritual springtime within herself that was bursting into flower, and she had no need, as have the travailing, often tortuous, artists of our darker, fogbound days, to search for symbols through which to express her inspiration. God's own symbol of the human body was enough for her, but, though she delighted in the ripple of sinew and muscle and the beauty of contour and bone formation, all were simply the vehicles of the spirit that came shining through them, as it shone through her.

A bevy of new Aspirants had arrived in the Novitiate that early autumn of 1921. One of them, something of an artist herself, homesick and miserable and wondering how soon she could run away, remembers, as a turning point in her early struggles, the day when a radiant young sister, prompted no doubt by the Novice Mistress' plaint that she had "a butterfly on a pin," appeared at the Novitiate door and invited her to come for a walk. On their return Sister Maribel took her into the Studio, where she gazed with delight upon the Epiphany group, still in the living clay, and felt that she was looking upon a new dawn of creation. That the "butterfly" not only revived but survived I have the best of reasons of knowing to be true. A few weeks later, to her great joy, she was called into help with the painting, when the clay originals had been cast in plaster by a firm of Italian craftsmen in London, and the "Christmas rush" was on to fulfil the many orders that had come in for sets of figures. Sister Maribel, with her passion for perfection in every detail, would allow of no shoddy, mass-produced work. Before painting, each newly cast plaster figure had to be gone over carefully with a tool and fine sandpaper to restore the cleanness of its lines that might have become blurred or roughened in the casting, a process known as "scratching and blowing," covering the worker with fine plaster dust, but ensuring for each figure the perfection of the original. Though she made full and trusting use of anyone with the slightest skill in her fingers, Sister Maribel always worked over the faces of the figures herself. They bore her unmistakable stamp, and each became a person, a character, in its own right. The coloring of the robes was never stereotyped. Full scope was always allowed for her helpers' inventiveness. If it was hard, exacting work, it was also tremendous fun.

However, Sister Maribel's boundless energies were by no means confined to the reproductions of the Crib figures. Responding to requests from different churches, she had modeled, during the same autumn of 1921, a seated Madonna, whose lips touch caressingly the upturned face of the Child on her lap. This was the largest figure that Sister Maribel had so far attempted, and the sheer weight and vulnerability of the clay made its transportation to London for casting too difficult and dangerous an undertaking to be contemplated.

Accordingly she and Sister Celia, deciding to do it themselves, ordered 150 pounds of gelatin and, while the Convent reeked with the smell thereof, boiled it down, made the mold, and took three casts with consummate success. One of these, packed in a large crate and accompanied by its watchful artificer, traveled by train to its destination in Plymouth.

The sculptor, Alec Miller, having seen some of her work, had written in appreciation of its "spirit and beauty" and "right feeling." So she turned to him now for advice, which he freely gave, as to methods, tools, and materials. She was preparing to carve, in Corsham stone for the Convent Chapel, the Madonna and Child which she had recently made in clay. "Remember," he told her, "that to carve in stone is not to copy the clay model, but to translate it into a new medium." She understood, and the difference in treatment between the two figures, though subtle, is marked. Alec Miller commended her on its "compactness," a great quality in her work, which he found "always delightful."

The architect, Ninian Comper, was, at that time, making certain alterations in Chapel, putting a baldachino and gilded pillars into the Sanctuary, and he apparently had made some criticism. Miller told her that she was not to be depressed.

"For Comper, no work is right unless it resembles that produced about 1350–1500. But traditions should be absorbed, not copied. So long as sculpture was a living art it changed. Since the eighteenth century it had known only revivals. Sometimes revivals of revivals. Keep to your own medium of expression. That is honesty, not heresy!"

She did.

It was while she was engrossed on this, her first essay in stone, that the news came of the sinking of the *Egypt*, after collision with a French trampboat in heavy fog off Brest, on the night of 20 May 1922, and that Sister Rhoda, who had sailed in her for India only the day before, had refused to take a place in one of the all too few and overcrowded boats, and had last been seen kneeling in prayer on the deck before the ship went down. So it came about that the statue was dedicated as her memorial, in a shrine at the West end of the Chapel, on All Saints' Day, that same year.

Orders came pouring in, not only for more and more sets of Crib figures, but also for fresh work. During the next twelve months, Sister Maribel carved in wood a statue of St Mary Magdalene for her old church in Munster Square, a large Christmas group for St Cyprian's, Clarence Gate, and also a crucifix for the convent garden, a strong six-foot figure which after fifty years, still mounts guard over the Community, living and departed, as it looks across the grass-covered graves to the Convent.

Quite suddenly came a new call. A war memorial was wanted for Rustenburg Church in the Transvaal, to take the form of a reredos and to be carved in marble. Because of the danger of breakage and the cost of freight for such heavy material, it seemed advisable, in this case too, for Mohammed to go to the Mountain, rather than the other way round. So, accordingly, on 28 December 1923, Sister Maribel sailed with three other Sisters for South Africa.

She was no sailor. She wrote home that "there were three stages of increasing despair. 1. I think I am going to die. 2. I hope I die soon. 3. I am horribly afraid I am going to live."

Happily, her "horrid" fears were realized; she recovered, and was soon amazing her Sisters by her enjoyment of second helpings with the best of them.

A disappointment was in store, however. For some reason a block of marble of the required size was unobtainable, and she had to content herself with modeling the three panels of the reredos in clay. The central one of these depicted the Crucifixion with Our Lady, St John, and St Mary Magdalene grouped around the Cross, while the side panels showed the watchers, the soldiers, and scribes. The casting process could only be done in Johannesburg, and she never forgot the day-long lorry drive there from Rustenburg, sitting hunched up beside the panels and keeping them damp with a watering can to prevent the clay from cracking in the blazing heat.

During the five months of her stay, she was kept hard at it to finish not only her main task, but also other requests that came in from churches in Johannesburg and Pietermarizburg, for Irene township, where Holy Cross, the Community's Mother House in South Africa, is situated. It was here that she stayed whenever she could.

Africa, that "land of far distances," vast, overarching skies and burning stars, and of friendly people, white and brown, won her heart, but because of those same people, also broke it. It was her first experience of apartheid. "They tell me I don't understand," she wrote. "I don't want to."

It was a sunburnt and glowing Sister Maribel, overjoyed to be home again, who returned on 22 May 1924. Then came a shock. In the church catalogue of a well-known and highly respectable London firm, appeared a quite unmistakable picture of her Christmas Bambino, which was being sold as their own. Clearly investigation was called for, and taking Bertie Herring with her for support and her original Baby as proof, Sister Maribel went up to London to make it.

Bertie, at this point, needs an introduction. His father was Convent carpenter and when, a few years earlier, Sister Maribel had asked the older Herring for a man with a two-handed saw to help her cut up a fallen lime tree into logs for subsequent carving when seasoned, he sent along Bertie, still in his teens, and they did the job together. When they had finished, Bertie burst out, "I do love your work. Do you think I could ever do it?" And so began a lifelong partnership. "The Firm of Maribel and Herring," they privately called themselves, though at that time neither could have foreseen its development.

Already young Herring had made himself useful in countless ways. He was keen to learn, and had all the natural aptitudes and instincts of a craftsman. Nothing could have pleased him more than to accompany her, as her private sleuth, on this expedition.

It transpired that the villains of the piece were the Italian casters who had pirated the Bambino, sold it to the firm in question, and then decamped. The shop manager who, in innocence and ignorance, had already sold two thousand of the little figures, was much distressed and immediately returned the few remaining ones, but warned her that, in future, all her work should be signed. Henceforward the initials CSMV became her trademark.

She and Bertie then searched London for the Italians' old workshop, where they retrieved the originals of the rest of the set, and Bertie broke up any molds he could find, so that they could not be used nefariously again.

This episode made abundantly clear the need for the Studio to be self-contained, if this kind of thing was not to be repeated. It must have its own caster. Bertie Herring, when approached, jumped at the offer of a few months' training under Mr Montecutelli, the great Italian caster of the day, who had cast many of the huge equestrian statues in Paris and in Rome and who was now working in London. He was as generous as his less reputable fellow-countrymen had been dishonest and was ready to take the young man on. Bertie proved an apt pupil, in whom Montecutelli's experienced eye detected the makings of a master craftsman.

Orders were pouring in for sets of the Crib figures, and over the following years young Herring must have cast hundreds, each cast turned out with the same meticulous care. After Sister Maribel and her small, fluctuating team of helpers had painted them, it was his job to see to the packing of them; thanks to his care, few, if any, were broken in transit.

But transport was a perennial difficulty, for travel by rail is always precarious. It so happened, on the rare occasion of a Sister dying away from home, that her body was brought down from London by road. Mother Isabel Mary, who, a few years before, had succeeded Mother Sophia in office, had an inspiration. She knew that there were some large figures which had to be got to London somehow, so, drawing Sister Maribel aside, she suggested that she should ask the men if they would take the cases up to town with them in the empty hearse on their return journey. They were only too pleased to oblige. Nothing could have been more convenient as to shape and size, and the seeds of an idea were sown. "So we prayed," Sister Maribel wrote later, "and lo! the father of one of our Novices offered us a Ford hearse for which he had no use. When I asked Mother Isabel Mary if we might accept, she laughed till she cried, and said that never before had she heard of anyone praying for a hearse and getting it! With the glass removed and three-ply wood substituted, 'Lizzie' did noble service as a van!"

Meanwhile, Sister Maribel turned to other tasks, including the first mahogany panel of her prolonged work on the Stations of the Cross, when quite suddenly, the whole course of her life was changed—election as Novice Mistress and Assistant General, 1931–1940, followed by a thirteen-year term as Mother General.

It was in that role, many years later, that she spoke of Bertie and their dual vocations. "If it had not been for him, it would not have been possible to spread far and wide the figures which were made solely to witness to the birth and life and death of our Lord Jesus Christ," she said. "It has been a silent mission work. Bertie and I made the figures and they spoke for us."

• *For her meditations on quietness and secluded tranquility, Sue Halpern visited several out-of-the-way locales, including the Trappist monastery in Kentucky where she stayed in the guest house and observed the monks from the balcony of the abbey church. A former Rhodes Scholar at Oxford, she writes for national magazines from her own secluded home in the Adirondack mountains of New York state.*

SUE HALPERN

Migrations in Solitude

Father Felix didn't read *The Seven Storey Mountain* until after he became a novice. He never made it all the way through another of Merton's popular works, *Seeds of Contemplation*. He became a monk not because of books but because he "kind of liked the thought of a life of prayer, where everything is arranged to allow you to live in prayer." The arrangement he is talking about is the seven offices. Seven times a day "you are pulled out of the busy-ness and given a fresh start, which permeates the whole day with a sense of values and a sense of presence." Monks at Gethsemani do four hours of manual or other non-spiritual work a day—in the bakery, in the fields (there are four hundred acres of farmland and a beef cattle herd), in the kitchen. For seventeen years, before becoming the retreat house chaplain, Father Felix worked in the infirmary, caring for sick and elderly monks. Labor, Silence, Prayer—day to day over forty years it has been pretty much the same. "It's a very good life," he says. "I'm lucky there is such a life." His faith, like his sincerity, is quiet. Not tentative—quiet. He doesn't say, "I believe this" or "I believe this and so should you." It is a faith so securely adhered to who he is that it *is* who he is—something on the order of Jung's "I don't believe, I know," where knowing is in fact being. When he says, "Basically we're a bunch of men living together... this is really a pretty normal way of life," it is possible to see past the celibacy and the silence and agree. Or to look at those squarely and agree. It is possible because he leaves *no doubt*—making your own theological misgivings seem petty and dim—that he is called to God.

- *Jim Bishop wrote of growing up as a police captain's son from Jersey City, of his years on the police beat for a Manhattan tabloid, the* Daily Mirror, *of his family and the Church. His abilities in drama and documentation are clearly seen in* The Day Christ Died *and* The Day Kennedy Was Shot. *Toward the end of his life he completed a biography entitled, appropriately,* The Bishop's Confession.

JIM BISHOP

Black Swans

The black swans of the classroom. They had neither feet nor legs. They floated silently, peering at students from behind white corrugations. The voices were clinical in detachment. Teaching nuns.

They were unpaid, bodiless creatures who mortgaged their souls in the task of taking heathens such as we and transmuting us into Christian gentlemen and ladies. They worked in miracles.

I attended a Roman Catholic primary school. It was a lesson in surviving fright. The teacher never had the time to exude love or compassion. The one she reserved for God, the second for the poor and the weak.

She was a cattle driver, a teacher, a judge, a passport to knowledge, the silent, lonely heart, the executioner. She seldom used a ruler to measure anything except the distance between a long overhand swing and a student's hand.

The difference between all of them was subtle. One was tall, like Agatha. Another was small, like Maria Alacoque. One was stout and red of face, like Alice Joseph. One was stately, like Helen Dolores. What they had in common was merciless devotion to teaching.

In retrospect I suggest that 30 percent of the time was given to discipline, 70 percent to studies. There were no hoodlums nor disorderly persons in class, because the slightest sound of movement, other than a cough, courted a birdlike attention, which presaged minor mayhem.

The youngest students were taught to be clean and composed. For the girls, this meant hair combed and ribboned, a starched dress or a skirt and blouse. For the boys it meant a jacket, shirt, and tie.

We were given pens and lined pads. We made endless circular tunnels on even lines. We executed slanted upright strokes. This was done to insure legible handwriting. It endured endlessly. We hated every moment of it.

There was no appeal. To be admonished, to be whacked with ruler or pointer was considered a matter of justice. Sometimes we ran home weeping.

There were two kinds of parents. Those who listened to the story and spanked the child for disobedience. And those who hurried to the teacher to complain. Sister Rose Patricia would explain the relationship between the laying on of hands and successful life to come. If that didn't work, she advised the parents to transfer the child to another school.

It became apparent in the third grade that there was nothing on earth powerful enough to stop the nuns from jamming lessons into our heads. We were going to learn to add and subtract small sums. We were going to learn to spell. We were going to understand that George Washington, with a ragtag army of undernourished farmers, did indeed accept the surrender of Lord Cornwallis at Yorktown. We were given to understand that, no matter how we turned in the class aisle, Canada was north, Mexico south, Europe to the east, and Asia to the west.

All they cared about were the fundamentals. We were taught

our prayers, our religion, about sin, tolerance for others, and punishment. We were doomed if we did this, touched that, stole a trinket, or disobeyed our parents. It was a no-win situation lasting eight years.

The black swans expected, when they dumped us out in the direction of the nearest high school, that we would lead our classes. We were their blotters. They had broken their lives and their hearts on us, and our future as physicians and attorneys and engineers occasioned no surprise.

And yet, in a shy way, we became their men and women. Later in life, some returned to class reunions to say hello. In the interim, the nuns became smaller, diffident, murmuring, "Oh, my, oh, my," when they saw the student's children.

They were always sure of their reward. It was at the end of a long road of faith. They believed when the rest of us were doubting. And if they feared for our safety, they prayed for us and didn't mention it.

I grew up to love one. God knows—and He may be the only one—how old she is. Sister Maria Alacoque. She taught me in the third grade. A note arrived from her yesterday. She and seven others were astounded that I had a career, a calling. "Jim," she writes, "do keep up the good work. I love your writings on Big John. He was wonderful."

Forget the religious aspects. By God, they were teachers.

• Born in New York City in 1931, Matthew
Bruccoli graduated from Yale and earned a
master's and doctorate at the University of
Virginia. He has been Professor of English
at the University of South Carolina since
1976. In addition to his biography of the
writer James Gould Cozzens, he has
published books of criticism on F Scott
Fitzgerald, Ernest Hemingway, and John
O'Hara.

MATTHEW JOSEPH BRUCCOLI

James Gould Cozzens: A Life Apart

During the summer of 1916 it was decided to send thirteen-year-old Jim Cozzens to boarding school, because, he suspected, his mother had found notes written to him by girls at the Staten Island Academy.

The Kent School in Connecticut recommended itself because it was High Church and because the fees were lower than for the better-known and older New England prep schools. Kent had been founded in 1906 by Frederick Herbert Sill. Born in 1874, he joined the Order of the Holy Cross, a celibate society of Episcopal monks, in 1900.

One of that legendary breed of headmasters whose schools were extensions of their personalities, Fr Sill established Kent "to provide at a minimum cost for boys of ability and character, who presumably upon graduation must be self-supporting, a combined academic and scientific course. Simplicity of life, self-reliance, and directness of purpose are to be especially encouraged." Located on the Housatonic River at the town of Kent, the school had some 160 students—or "fellows," as they referred to themselves.

Kent boasted of its self-government system but Fr Sill supervised every aspect of its life, and the enrollment was small enough for him to know every fellow. The familiar cry at Kent was "the old man's on a rampage!" At these times Pater—as he was known to students and faculty—would explode into anger and go through the buildings seeking malefactors. Despite his sometimes arbitrary or outrageous behavior, Fr Sill had an intuitive genius for knowing what was right for Kent. "He felt the feelings of a boy. He could accept as real the values of a boy. A boy's wants were obvious to him; a boy's intentions were readily forseeable." Cozzens later described him very carefully in the character of Dr Holt in a series of short stories about the Durham School, which was Kent.

"Dr Holt had a magnificent, solid, convex profile," he wrote. "The type is often small-boned, intellectual, but Dr Holt's face was like something outstanding and lordly cut from a cliff. His blue eyes, keen, haughty and wise, waited, ready to leap. His tangled blond eyebrows—these were a sandy, strong blond, and similar hairs grew out of his massive nostrils—resembled somehow the illustrations in the fourth-form Caesar, showing a cross section of the Gallic defenses—ditch, glacis, and a hedge of uprooted trees. Rather round-shouldered, he was not tall enough to have a hollow appearance. He was intensely solid; a considered, terrible energy. Also, he was slightly deaf. This seemed sometimes a stratagem, for whatever it was disastrous or expedient for him to hear, he heard. Involved explanations, trembling evasions, and artless falsehoods he could not hear. He roared for their repetition—a task beyond many a guilty conscience."

This was the man who dominated Jim Cozzens's days for six years at Kent.

Fr Sill endeavored to keep the fellows too busy to get into trouble. There was no social life off the school grounds, and permission was needed to cross the bridge into town. The religious atmosphere was strong but not overpowering. Attendance at chapel and Sunday services was mandatory, and Fr Sill heard voluntary confessions. There was a stream of visiting missionaries, bishops, and monks. Pater, who wore the white habit and plump wooden cross of his order, taught required classes in sacred studies. A favorite theme of his discourse was "Can Cosmos Have Chaos for Its Crown?"

Jim loved Kent in his own way; but he was not the familiar case of the old boy who loves his school for the rest of his life because he was happy and admired there. An indifferent scholar, he violated the rules and rejected the life of muscular Christianity— not because he was a natural rebel, but because his own values were the only ones that mattered to him. The prefects were authorized to administer corporal punishment in cases of incorrigible recalcitrance. Jim was paddled for reading indoors during a flu epidemic when Fr Sill had ordered the fellows to stay out in the fresh air.

Jim's first major crisis with Fr Sill came when he was 16, after a summer 1919 canoe trip on Lake George during which he read Thomas Paine's *The Age of Reason*. He returned to start his fourth-form year at Kent and informed Pater that he could no longer attend chapel because he did not believe in God. When Jim declined to discuss his loss of faith, Fr Sill roared, "Get out of this room! I'm sick of the sight of you! Report yourself on detention for a month. If you're absent from chapel, the prefects will take care of it. Get out of my sight!"

Jim did not return to the fold, although he conformed to Kent's religious practice and maintained a lifelong interest in the Church.

Years later, on June 21, 1930, the *Saturday Evening Post* published Jim's story, *Someday You'll Be Sorry*, recognizably about Kent and Fr Sill. It told of a very successful alumnus, once the target of the Headmaster's displeasure, accepting the invitation to speak at a fund-raising dinner, planning to use the occasion to tell off the Headmaster. When the moment comes, the speaker cannot betray the roomful of people who admire him. Instead of denouncing his old teacher he pledges a large sum of money. "It took a long time, but the account was squared." Old-boy Cozzens squared his own account with Fr Sill in the short stories—not by providing a characterization of the Headmaster at his roaring worst, but through revealing Kent at its best.

In 1978, widely acclaimed as a writer and pictured on the cover of *Time* but nonetheless widowed and ill with cancer, James Gould Cozzens confided to his journal that he had decided to wait a year before killing himself and added that "only subliminally I suspect the ghost of Fr Sill in the boy still in me will give me crap about 'Kent boys don't quit.' " He died less than four months later.

• As the son of a doctor and himself a
physican, Richard Selzer's essays often center
on medicine and the medical metaphor:
surgery as the red flower that blooms among
the leaves and thorns of the rest of medicine,
the heart as pure theater throbbing in its
cage as palpably as any nightingale, the liver
as that great maroon snail, liver patients as
wearers of the yellow livery of cirrhosis.

RICHARD SELZER

Hospital: A Meditation

My earliest recollections of a hospital were of St Mary's, in a town
in upstate New York. Actually, that was its nickname, short for St
Mary, Consoler of the Afflicted, or as my father liked to say (and
make me say), Maria Consolatrix Afflictorum. He was of the conservative branch of atheism, and insisted on the Latin. The year
was 1932. He was a general practitioner there during the Depression, and the whole town was, as Lyndon B Johnson might put it,
stone-sucking poor.

St Mary's Hospital was a three-story, red-brick building built
in the 1890s, a long rectangle with two pavilions, or wings, on
each side. Because it was operated and staffed by an order of nuns
called Sisters of Mercy, that building was winged in more ways
than one. It was situated halfway up the slope of a steep hill from
which you could look down over the town. Ever since, I have
thought that halfway up a hillside is just where a hospital belongs—
midway between a cathedral on the top and a jailhouse at the foot,
in touch with both the sacred and the profane. Whether it was

prophetic or simply a matter of logistics, the cemetery was right up the street. From the solarium on the second floor, you could watch the smoke from the crematorium chimney rise and diffuse over the city as the dead insisted upon mixing with the living. In summer, with the windows open, you could even catch a whiff—a compelling early lesson in death, resurrection, and ecology.

Now and then, my father would take me along when he made his rounds. I can still close my eyes and smell that blend of starch, candle wax, ashes, and roses that permeated the building. It is an odor I have not since recovered in a lifetime of hospitals; an odor of sanctity, I think. The nuns ran the place as if it were a flagship on the eve of a naval battle. That is to say, with military precision. Here, if nowhere else, cleanliness was next to godliness. The polished floors wore a fanatic gleam. Dirt was rooted out as if it were sin. If my years be Methuselan, I shall never forget Sister Michael's evening inspection of the long marble corridor. Behind her limped a wretched porter who had spent the day washing and waxing. I remember the stiff white wings of her cornet slicing the gloom, the crusader's curve of her nostrils, her eyes that reconnoitered every corner, then turned upon the miscreant with the glare of black olives as she pointed to a bit of smudge invisible to me. With the student nurses, she was equally exacting. Like that precise princess in the fairy tale, the one who was put out of sorts by a rose leaf out of place in the garden, just so did Sister Michael appear in the doorway of a ward, sniff once or twice, and go directly to the very bed where one corner of a sheet had not been tucked to ferocity.

The habit of the Sisters of Mercy was black and full, and it fell to within an inch and a half of the floor. From a cord about the waist a black rosary hung. The wimple was topped by a starched white cornet with a broad lateral flap on either side of the head. A nun alone was a sailboat; two, side by side, a regatta; three, a whole armada. These nuns did not walk; they skimmed; they hovered. Free of the drag of gravity by which the rest of us are rooted to the earth, they floated quickly and noiselessly, save for the soft click of wooden beads tossing among the folds of their

8

habits. With each step, the black nose of a shoe would peek from beneath the hem, then dart back inside the flaring recesses, as though each was sheltering a family of mice. More than once, in the springtime, I sat in the many-windowed solarium filled with vases of lilacs or peonies and gazed down the long hall in full expectation that the very next thing I would see coming toward me would be Maria Consolatrix Afflictorum Herself, to whom I would, Oh, Yes! I would hold out my own wounded heart. The reading material there was religious—variations on the catechism, news from missionaries.

As severe as Sister Michael was with the porter and the students, just so kindly did she move among the sick. The quality of mercy, before leaving the world of medicine, lingered among those nuns. How different they were from the doctors who stepped importantly among the puddles of patients. Especially the surgeons, each of whom was convinced that after he left the ward his disembodied radiance lingered on. My father was the Sisters' favorite. Their affection was based on his good-humored teasing, to which they responded with a commotion of cornets and rolling up of eyes. "Commercing with the skies," my father called it. With what wit and gallantry he returned to these laborious virgins a glimmer of their long-forsworn sexuality. When I was 12, my father lay dying in their hospital. Long before my eyes had had their fill of him I remember them grouped like lamps in the darkened room, his face greying, theirs glowing with an imperturbable golden light.

Years later, on vacations from college, I worked as an orderly at St Mary's; on my first night, I was told to wheel a stretcher quickly from the Emergency Room to the Operating Room. My charge was a young woman who, I was told, was hemorrhaging briskly. With one hand holding a bottle of saline aloft and the other pushing, I set off at a speed just short of reckless endangerment, only to find the single working elevator was in use. Minutes went by and still the elevator didn't come. I began to despair. From the head of the stretcher rose moan after moan to break the heart of Caligula. Was the red stain on the sheet spreading? A

Sister of Mercy arrived, also to wait for the elevator. At last I heard from the upper regions of the shaft the door slide shut, the gears engage, and the car set in motion. Like a sentry on the *qui vive* I prepared to storm and capture that elevator and rescue my first patient from death, only to watch the car pass without stopping. Its slow disappearance remains one of the most sickening events of my life. At the best of times, I do not exhibit a phlegmatic temperament. This was not the best of times. I ran at the door of the elevator. Again and again I kicked and pounded it, and I cursed it much as Jesus cursed the fig tree that bore no fruit. Damn elevator, I cried. May your cables rust, your gears be stripped, your door go unhinged so that never again shall you know the bliss of ascension or descent. To which the Sister of Mercy responded by reaching for her beads and beginning to pray. She hadn't gotten past bead one when the elevator appeared out of nowhere, and we all rose up to a happy ending.

That was the trouble with working at St Mary's. You were always at risk of having Maria Consolatrix Afflictorum called in for a second opinion. Which kept a permanent sheepish expression on the face of the heathen.

• V V Harrison *attended Sacred Heart
academies in Louisiana, Pennsylvania, and
New York City, and also studied at Sacred
Heart's Manhattanville College. She is a
freelance writer in Washington, DC.*

V V HARRISON

Changing Habits

Almost every child of the Sacred Heart had a favorite nun, especially at boarding school—one nun who stood apart from the others, with whom, although the rule did not permit, a special relationship developed. She was the one you looked for in the communion line each morning at Mass, the one you followed around and tried to find out things about—where she had lived and had gone to school, whether her hair had been curly or straight, if she had ever been in love or kissed a boy. She was the one you confided in when you thought you couldn't survive another day; and when you did something to displease her, your betrayal made you feel loathsome and unworthy. She mended your blazer when it was torn, laughed at your antics—often designed to catch her attention—and when she told you personal, private things you kept them proudly to yourself, savoring each one. For to know a little about a nun was to think you knew a lot, but the thing you were surest of, and the thing you were never allowed to say, was how much you loved her.

The nuns' past lives were closely guarded secrets, and there was much conjecture as to whether they had been born in the convent or had been forced there by an unspeakable act of treachery or tragedy. For some students it was unimaginable that the nuns had freely chosen to shut themselves off from all forms of pleasure, to wear a habit, to live lives of prayer and mortification, and to forever cut themselves off from the outside world. I was one of those. It was always a challenge to put the nuns through what we thought were subtle inquisitions to cull a few fragmented facts. In most instances our imaginations worked overtime to fill in the missing pieces, injecting drama and intrigue whenever possible. In retrospect, I am not sure which things Mother Daley told me about her past life and which I invented to satisfy my own illusions.

She was one of the many nuns we called Mother, who wrote RSCJ (Religieuse du Sacré Coeur de Jésus) after her name, who had renounced all worldly pleasures, who because she was cloistered would never go home again, eat in a restaurant, drive a car, or take a vacation, to whom we were instructed to say "Happy Christmas" instead of "Merry" and to close our letters "Your loving child," no matter how old we got.

When I first met Mother Margaret Daley in the fall of 1959, she wore the crisp, traditional Sacred Heart habit with fluted white bonnet and thin black veil. She exuded a comfortable confidence, skimming the polished corridors gracefully, floating like a hydrofoil on a lake. The long, black gathered skirt fit her trim figure perfectly, and the coif held mischievous hazel eyes and a broad, thin-lipped smile. If the Society of the Sacred Heart had a recruitment poster, Mother Daley could easily have been the model.

I fell under her spell the first time we talked together in a large linen closet on a top floor of the school, where as captain of the field hockey team I was doling out gym suits to the varsity squad. Mother Daley was supervising the procedure, chatting easily with us, punctuating sharp observations with laughter, good-naturedly joining the confusion of pairing each tunic with matching bloomers and belt. After the team had been properly outfitted and dispersed, I stayed behind with her to tidy up, confiding that my position as varsity goalie was a source of embarrassment because I had replaced the fattest girl in the school. She laughed and then posed a serious question, "What do you plan to do with your senior year?"

I closed the closet door and walked with her down the hall.

"Mother, you don't make any plans at this school," I replied with my usual dramatic flair. "Every hour of every day is mapped out in a book in Mother Tobin's office. The only difference between this place and Holmesburg [a nearby prison] is that we have to pay to go here and the food is worse."

She smiled, shook her head, and picked up speed, leaving me trailing behind. Midway down the corridor she stopped, twirled around on the heels of her black oxfords, and waited.

"You know," she said when I had caught up, "a lot of men in prison work hard to take advantage of the opportunities that come their way. The smart ones even come out with degrees sometimes. Think about it." Then she was off, leaving me to ponder her words and wonder if she had already gotten wind of my dismal academic record.

So it began, Mother Daley countering my flippant, sarcastic remarks, making her point, leaving me with the challenge, forcing me to *think*.

She had entered the Society of the Sacred Heart in September 1951, one year after her graduation from Manhattan College in New York City. She told me that, like St Madeleine Sophie, the foundress, she had wanted to be a nun even before she knew what a nun did. "I never had a choice about it," she said as we walked together at evening recreation.

"But how were you sure, Mother?" I asked, hoping she would elaborate. Instead she offered only one of her mystery smiles to reconfirm the obvious.

"I just knew, that's all."

That was all for the moment, but it was enough to keep me coming back to dig for more details.

More than other religious orders for women, the Society of the Sacred Heart filled its ranks with daughters of affluent, prominent Catholic families. It was a rare novice at Kenwood who had not completed four years of college. The girls who walked down the King's Highway (the corridor that connected the new novitiate building with the old and that for many became the symbolic passageway from the secular world to the cloister) were for the most part well traveled, well heeled, and gently bred. Many left mink coats, convertible cars, and trust funds behind when they entered the convent. There were some who were rumored to have left a trail of broken hearts as well. Naturally, I assumed Mother Daley was one of these.

"Sometimes I invited friends from the wrong side of the tracks home for dinner," Mother Daley once told me, as I pressed close to her side waiting for the next revelation. "My mother would be furious, but they were my friends, and where they lived had nothing to do with how I felt about them."

Of course, it had everything to do with how I felt about Mother Daley, who seemed to me as close to perfection as God intended any human. She told me she had once gone to a coming-out party and left when she discovered a group of girls looking at the labels in the guests' coats.

Often between classes we'd stand in the hall and spend a few minutes exchanging views on various school activities, and occasionally I'd give her something I had read or written as she glided by on her way to chapel or into the cloister. Almost every night I attempted to sneak past Mother Guerrieri, one of the nuns who patrolled the halls, in order to see Mother Daley in the dormitory down the corridor. I knew I was off limits and that the rule of silence was in effect, but Mother Daley usually smiled when she saw me, knowing that Mother Guerrieri would not be far behind to shoo me out.

"But Mother Guerrieri," I'd protest, "I am here on official business. I need to talk with Mother Daley." But Mother Guerrieri would have none of it and would silently beckon to me with her large index finger as Mother Daley darted behind the white-curtained cubicles where her charges were preparing for bed.

Like many of the younger nuns, Mother Daley had multiple duties, and like the children she watched over, she slept in a dormitory cubicle, with a white bedspread covering the iron bed and with a crucifix on the pillow. Often she was wakened in the night and rehabited herself to tend to a sick child or to check on a restless one. She rose at 5 A.M. every day to meditate, say her prayers, and prepare for the long day ahead.

Although she was never officially my teacher, Mother Daley taught me many things. She counseled me on what to read, introducing me to existentialism, Kierkegaard, Emily Dickinson, T S Eliot, and Antoine de Saint-Exupéry. As for religion, she advised me to "think calmly about God and not try to know Him all at once." When I returned from Christmas vacation with a book by Jean-Paul Sartre, whom she had not recommended, she did not confiscate it, as many others would have done, but left a note in my desk that said, "Please give God the same chance you give Sartre."

I watched her pray at morning Mass and envied her piety, which seemed so sure and constant beside my own religious doubts and proclivity to ridicule unquestioned faith. I could not help being impressed by the strong, visible example she set of uncompromising commitment to the unseen. For three years I remained mystified by, but admiring of, the pact between the nuns and their God, which appeared to produce not only visible tranquility but a peace of mind and heart that was inspiring to witness and impossible to ignore. Like many of the nuns, Mother Daley indeed wore, as Thomas Merton wrote, "the mild yoke of Christ's service."

Before her arrival, my interest in religious vocations had been heightened by my talks with Mother Tobin, the Mistress General, and with Mother Geraldine Hurley, who was for two years my dormitory mistress. Mother Hurley was a young nun who had not yet been to Rome to make her final vows and receive her cross and ring. Artistic, articulate, and amusing, she taught in the school and worked on her master's degree in philosophy. St Augustine was her hero and I was the thorn in her side. She was constantly pained by my slovenly housekeeping ways, so much so that when I returned for my senior year she had designed a card with a special message beautifully lettered in black italic script. It was perched on top of my bureau and remained there for the entire year. On the card was a quotation about *order* being essential to *life*. I pretended to be insulted, but in fact I was pleased that she had gone to such trouble to get her message across.

Mother Hurley was a wonderfully tolerant nun who was in the first stages of her love affair with God. We teased her constantly about *Him*, made up a song with lyrics that began, "Oh, Geraldine, you're a little bit like every nun I've ever seen,/ When you wandered into my room last night, you tried to give me an awful fright." She only smiled and shook her head.

When Reverend Mother Agnes Barry, sister of playwright Philip Barry, visited the school as Vicar General, I left a note inside one of my messy bureau drawers that read, "Dear Reverend Mother, don't judge a book by its cover." To my great disappointment Mother Hurley found it before Reverend Mother Barry did, and she called me out of study hall. "I should be very angry about that," she said, handing me the note, "but I am only disappointed that you were willing to jeopardize the effort this school has made to get ready for Reverend Mother Vicar's visit."

"That's why I did it," I confessed. "Under normal circumstances this place is run like a dictatorship, but when someone important is visiting, it turns into something even worse."

Mother Hurley smiled at me. "Have you ever thought about taking up the law?" she asked. Then she told me she would not report the note but advised me to try to use better judgment in the future.

"You'll have plenty of time to speak out against things you consider unjust in the world after you graduate," she said. "But Mother . . ." "Enough now," she said gently, "go back and try to concentrate on your homework." And I went back to study hall, not to study, but to write out a list of things I thought were inequitable about life at the Sacred Heart.

Sometimes, after the bell for lights out had rung, I would slip out into the corridor and ask Mother Hurley to let me help her wash down the bathroom floor.

"VV, go back to your room."

"But Mother, I can't sleep."

"All right, but only for five minutes."

"How did you know you wanted to be a nun, Mother?"

"How do people know they want to be doctors or nurses or soldiers?"

"Nobody wants to be a soldier, Mother."

"Read the life of General Patton."

"Is being in love with God like being in love with a real person? I mean a feeling, touching person."

"Do you ever think about wanting to be a nun, dear?"

"No, Mother. Do you ever think about not wanting to be one?"

"Five minutes is up. Now go to bed before we both get into trouble."

Then I would slink back into my room, silently slip between the cool sheets of my bed, and wonder how it was possible to live like Mothers Hurley, Daley, and Tobin, and appear to be so happy.

The night before my graduation, while my roommates packed their suitcases, joyously anticipating the next day's events, I sat on a windowsill outside Mother Daley's dormitory.

The outline of her white cap and silver cross was all I could see moving toward me in the darkness. It was then that I felt the surge of sadness I had sought during the previous days of preliminary graduation activities.

"I don't want to leave," I said quietly.

"That's only the way you feel tonight," she assured me. "It's the thing you have talked most about wanting this entire year."

I moved off the windowsill and we walked past the infirmary to the edge of the wide hallway that split into a double corridor.

"I think that you have grown in many ways these last months," she said. "From now on I think you will understand many of the things you have been worried about. Just remember, never be afraid to be the best you can be."

Before she could say any more, I threw my arms around her neck and sobbed. In that moment, all my reserve and the unwritten edict of never touching a nun vanished. I wished I could take her into the world with me, for I did not believe I could be the best I could be without her.

As we stood together, my tears dripped onto her habit, I felt none of the elation I expected to feel on my last night at school. All the anger and rebellion had disappeared into some foreign past from which I was momentarily removed. Mother Daley patted my back and I began to regain my composure. When I stepped away from her embrace, she squeezed my hands.

"We'll talk more tomorrow," she said, and for the last time I walked down the Holy Angels side of the split corridor toward my room.

The following morning, when I stood for the final time with my classmates, it was raining. There had been no opportunity for Mother Daley and me to resume our conversation, but what had been said was sufficient to shore me up for the remaining hours.

Clad identically in stiff white piqué dresses, laurel wreaths, and white gloves, we graduates filed into the chapel singing the Sacred Heart hymn: "Jesus be our King and Leader/Grant us in Thy toils a part,/ Are we not Thy chosen soldiers/ Children of Thy Sacred Heart." By the time we filed out again, clutching red leather folders that held the coveted diplomas, my friend Grace was crying and so was I.

"I don't know why I'm crying," she sobbed. "I hated this miserable place." And the irony of it all made us giggle.

Cars driven by brothers and fathers took turns parking in the circular driveway below the porch of the main building. Trunk tops slammed down in a series of crescendos. The rain had stopped, and beyond the lake there was a rainbow. My father pulled his station wagon up and removed his jacket before hauling my luggage into the back.

The nuns had gathered in clusters on the porch, their white handkerchiefs at the ready for waving goodbye. I ran up the stairs for a last round of farewells. Mothers Tobin, Hurley, Carmody, and others who had been such a significant part of my life at the

Sacred Heart embraced me and looked surprisingly pleased. When I reached Mother Daley she took my hand.

"I am ready to go now," I said.

"I never doubted it for a minute," she replied, and then she laughed and hugged me.

CAMEOS

• *Born in 1931 and a veteran of the Royal
Navy, Geoffrey Moorhouse writes for* The
Guardian *and other publications on wide-
ranging assignments, from cruising in a
Polaris submarine to climbing the
Matterhorn.*

GEOFFREY MOORHOUSE

Against All Reason

[The religious life] is so broad that it can have a Dominican
clambering into bed after a long evening's wrangle with university
students at about the same time that a convent of nuns is rising to
chant the night office. It contains both Benedictines living in the
priceless treasury of Kremamunster and Petits Freres subsisting in
the gaslit slums of Leeds as well as Spanish Carthusians to whom
the infallibility of the pope is still almost an article of faith and
French Protestants of Taize who have never believed this and to
whom it is not even a matter worth debating with Catholics any
more.

There is one element above all others, above the poverty, the
chastity, and the obedience which all profess, which spans it from
side to side and from end to end, which holds it together and gives
it a unity. It is as vital to the Capuchin friars who are bearded in
imitation of St Francis and Christ himself as it is to the Trappist
monks who are tonsured in a symbolic reference to the crown of
thorns. It is as central to the life of a Brigittine nun, whose habit
is grey, whose shoulders and face are framed in a white linen
wimple, whose head is veiled in black with a white linen crown in
the form of a cross with five red drops on it, as it is to a Daughter

of the Heart of Mary, who does not look like a nun at all because she dresses in ordinary clothes. One thing alone supports those who falter in the religious life and kindles fervor in those who live it confidently to the end of their days. That is prayer.

• *Whatever the desire for selflessness,*
strong individualistic devotion
still shines through in the lives of
the prominent and the humble in
every monastic household, as seen
in these excerpts from The Nun's
Story.

KATHRYN HULME

Three Graces

On Sister Margarita, Mistress of Postulants:
Gabrielle looked at the austerely beautiful face of Sister Margarita
and knew that she must be looking at *une Règle Vivante*, a Living
Rule, of whom it was said that if the Holy Rule of the Order were
ever destroyed or lost from the printed record, it could be recaptured
in entirety by studying such a perfect nun. Sister Margarita's
immense coif starched stiff as a shell and curving shell-like about
the ageless Flemish face turned, almost imperceptibly, as the
Mistress examined her new postulants. She spoke in a voice
exactly pitched to reach to the edge of the group and not a breath
beyond. She turned and opened, as though it were a soundless
panel of felt, a heavy oak door, and Gabrielle saw how one hand
dropped over the ring of keys hanging from her leather belt so they
would not clink together as she moved.

On the Reverend Mother Emmanuel:
She was tall and spare. Her plain face had a carved simplicity, like
an early Flemish primitive, but when she smiled, there was a
sudden beauty cast over the countenance that made you catch your

breath. She gave her exhortation in Flemish. For the farm girls, Gabrielle thought, and she knew how they must love the Reverend Mother for her robust accent in their native tongue. As Gabrielle listened she studied the woman who, during her religious life, had served as missionary in India, as teacher in Poland, as supervisor of the psychiatric institutions of the Order, including the home for uneducable idiot children which broke most nuns after a tour of duty there. She knew the Superior held degrees in philosophy, the humanities, and was a diplomaed nurse besides. Every six years when she visited the missions all the way from the Great Wall of China to the Himalayas, she could call every nun by name without prompting from the local Mothers Superior. She's not one woman, Gabrielle thought, she's a multitude of women. The Superior General's right hand, knife-thin and long, appeared from beneath her scapular. She made the sign of the cross over them, a compact gesture without any energy-wasting sweep, gave them her benediction in Latin and sat down.

On Sister Eudoxie, the Vestiaire:
Gabrielle had never before been inside the cavelike workroom where the old nun, known as the Cyclopean eye of the community, had spent the half-century of her cloistered life mending and altering the habits of nuns and supervising a large staff of novices and postulants who mended hospital linens. Save for the obligatory attendance at meals and devotions, Sister Eudoxie was seldom seen outside her silent workroom; she knew, nevertheless, nearly all there was to know about the private lives of her sisters. She could read in any garment she mended the total life of the one to whom it belonged and, sight unseen, could judge that nun's perfections and faults. A worn place on the back of a skirt hem told her that the wearer was careless about lifting her skirt from the rear when descending stairs, a thoughtless waste of good material which translated instantly into an imperfection against poverty. Sister Eudoxie personified the Holy Rule even more than the gracious living images of it embodied in the Superiors, and it was whispered along the young nuns that she had, in addition to

the rule, all its bylaws, bibliographies, and historical references bound into her venerable frame. The Vestiaire's eyes, sharp as the needles she threaded without aid of spectacles, looked up at her and seemed to penetrate her habit right down to the drawstrings of stockings and *serre-tete*, testing their tensions. For half a century in this same small corner of the immense convent world, this sister had been content to serve the Lord with her thimble, taking in the skirt bands of struggling young ones and letting them out years after when struggle reaches the equilibrium of adjustment that allows a little fat to gather at the waist. Up and down those overhead stairs whole generations of nuns have passed on their ways to schools and hospitals all over Belgium and beyond, to India, Africa, the Orient, and all that this great pageant of Christ's work being carried to the world has meant for this old nun has been an endless succession of wicker hampers filled with clothes to be mended. Then Gabrielle bowed and withdrew from the presence of the *monument historique*, a self-sacrifice so complete that it stunned her. As she closed the door behind her, she prayed God to give her a wider horizon for her own sacrifice to Him.

• A former nun, Mary Gilligan Wong's order is fictionalized as the Sisters of Blessing; she withdrew in 1968 after seven years in the community and is now a wife and mother with a career as a clinical psychologist.

MARY GILLIGAN WONG

Nun

Sister Helen Clarita was a legend in the order because of her extraordinary success as a boys' teacher.

"Herbert and Joseph I especially remember," she tells me. "I had them in the second grade, Joseph a rather quiet boy but Herbert a terror. Recently they came to see me. Both must be in their 50s now. Joseph was as shy and polite as always, but that Herbert was his old scoundrel self!"

After a while she asks me to hand her a glass of water and when I do, she sticks her finger into it and then pulls it out slowly. Thinking that her sharp mind is beginning to go at last, I am dismayed. More seriously than I've ever seen her, she says, "There, Sister, you see the effect my finger has on the water? That's about the effect a teacher, even a very good one, has on the lives of her pupils."

Some weeks afterward I am working in the infirmary the morning Sister Helen Clarita dies. Soon the word of her death will go out to all the Herberts and Josephs of her half-century of teaching, and they will fill the church to overflowing at her funeral.

When she opens her eyes just a crack she sees me kneeling at the door and beckons me to her side. A bony hand clasps mine one last time as a twitch of pain moves through her body. She opens her eyes and looks directly at mine. I am startled by the look of tranquility and peace I see there, and I bend close to hear her whispered legacy. "About the water, Sister: we can never change the world; we can only change ourselves."

A few minutes later I am again kneeling outside the door when the room is suddenly filled with a strange silence. Morning sun streams in at the window, and through swimming eyes I stare at a half-filled water glass that sits on Sister Helen Clarita's night table. In her graciousness my sister has taught me this one last lesson: that the surrender of death holds no terror for one who has been surrendering—changing herself, not the world—all her life.

- *Frequent, fervent prayer is central*
to each of the lives briefly glimpsed
in these sketches and miniatures that,
taken together, compose a broad canvas
of the religious life as it is
lived out in its farthest corners,
in many tasks and thoughts.

From *This Is My Beloved* by Mother Catherine Thomas

For the Religious it is her pleasure no longer to do her own will. It is her pleasure and joy to do the will of her Beloved. It is, or can be, that simple. A Carmelite nun should be, by the very nature of her vocation, a specialist in prayer. Or, to give it a more modern twist, she is a career woman in the field of prayer and contemplation.

From *Once There Was a Nun* by Mary McCarran with Ruth Montgomery

Speaking ever so gently, Mother Aloyese said, "The life you have entered is new and strange, but day by day as each new thing comes along, just remember that God is holding your hand, and He will show you the way. Obedience is your guiding star." She wrote those last few words on a small piece of paper, told me to keep it in my pocket, and added with a smile, "Those are pretty big pockets, aren't they, for such a little sister?"

From *Black Narcissus* by Rumer Godden

One of the most important things in Sister Briony's life were her keys. Waking, her life was bound by them, and sleeping, her thoughts were dogged by them and she had always the comfortable feeling of their weight by her side. She was never quite sure of them though, and if you saw her lips silently moving while her fingers were busy . . . you were never quite sure if she was saying her prayers or counting her keys.

From *Those Whom God Chooses* by Barbara and Grey Villet

"The true vocation starts to be settled on the day a girl looks back over the wall and sees a young woman her own age in pretty clothes wheeling a baby carriage past the convent," says the Mistress of Postulants for the Missionary Society of Mary. "Then her heart sinks, and she knows what it is that God is really asking of her. It's then she finds out if she has a true calling and the makings of a good Religious."

From *With Love and Laughter* by Sister Maryanna

I never tire of singing my own "Manhattan Magnificat." Often I look out of my sixth-floor window at midnight or an early hour of the morning at the squares of gold and topaz and I pray for all the worry-weary souls behind those windows—and the glad and happy ones, too. For there is a jauntiness in this sprawling metropolis. You hear it in the cheep of sparrows in the park, the laughter of children in playgrounds, the banter of taxi drivers lightly insulting other motorists, and it is truer than that which glitters in the night spots or theaters, where visitors so often seek it.

From *Sisters at the World's Fair* by Mort Young

The aged nuns struck out across the grounds, looking at the wonder of it all and seeming to passersby like gentle, tired birds whose wings no longer had the strength to lift them beyond the clouds. It was an illusion. It was only their hurt bodies that were earthbound.

From *Father Algy, SSF* by Robert Cecil Mortimer

This was a splendid life. Splendid in its obscurity and humility, splendid in its strength and charity, splendid in its achievements that are in the lives of men and women who are established in the faith and love of God and whereby he left upon society a deeper and more permanent mark than many of the acknowledged and great ones of our time.

From *Write the Vision Down* by Sister Louise Sharum

Sister Zita, a short little nun from Germany who never quite mastered English, often handed novices dish towels as she said, "Take me out and hang me up and let the vind blow me through." Another special nun, also from Germany, Sister Ferdinand, received a sales slip on which had been written, "Compliments of . . ." She replied indignantly, "I ordered no compliments, and I pay for no compliments."

From *Old Habits* by Joe Starkey

"Sister George!" said the young Sister. "Her, I remember. She played the organ well into her 70s. We still have the old one. If I ever win the lottery, I'm going to buy a new one in her memory." Sister George, I recalled, was a refined old woman who looked and sang like Hermione Gingold. "All togethah gayles," she would exhort the choir as she pounded and stomped away at an ancient organ whose innards snorted like the bellows of hell. (*New York Times*, 29 September 1991)

From *The Diary of an African Nun* by Alice Walker

The sight of a black nun strikes visitors' sentimentality, and as I am unalterably rooted in native ground, they consider me a work of primitive art, housed in magical color, the incarnation of civilization, antiheathenism and the fruit of a triumphing idea.... I am as I should be. *Gloria Deum. Gloria in excelsis Deo.*

From *Merton* by Monica Furlong

At Gethsemani the first news received of Thomas Merton's death was a cable from the American embassy. Dom Flavian summoned Brother Patrick Hart to his office and they waited for two hours for confirmation, hoping the whole thing might turn out to be a mistake. By noon they had learned that Merton was indeed dead in Bangkok. Dom Flavian announced the news to the community in the refectory. Ironically, one of the oldest fathers had come in to find a postcard from Merton awaiting him at table. The body was met at Louisville by Dom Flavian and a group of monks, and the casket was opened and the body identified. The remains arrived at Gethsemani early on the afternoon of December 17. Monks and friends chanted the funeral liturgy in the church, and he was buried at dusk in the monastic cemetery under a light snowfall. He had, after all, returned home in time for Christmas.

On the restoration of Leonardo da Vinci's 1498 refectory fresco *The Last Supper*

Imagine 500 friars eating 500 plates of steaming minestrone every night—that's pollution! (Gisberto Martelli, Superintendent of Monuments, Milan, in the *New York Times*, 20 August 1980)

FICTION

• *"It was a gift from God, a distilled
grammar of faith and practice, a treasure
great and always ready: he loved the taste of
the phrase in his mouth,"* writes Charles
Turner *of a priest's use of the Book of
Common Prayer that is the pattern for
Turner's simplicity of style. This excerpt
from his novel is based on Memphis' yellow
fever epidemic of 1878.*

CHARLES TURNER

The Celebrant

At the convent, too, the talk was of Memphis.

Sister Constance and Sister Thecla, who had been in Peeks-
kill for a rest in that summer of 1878, had hurriedly "thrown their
things together" and returned to the South two weeks ago, at the
first report of the fever.

"There was no stopping them," Mother Harriet said.

Now, on this Wednesday morning, the Eucharistic celebration
was over. It was the last of the morning walk. Ahead of Mother
Harriet and Fr Louis Schuyler went the covey of nuns, a wind
lapping at their habits.

"But I know you," Louis said. "You wouldn't have kept them
from their duty."

"I don't know. I think I was about to try. The danger is so
great, even for persons who are acclimated. I'm not convinced the
love of Christ demanded their scurrying off to that city of death."

Not a bird cried out. The hill was quiet, save for the breath of
wind.

Louis clasped his hands behind him. "You will see your children again."

"God knows," Mother Harriet said.

"Yes," Louis said. He felt somewhat reproved.

"And that's what it is—a city of death. I'm beginning to wonder if we shouldn't close the school there, for good. It's hopeless. Every summer is a fear."

Sister Catherine, the youngest of the nuns, had reached the house already and now was heading back along the path, sailing. She skirted the others and they turned with questions in their eyes. Louis saw the telegram in her hand.

"Mother," Sister Catherine said, presenting the envelope.

"What have we?" the Superior said. She sounded drained all of a sudden.

"Good news, I pray."

"And I," Louis said.

Mother Harriet opened the envelope and strolled away, off to herself, to the trees, to read the message. Sister Catherine stood with Louis. Some of the others had started for Mother Harriet, but they stopped short and honored her privacy. The Superior seemed to lose inches from her shoulders while she surrendered to the telegram. When she returned to the group, she managed her posture again.

"It is word from the Sisters in Memphis," she said. "It is not encouraging. The Reverend Dr Harris is seriously ill with yellow fever."

"The Dean?" Louis asked.

"The Dean."

Someone asked, "What about the Sisters?"

Mother Harriet said, "The Reverend Mr Parsons also has been stricken."

"No," Louis said.

"What about the Sisters?" another asked.

"They take no thought of themselves. I suspect that several are down."

Mother Harriet handed the telegram to Louis. He read it for

himself. The last line stabbed at him. *There is no other priest of our church in Memphis.*

"They are without the Sacrament," he said.

He found that he was alone.

Mother Harriet was on her way again, angling for the porch. She was in the lead now, hushed, and her wake was a rush of shadows. Louis read the last line again and then walked slowly with his thoughts. The Sisters in Memphis needed a priest. And they needed help. People were suffering, people were dying. He felt the Lord's hand upon him. It was as simple and as fixed as that.

Within days, Louis was in Memphis.

Upstairs, at the Sister-house, a bed dominated a room. The flattened occupant was asking, "Who is there?"

"My Sister, Father Schuyler is with us now," said Sister Clare, the nun who had come to greet him. "Father, our Sister Superior."

A hand, as if remembering its youth and health, roused from the bed-sheet. Louis moved in and took the fingers into his. The flame in the room was low and Sister Constance seemed to miss when she looked up for him. At the same time, but not at all because of the poor light, he was unable to find the Sister Constance he had met on several occasions. Why, she had been no more than 35 when they had first met, if that.

"O Lord, open thou our lips," he said.

"And our mouth shall show forth thy praise." Sister Constance was remarkably clear with the words.

"O Lord, make speed to save us," he said.

"O Lord, make haste to help us."

Never had the versicle and response been more apropos, he thought.

He thought it best to cut short the visit and was on his way to the stairs when, from a door down the hall, there burst toward him a nun bent on escape, delirious, and behind her came another nun, gaining on her, fetching her. "Thecla, Thecla—you *must* be quiet. Come back to bed now. Be a dear."

So that was Sister Thecla.

She cried, "I see the Lord!"

"No, Sister," her captor said, "that is only the young priest from the North."

Louis awoke at dawn, with an ache that ran the length of him. Had Dr Dalzell not given him charge of an early Eucharist, he would have dropped to the blankets again, regardless of the hard floor. The morning into which he was moving had a rigidity of its own.

The assemblage at the altar rail was like a depleted, linear army. There were but five mouths, and his own, for Bread and Wine. First in the row was Sister Ruth, her thanksgiving strained but recognizable. Next was Sister Clare, who wore her composure as a bride would wear white. Then there was Sister Frances, who simply looked hungry. "She tends the orphan asylum down the road," Sister Clare had informed him. Shoulder to shoulder the Sisters knelt. Down further was the Sisters' friend and helper, Mrs Bullock, whose hands told more of her life than her lips ever would. Behind the kneeling figures, the nave yawned emptily.

Sister Clare accompanied Louis on the rounds to the infirm ones. After communicating with the Dean, Louis went to Sister Constance. She had lasted the night—that was about all that could be said. Her responses were far away now. The situation in Sister Hughetta's room turned awkward and beyond help, with vomit preventing the Sacrament. Dealing with Sister Thecla was impossible too, for she was swatting at a dream of bats around her bed and would not be stilled.

He started back to the Cathedral. A sense of failure hounded him as he walked. The bell began to toll and he gave himself immediately to another sadness, one which was kinder by far. There was no question in his mind, Sister Constance was with her Bridegroom. Mud squashed between the boards in the street. On and on the death rang out through the watery morning.

Sister Clare let him in the Sister-house. She looked like a slapped little girl yet to deliver tears, and she was silent to everything he found himself saying. They stood at the foot of the stairs. She held to the newel. She directed toward him the sort of blankness she might have bestowed upon a forward stranger who had wandered in. The last peal faded, seemed to travel off above the trees, and Louis realized that he should lower his voice, maybe even forsake for the moment this business of trying to speak comfort. He wondered if he would ever feel expert at any of the duties to which God had put him.

Down the stairs came Dr Dalzell.

"You were here with her?" Louis asked him.

"God brought me here in time."

"I'm thankful of that."

Sister Clare got her voice to work. "Yes, the doctor read the commendatory prayer."

Now Sister Ruth was descending. "My sister, I'm useless," she said, "and so ashamed. Mrs Bullock is robing Sister in her habit and needs help. I'm sorry, it's a grace I don't have."

Sister Clare gathered herself and started up. At one point she turned to them and said, as though a tonic were taking effect, " 'Hosanna,' that was her last word, clear as could be."

Louis fed on the thought.

As for Dean Harris, he had dressed himself and was almost out of the room when Louis got there. One end of his collar was wild, erect at an angle in the back, and his coat hung loosely, making steep slopes of his shoulders.

Louis stood in the doorway.

"Not Constance," the Dean said.

"The Lord has taken her," Louis said.

"I saw her face at the first sound."

"It was only a matter of time."

"I must go to the others." With obvious determination, the Dean took a step.

"Back to bed for you, Father," Louis said, trying a new voice. "You are not fit. I am certain that Dr Dalzell would have you remain here and build your strength."

Moments went by with Louis unsure of what to say, and then he found that all he had to do was listen, for the Dean began to recount the worth of the woman who had died—what she had done with the school, how it had grown because of her. The Dean spoke hoarsely now, his debility seeming to intensify the emotion in his words. Everybody, according to him, had been touched by her radiance. She had led the girls in laughter with the same heart that she had led them in prayers. But that was not to suggest slackness, and he indicated how stern she was on occasion. Louis almost got a whiff of chalk and slate. The students having vanished before his arrival, this was the first time he had received a sense of the school as something that had a real life. For that matter, even though he had met her in New York when she was well, this perhaps was the first time he had glimpsed through to more than the *idea* of Sister Constance, to the material of the actual person.

"If I ever saw a woman," the Dean was saying, "whose will it was to do the will of God—"

Later that week, Sister Ruth called Louis out to see the sunset. He had finished the egg that was supper. They went out to the street for the view, where the trees were not a hindrance, where the way was straight to the fire.

"The glory of the Lord shall be revealed," Sister Ruth said, in awe.

"And to think we see darkly here," Louis said.

"It's only a matter of time for Sister Thecla."

Indeed, the time was short for Sister Thecla. When the hour came, a bell tolled in the distance behind them.

"I see the Lord!" Sister Thecla had cried that night in the upstairs hall. Now Louis heard her again. There were no arms to restrain her this time, there was no voice to deny the validity of her sight. And the turbulence of bats, against which she had fought when he tried to give her communion, had suddenly become a swarm of angels defining with motion the Perfect Stillness of the Throne of Heaven.

[The fever claimed four Sisters—Thecla, Ruth, Constance, and Frances—as well as Nannie Bullock and Father Schuyler plus twelve Roman Catholic priests and thirty-four religious.]

• Born in Sussex in 1907 and brought up in India, Mrs Rumer Haynes Dixon, known professionally as Rumer Godden, wrote most of Black Narcissus in a cabin she shared with her children while crossing the Atlantic in 1939. The story of Anglican nuns in the Himalayas, it has never gone out of print and in 1946 was made into a widely acclaimed film.

RUMER GODDEN

Black Narcissus

The Sisters had left Darjeeling in the last week of October. They had come to settle in the General's Palace at Mopu, which was now to be known as the Convent of St Faith.

Last year it had been called St Saviour's School; but when the Brotherhood left after only staying five months, it lapsed into "the Palace" again. The natives had never called it anything else; they had hardly noticed the Brothers except, when they met them out walking, to wonder how they grew such beards on their faces; their own chins were quite hairless though they had long pigtails, and they thought the Brothers must be very senseless to grow hair down their fronts instead of down their backs where it was needed to shield them from the sun. There had been only two pupils in the school; one was the General's nephew and the other the son of his cook.

The General had sent two men to show the Sisters the way, and Fr Roberts had lent them his interpreter clerk. Fr Roberts seemed very anxious about them altogether.

"What is he afraid of?" asked Sister Blanche. "I think these hills are lovely."

"He thinks we may be lonely."

"Lonely. When we're all together? How could we be?" But outside the town, they did seem a very small cavalcade as they rode away to the hills.

They rode on Bhotiya ponies that were small and thickset like barbs, and sat swaying in their saddles, their veils tucked under them. They looked very tall in their veils and topees, the animals very small and the grooms laughed out loud and said, "These are women like the snows, tall and white, overtopping everything."

One man said, "I think they're like a row of teeth. I can't see any difference between them and they'll eat into the countryside and want to know everything and after everything. I was peon at the Baptist Mission and I know."

"Oh no, they won't," said a very young groom. "I know all about them. These are real Jesus Christ ladies like the Convent ladies here. They only teach the women and children and that doesn't matter, does it?"

Sister Clodagh rode on in front with the clerk. It was easy to see that she had been on a horse before and the others watched her enviously as she sat, upright and easy, bending her head to talk to the clerk, sometimes half turning round to see if they were all following. They rode up one after the other along the path, but Sister Blanche's pony kept hurrying to push to the front and Sister Ruth screamed every time it came near her. She was terribly nervous; when her pony flicked an ear at a fly, she thought it was going to bolt and when it tucked its hoof up neatly over a stone, she cried out that it was going to kick; the grooms walked negligently along at the back, laughing and talking, their blankets over their shoulders. Hers was a bowlegged small man in a black fur hat and when she called out to him he smiled at her, but stayed exactly where he was.

Behind the grooms were the porters whom they had overtaken already, fifty or sixty of them, some carrying enormous loads; they were gradually left behind and the ponies and the laughing grooms went down and down, into the forest between the hills.

They spent the night in the Rest House at Goontu, a market village above the forest. There was a long market-ground of beaten earth with booths standing empty for the next market-day and hens like bantams wandering under their planked boards. The Rest House was a whitewashed bungalow with a red tin roof; as they came up to it, they heard the squawking of chickens being killed for their supper and the caretaker came up to salaam them with the chopper in his hand. There was a temple at Goontu and the bells rang persistently from sunset until the middle of the night; the clerk told the Sisters that they would hear them at Mopu.

"Are we nearly there then?" asked Sister Blanche.

"We have to go up there," said the clerk, pointing to the hill that shut off the North's sky above them, "and down a little, up again, higher and higher, and then down, down, down."

They stood in front of the Rest House, looking at the silent great hill they had to cross.

On the afternoon of the second day they rode through the last stretch of forest; they were aching and sore and stiff. All day they had been climbing up so steeply that they were slipping over their ponies' tails, or going down at such an angle that they could almost have fallen between their ears. Now Sister Blanche's pony walked in its place and the grooms had stopped their laughing; they hung on to the ponies' tails and had tied leaves round their foreheads to catch the sweat.

The nuns' heads nodded above the ponies, they rode in a shade of green dark sleep; the ponies' hooves sounded monotonously on the stones, their tails hung in the grooms' hands, too tired to twitch at the flies.

Then round the bend, almost on top of them, swept a party of horsemen; suddenly they were in a sea of manes and rearing heads and clatter and shouting; legs brushed theirs rudely and their ponies were buffeted and kicked. Sister Ruth screamed and a horse began a wild-pitched neighing. At last the grooms separated the ponies and helped the nuns down from their saddles, and the pandemonium died down. Sister Ruth looked as she might faint; she stared at the horses, her green eyes bright with fright, and her little groom stood beside her, patting his pony's neck, telling her not to be afraid. They all called reassuringly to her, but Sister Clodagh said briskly, "Come along Sister. It's over now. You weren't in any danger, you know; that pony's as steady as a donkey."

"How she loves to exaggerate," thought Sister Clodagh as she watched the horses, which were different from any she had seen. They had swept up the path and now the men could not get them to stand; they had galloped up the hill and still they swung and dodged as they tried to hold them. They were only ponies, like the Bhotiyas, white and nursery-dappled, but their nostrils were wider, their necks thicker, their tails more sweepingly curved, they were eager and powerful as they moved. "They are stallions you see," said the clerk. "The General has sent them to welcome you."

"They might have done it more tenderly," said Sister Clodagh. She had been in front and met their full force.

"They did not mean to do it so fast," said the clerk. "These horses gallop uphill. They are saying," he added ingratiatingly, "the men are saying, that the Lady-Sahib sits her horse like a man."

The General had sent tea and, as he knew very well how to please and excite Europeans, he had told his men to serve it in handleless wine cups made of soapstone.

Sister Ruth was positive they were jade. "Mutton-fat jade," she said. She always knew everything.

They sat on their saddles, which the men had taken off their ponies and put for them on the grass, drinking the General's tea and trying to eat his cakes, which were very elaborate and very dry. They were tired and the shade of the forest was greener and more pleasant than anything their eyes had seen for months; and, because outside the weather was sunny, the hill butterflies with wings like sulphur were flying through the forest and, where the yellow ones flew, the white ones followed. They seemed more beautiful than flowers to the nuns as they looked after them through the leaves; each sat with her thoughts round her like a cloak and after a while no one spoke; they were too tired.

Sister Briony sat on her saddle with her knees apart, her elbows on her knees; she was eating a cake with her handkerchief spread on her chest to catch the crumbs. She wondered pleasantly about the baggage and the porters who had straggled in so late the night before, poor things, and about their new quarters and particularly that Sister Clodagh had said that there were plenty of cupboards. Sister Briony had been chatelaine at many convents from Wanstead to Lahore, and she could have told you every detail of every cupboard in them and how many keys they each had. . . .

She was glad she was going with Sister Clodagh, quite apart from the cupboards. "If there's one person I do admire," said Sister Briony often, "it's Sister Clodagh. I have, really I have, a great admiration for her." She was the oldest Sister, but Sister Clodagh had passed her long ago; she could remember the brilliant little Clodagh, who had come all the way from Ireland, in her last years at school.

Sister Blanche was talking again. She was a chatterbox and dimples chased round her mouth like the butterflies through the wood; she was still pretty though her face was beginning to fade and she was not as plump as she had been, but the girls' name for her, Sister Honey, still suited her and they came to her like flies round a honey pot. Everyone was fond of sentimental Sister Honey.

"Why Sister Blanche?" Sister Clodagh had asked when she was given her list of names.

"Sister Honey?" said Mother Dorothea, the Mother Provincial. "I think you'll need Sister Honey. She's popular. You'll need to be popular."

Sister Clodagh said nothing to that—there was nothing to say—but she asked, "Why Sister Ruth?"

No one wanted Sister Ruth. She was an uncomfortable person. She was young and oddly noticeable, with high cheekbones and a narrow forehead and eyes that were green and brilliant with lashes that were so light and fine that they hardly showed;

they gave her a peculiarly intent look; and her teeth stuck out a little, which enhanced it. She had a way of talking that was quick and flickering and she seemed to hang upon your words, waiting for the moment when she could interrupt and talk again herself. She had come to them with a reputation for cleverness but in the Order they had many teachers, some of them with high qualifications like Sister Clodagh herself, and Sister Ruth found she was given only a junior teacher's work and she resented it.

"She's a problem," said Reverend Mother. "I'm afraid she'll be a problem for you. Of course, she hasn't been well and I think in a cooler climate and with a smaller community she'll be better, especially as she'll have to take responsibility. That's what she needs. That's my chief reason for sending her. Give her responsibility, Sister; she badly wants importance."

"That's what I feel, too," Sister Clodagh had answered. "She always wants to be important and to make herself felt." It seemed to her that there was an undesirable quality in Sister Ruth, something that showed in all her work, clever though it undeniably was. It was even in the dolls she had dressed for the Fete, that made the others look like clothes-pegs; she remembered the poise and smugness, the complete take-in of those dolls, and said, "Is it a good thing to let her feel important? I feel she should learn—"

"She's more easily led than driven," Reverend Mother cut her short. "Be careful of her. Spare her some of your own importance—if you can."

Sister Clodagh was startled. Reverend Mother was looking at her; her face was such a network of lines that it was hard to make out her expression, but for a moment Sister Clodagh thought that she was looking at her as if she were displeased with her and at the same time was sorry for her. *Sorry* for her.

Mother Dorothea was 81 and as dry and unexpected as snuff; her bones were small and exposed like a bat's and she weighed no more than a child of ten, but there was no one in the Order more feared and respected. Sister Clodagh had a tall and supple figure and her face was smooth and serene, with beautiful grey eyes. She had white hands and almond-shaped nails and a voice that was cold and sweet. She had just been made the youngest Sister Superior in the Order.

She asked, "Mother, are you sorry that I've been appointed to take charge at St Faith's?"

Mother Dorothea laid a hideous old hand on her arm. "Yes," she said. "I don't think you're ready for it and I think you'll be too lonely."

"Why should I be lonely? It will be the same for me as for the others."

"If I thought that, I shouldn't worry so much, but I'm afraid you won't let it be."

"I don't understand."

"What's good enough for us," said Mother Dorothea, "isn't quite good enough for you, is it?"

That was nasty. Mother Dorothea had said some very nasty things. "Remember a community isn't a class of girls. The Sisters won't be as easy to manage—nor to impress. If you want advice, and I hope you will want it . . ." "Don't despise your Sisters. You're a little inclined to do that . . ." "Remember the Superior of all is the servant of all . . ."

"You think I'm being nasty, don't you?" she said at the end. "I wish it were any use. Well, you're going and that's a fact. Don't be afraid to say that you want to come back, and don't forget to enjoy yourself."

That was an odd thing to say. She might have said almost anything else but that. They were going into the wilderness, to pioneer, to endure, to work; but surely not to enjoy themselves. She could not forget Mother Dorothea saying that.

Yet, now that they were close to it, she remembered again how much she had enjoyed that night she had spent in the Palace at Mopu when she had come up to inspect it with Sister Laura a month ago. She had not forgotten it since. It was extraordinary how she had remembered it; the feeling of the house and the strange thoughts she had when the General's agent, Mr Dean, showed them over it. It had reminded her of Ireland. Why, when it was entirely different? Was it the unaccustomed greenness, or the stillness of the house after the wind outside? Now, in the forest, she had a longing to feel that wind again.

She began to tell the Sisters again about Mopu. She told them about the Palace, that was only a ramshackle house facing the Himalayas; it had come as a direct answer to their prayers she said, an answer to their need. They all knew that their Order had no cool place to go to from the Plains; there was no room for them, as every hill station had its Convent; "—and this isn't only fortunate for us. The people must need us here. There isn't a school or a hospital, not even a doctor nearer than Goontu."

While she was speaking, it seemed to her that she was standing on the terrace at Mopu in the wind. She caught at that and dragged it in. "Sister Laura isn't with us today but she could tell you that, as we stood on the terrace and saw what you will presently see, we felt it was an inspiration to be there."

Sister Briony and Sister Honey listened with even their breath following hers, but Sister Phillippa smiled as if to herself and Sister Ruth said, "I wonder why the Brothers left so soon."

"How lucky we are," said Sister Honey, "to be going to such a beautiful place."

"But I should like to know," said Sister Ruth, "why the Brothers went away so soon."

Sister Clodagh frowned. She had asked Mr Dean that question herself and he had looked at her as if he were going to tell her, and then shrugged his shoulders and said, "The school wasn't a success."

"No? They have a very great reputation for their teaching."

He had not answered that, but he turned to her and said, "It's an impossible place to put a nunnery."

She said blandly, purposely not drawing him out, "Difficult, but surely not impossible. Nothing is impossible." She tried not to remember what he had said to that.

She told herself that it was because he did not want them there. That was true. She had felt it while he was showing them over the house and garden; apart from his rudeness, he was hostile as soon as they came inside the grounds, he and the old caretaker,

Angu Ayah. Usually Sister Clodagh did not notice servants very much, but that old woman had made an impression like an impact on her.

She picked up one of the wine cups from the tray. It was cold and thick and grey-green between her fingers. It had a rancid smell that they had noticed as they drank the tea, but she liked its shape and, in spite of its smell and coldness, she liked to hold it in her hand.

She looked at the men sitting and gossiping. One of them had taken off his crown of leaves and stuck a twig of them behind his ear; the green brought out the color of his cheek and it looked as if it would be warm to touch. How often had she touched Con's cheek and found it smooth and warm; like the feel of his fingers. His fingers used to play with her hair behind her ear. "Your hair's like honey and satin, Clo. Don't you ever cut it off." She shut her eyes. The knuckles of the hand that held the cup were stretched and white.

All last night at Goontu she had lain awake thinking that they should not have come. She should not have let them come. She had been sent to report on the house and advise on her Order's accepting or refusing the General's offer, and last night she had tossed and turned on the Rest House bed, thinking she had not reported quite truthfully. That uneasy conviction was with her still. Was it a conviction or only a dream? She did not want to answer that question and now Sister Ruth had asked, "Why did the Brothers leave so soon?"

The young groom stood up stretching and, taking out his leaves, he shook them carefully and gave them to Sister Phillippa. They had rough white flowers on them like daphne; Sister Phillippa was so surprised that she blushed.

Sister Clodagh put the cup down on the tray and rose, brushing her habit. "Now how did he know that you are the garden Sister?" she said.

The path led out from the forest and young plantations on to the bare hill where the light dazzled their eyes. They saw the great slope of hill and the valley and hills rising across the gulf to the clouds; then they saw what they had missed at first, because they had not looked so high. Across the North, the Himalayas were showing with the peak Kanchenjungha straight before them. They recognized Kanchenjungha but no one remarked on it; but as they stared, they and the hill they stood on seemed to dwindle.

The wind blew, the ponies shifted; a groom blew his nose on his fingers and still these strange white women sat staring at the snows.

"Kanchenjungha reminds me," said Sister Phillippa, "of the Chinese house god that always sits in front of the door." As she said it she looked over her shoulder. The others followed her gaze and, moving together, reined their ponies back on the path.

Under a deodar tree, solitary among the saplings, a man sat on the ground on a red deerskin spotted with white. The color of the skin and his hands and face and clothes blended with the color and twistings of the roots of the tree, so that it was easy to see why they had not noticed him before. By his robe and the wooden beads round his neck, they knew he was a Holy Man, a Sunnyasi; there, at the foot of the tree, was the platform of whitewashed earth and string of marigolds that marked his shrine. Among the roots was his bowl of polished wood and his staff, and against the tree leant a hut. He sat cross-legged and took as little notice of them as if they were flies; his head did not move, nor his eyes. In the teeth of the wind he seemed to have on nothing but his cloth robe, his arms and chest were bare and his head was shaved.

Sister Phillippa's voice seemed to ring on the air, and the clatter of the ponies' hooves and the creaking of their saddles. They felt curiously abashed and silently followed one another down the path.

• Ordinarily a novelist of the contemporary scene in which religious often figure, Brian Moore here turns his attention to Jesuit missionaries in the Canadian wilderness of the seventeenth century. His best-known book, centered in Belfast, is The Lonely Passion of Judith Hearne.

BRIAN MOORE

Black Robe

The mirror, oval in shape and encased in a wooden frame, had been dropped last year by one of the Savages' children whom he had taken as a pupil. Now it was cracked in a spider web of tiny sections, which split and altered his image as he moved in front of it. Reflected, the face which examined him from the web of slivered glass seemed the work of an indifferent caricaturist who had tinted his beard gray, enlarged and discolored his right eye, and drawn the left side of his face in a lopsided, lifeless manner, the mouth's corner turned up in a stiff rictus which parodied a grin.

He looked in the mirror through no motive of fear or hope, or even of disgust. He studied the left side of his face as his brain issued the simple commands of speech. It came, but he was not sure that the sounds could be comprehended. With his good right arm, he steadied himself on the makeshift crutch and then, with great care, dragged himself through to the second room of this longhouse, which he and Fr René Duval had partitioned off in sections to form the residence of the Jesuit mission of Ihonatiria of Canada.

177

The second room had been their kitchen and workroom and a classroom for the children they had taught. Now, its kettles and pans, its tables and rough benches seemed like exhibits in some museum of former times. Water which had leaked in under the loose doorjamb covered this part of the floor with a thin film of ice, making it necessary for him to hammer and crack it before he trusted his moribund body on its treacherous sheen. He moved to the large wooden chest in which the corn biscuit was stored. Each day he ate biscuit and drank water which was now bad-tasting, lying in a pail covered with a film of dead midges. He gave thanks before he ate, saying the words he had always said. When he had finished he sat for a long time, half listening for Joseph's footsteps. But Joseph, whom he had christened as the first of his converts— even Joseph no longer came. It was as Joseph had predicted. No one would come any more into this house. The village waited for his death.

Today, straining to hear sounds, he thought of former days when he had striven for silence. The residence had been built inside the palisades erected by the village to protect the community against enemies, but he had asked that it be placed as far as possible from the other dwellings. He had asked this so that he and Fr Duval would have quiet for their devotions and studies. He had not known until the fever came that, like so many of his requests, the Savages interpreted this as hostile behavior. The Savages distrusted privacy. In time of illness, noise and company were thought essential to drive out evil spirits. When the fever had first come upon him and then on Fr Duval, the villagers had crowded in with advice, beating drums and offering ritual cures. He turned them away and asked for silence. It was a fever of a sort he had known in France, a fever brought on by a sudden chill. After fourteen days he was rid of it, and Fr Duval, being younger and stronger, threw it off in half that time.

Then the fever spread. Unluckily, the first to die was a young woman who last year had refused their efforts to convert her. Her family said it was the Blackrobes' revenge. Since then more than thirty men, women, and children had caught it and perished. At first, the village did not believe the young woman's family, and he and Fr Duval had been welcome as they went about dispensing herbs and other simple medicament from their pharmacy. They were welcome because the Savages knew that they had thrown off the fever. No one else had done so. Therefore they must be sorcerers of strength. But at that time, he and Fr Duval, seeking to baptize those who were about to die, had said in all innocence that baptism would lead their souls to heaven. The Savages reacted with alarm. They had hoped that baptism would cure the fever. Now, they said, the Blackrobes did not promise a cure but performed an act which led to the sick person's death.

That decision on the part of the Savages caused a council meeting. It took place, he thought, on the week when he suffered his second and crippling stroke. But he could not be sure. No, it must have been later than that. Yes, he remembered clearly the day he heard drums outside the residence and, on going to ask the cause, found Fr Duval's body, his head split by an ax, thrown into the doorway. He had carried Fr Duval into the small chapel, which was partitioned off next to the kitchen. It was as he laid the body down before the altar that he fell and lost consciousness. And woke to the bad paralysis on his left side. How long ago was that? He was not sure. If the stench from the chapel was any guide, it was many weeks ago. The smell had been dreadful for a while, but now it was much less pungent. He had dragged himself into the chapel several times. The host was still in the tabernacle. Christ was present and watched over poor Fr Duval's remains.

On the day after his stroke, he had managed, with a make-shift crutch, to go outside the residence. All hid from him. He called out, asking for someone to come and help him bury his dead. But no one came. A week later, Taretandé, the leader of the village, came with the senior men to visit him and told him that the warrior who had killed Fr Duval had, next day, been stricken with the fever and had died. It was proof, Taretandé said, that the cure of the sickness lay in the Jesuits' hands. Taretandé asked him to forgive the village for the death of Fr Duval. As a sign of his forgiveness, they asked him to lift the fever. When he told them there was nothing to forgive and that the fever was the will of God, they withdrew at once. Later, Joseph, come to him under the cover of darkness, told him that the council had ordered that no one cross his path. It was said that he willed the death of the village but that their own sorcerers had stricken him with the falling sickness and soon he would die. Meantime, the people waited. In his death they saw their deliverance.

Now, when he had finished his biscuit, he felt for his crutch and cautiously propped himself up, preparing to make the difficult journey across the kitchen to the chapel. He did not enter the chapel but, as usual, sat himself down just outside the doorway. From there he would see the statuette of the Virgin, which sat in a niche to the left of the altar. He could also see the tabernacle. The squeaking sound below the altar was the sound of mice. He prayed, as every morning, for the soul of Fr Duval, a soul which did not need his prayers, he was sure, for Fr Duval must now sit at the right hand of God in heaven, the first martyr of the Ihonatiria mission.

When he had finished his prayers, he allowed himself to think of Paris. He had been born forty-four years before in the Rue St Jacques, and now the Seine, the Ile de la Cité, the markets of the Marais, the nave of the Church of St-Germain-des-Près where as a boy he had dedicated his life to God, the streets, the sounds, the hawkers, the feast-day processions all paraded once again across the retina of his mind. Sometimes he heard the music of Palestrina played on his mother's spinet. And sometimes he saw his father's body, covered in black velvet, carried high on a bier through the crowded gravestones of the Cemetery of the Innocents to be buried with pomp and circumstance in the place where his father's father lay. At other times, as in a dream, he saw a grave marker in the Order's cemetery at Rheims, a marker which bore his name and this year's date: *Fernand Jerome, SJ, 1591–1635*. The stone marker was worn with age and greened with moss. A certain peace entered his reverie when he looked on this marker, evidence that he had lived and died. For in this emptiness now that René Duval was dead, it was the aloneness of his fate which caused him, at night, to fall into a trembling as though his fever had returned. The Savages, once so noisy, were totally silent. Had they abandoned the village? Had they taken their dead and dying and moved to some other place? Perhaps he was surrounded by empty dwellings. Winter was at hand. Without a fire, he would perish of the cold.

But today, as he dozed in his accustomed place facing the small simple tabernacle on the altar which contained the body and blood of his Savior, he fancied that, in his reverie, someone called his name.

"Fr Jerome? Fr Jerome?"

It was a fancy, he was sure. The Savages did not use his French name. They called him Andehoua. But again, clearly, he seemed to hear it.

"Fr Jerome?"

Stumbling, he hoisted himself up on his crutch and, warning himself to patience, began the careful trajectory toward the doorway of the residence. Again he heard his name. And then the voice, in French, called, "Fr Duval? Are you there?"

On either side of Fr Laforgue the dwellings seemed deserted, but wisps of smoke from the openings in the roofs of the habitations warned him that he was being watched. Occasionally a dog ran up to sniff at him, and twice he saw children peering at him from the skin-covered doorways, before some hand plucked them inside. He had left his canoe at the landing place. Some twenty other canoes were beached there. He walked on. He had almost covered the entire area enclosed by the palisades when he saw, ahead, a longhouse, built like the others but with a wooden doorway and, on its roof, a small wooden cross. At once, approaching it in excitement, he called out, "Fr Jerome? Fr Jerome?" There was no answer. He quickened his pace, going up to the door, his heart hammering in anxiety, "Fr Jerome?"

He tried the latch. The doorway was not locked. Surely this must be the residence? He opened and peered in. "Fr Duval? Are you there?" Inside, he was met by a foul charnel-house smell which made him gag. In the darkness of the interior, there moved, unsteadily, a tall bulky figure. It spoke in a voice like the hollow echo in a sea cave. "Are you . . . ?" it said. "Are you there? Do I really see you?"

Taretandé and Sangwati were in the fields when the messenger arrived. "A Blackrobe has come. He wears a long cloak and carries *raquettes* on his back. He has been beaten and his right hand lacks a finger. He came alone in a canoe."

"Where is he now?"

"He walked through the village. No one greeted him. He called out in the Norman tongue and all hid from him. He went to the Blackrobe's longhouse. He entered. Then I came here."

"And Ondesson, where is Ondesson?"

"I think they went to hunt."

"Find him," Taretandé said. "We must call the council. Join us by the river in the meeting place."

When the messenger had gone, Taretandé looked at Sangwati. They were brothers, born of the same mother, and did not need to hide from each other.

"If another one has come, and alone, it is not natural," Taretandé said.

"They are sorcerers," said Sangwati.

"More than sorcerers, they are witches. They are not men but evil spirits."

"You were the one who said we should not kill Andehoua but let him be, as he is dying of the falling sickness."

"I know," said Taretandé. "Ondesson will hold it against me. He would have killed him as the other Blackrobe was killed. One hatchet stroke."

"But even if you had killed Andehoua," Sangwati said, "who's to say this other would not have come?"

"You are right," said Taretandé. "They are not men but evil spirits. What can we do against them?"

They had been working with ten other men and boys in the fields, but now they took their leave and went to join the council members in the meeting place. It was a clearing in the woods not far from the village. When Taretandé and his brother arrived, Ondesson and the seven other council members were already assembled. All had been told the news.

Ondesson was the war chief. In the past he had deferred to Taretandé, who was chief in council. But today it was as though Ondesson had prepared a war party and was ready to set out. As Taretandé and his brother entered the circle, Ondesson said, "There is one solution. Both Blackrobes must be killed."

"And how many days have you been alone?" Fr Laforgue asked, when the older priest had finished.

Fr Jerome did not answer. "First," he said, "you know what must be done."

"No, Father."

"The body is the temple of the Holy Ghost. That must be your first task."

"The body is in the chapel?" Fr Laforgue asked.

"Yes. By the altar. Those are now the remains of a martyr of the Church."

Fr Laforgue stared at the pale paralyzed face, the enlarged discolored eye, the heavy grey beard. He thought of a painting he had seen in the cathedral in Salamanca, a saint's face but with a look of madness.

"Day and night, I have wondered how I could inter his remains," the sick priest said. "So let that be your first task. Afterward, you must find the leaders of the village. You speak the Huron tongue?"

"Yes. Not as you do, but I have studied it for two years."

"We must speak with them once more. We must convince them that this fever is not our doing. The Savages are under the spell of their sorcerers. And the sorcerers speak against us. Now, go. You will find a shovel and an ax in the outer room. The floor of the chapel is of earth. We cannot have a coffin, but we can bury him in God's presence. When you have dug the grave and interred him, call me. I will say the prayers for the dead."

Fr Laforgue rose and went to the outer room. The stench was less overpowering there. He took a shovel and an ax and went into the chapel. As he crossed the threshold he made the sign of the cross and genuflected to the altar. As he rose from his knees he saw, sprawled beneath the tabernacle, the corpse of Fr Duval, an arm thrown out as in a grotesque gesture of welcome. The face was already in a state of putrescence.

He looked away, then forced himself to look again. This was, as Fr Jerome had said, the body of a Christian martyr. He saw the matted hair, the skull split by a hatchet, the dried blood and congealed fluids. Quickly, he picked a burial place and began to hack at the earthen floor. He threw off his cloak and unbuttoned his cassock and, in the dreadful stench, working like a man possessed, within an hour he had dug a rough trench, six feet long by three feet wide. He went to the corpse and, taking it by the heels, dragged it toward the grave. As he did, to his horror he saw the head, already split, come apart at the base of the skull as though it would separate into two halves. But then, with a lurch, he pulled the body into the trench. He stood, panting, and wiped his brow with the cuff of his robe. As he did, he heard a sound behind him.

A Savage watched him from the doorway. The Savage wore a long beaver cloak over a tunic and leggings of deerskin. His face was painted black on one side, red on the other, and his hair, elaborately arranged, was cut short on the one side and fell in a long braid on the other. Around his neck he wore a ruff of feathers, and bead bracelets decorated both of his arms. He carried no weapon.

"Come with me, sorcerer," the Savage said. "And be quiet." He spoke in the Huron tongue. He beckoned, and Fr Laforgue followed him out into the kitchen of the residence. There, Fr Jerome stood, tottering on his makeshift crutch. "Take his arm," the Savage said to Fr Laforgue. "Help him."

Fr Laforgue went to the sick priest's assistance and together, slowly, they made their way to the front door of the residence. The door was open, and outside they could see several Savage men, painted and wearing robes of ceremony. The Savage who had come to fetch them signaled to these men.

"He is Taretandé," Fr Jerome said, in French. "He is their leader."

The Savages at once surrounded the two priests. Drums began to beat. Men and women, children and dogs came suddenly from all the longhouses, in a din of noise and excitement. Yelling and screaming they marched with the priests toward the largest long-house, the place of assembly.

Fr Laforgue, half carrying the sick priest, made slow progress in the din. When they entered the longhouse, he felt the para-lyzed body sag and become almost a dead weight. He looked at Fr Jerome. The priest seemed to have fainted. "Fr Jerome?"

The sick man rallied and opened his eyes. In the uproar Fr Laforgue could not make out the words formed by the half-paralyzed mouth. He leaned toward the priest's lips and heard, "Did you—did you bury him?"

"It's begun," Fr Laforgue said. "I will finish later."

Ahead, a tall, heavily built Savage stood with three others, painted for war. All three carried heavy clubs.

"Ondesson," said the sick priest, nodding to this Savage. "Ondesson, we must speak together."

"Shut your hairy face," the Savage said, and laughed. "Are we all assembled?"

A roar went up from the crowd. People scrambled up on the sleeping platforms as though taking their seats at a performance. Fr Laforgue, remembering that other time of torture, in the long-house of the Iroquois, felt himself tense. Was this a parley, or was it what he feared?

"Come! You!" shouted Ondesson, beckoning to Taretandé, the council leader. "Tell them."

Taretandé bowed to the war leader, as though in thanks, then turned to face Fr Laforgue and Fr Jerome. "Fifty-three are dead," he said. "Men, women, children. Fifty-three you have killed, of our people. And every night more sicken and die. No one lives once this fever comes upon them. No one who is a man like other men." He pointed to Fr Jerome. "But *you* lived. You and the other witch. Both of you had the fever and lived." He turned to the crowd. "Today, I went into their longhouse. I went into that place, shut off, where they keep pieces of a corpse in a little box, a corpse they brought from France. And what did I find? This new one, this new witch who came alone to this place, was there, digging in the ground. And in the place where he dug, there were the guts and head and body of the one we killed. He was hiding him under the ground so that some new spell can be made."

There was a silence; then, suddenly, men and women began to moan and cry as in pain or terror.

"These are not men," Taretandé said. "They are witches. They must be killed as a witch is killed."

A roar went up. Fr Jerome raised his crutch, waving it as though asking permission to speak. As he did, Ondesson, the war chief, banged suddenly on the ground with his club. "They are men and they will die like men! We will caress them. We will take strips of their flesh, roast it on the flames and make them eat it. We will remove their fingers, one by one. We will cut out their hearts and give their bowels to the dogs. We will cut off their heads and their hands and their feet."

"Wait!" Fr Jerome managed, despite his hoarse paralyzed speech, to make the word sound clear above the din. At once, the yelling ceased. "You must not do this," the sick priest shouted. "If you do, God will punish you! Do you hear me? God will punish you!"

"Prepare the coals," said Ondesson. "We will start with the coals."

At that, the din began again, rising to pandemonium. Three women ran to the fires and scooped up hot coals on birch-bark platters. They presented the coals to Ondesson.

"Strip the prisoners," he commanded.

At that, two warriors ran up to the priests. As they began to pull at the cassocks, ripping the buttons, the light died in the longhouse as though someone had blown out a candle. All looked up at the openings in the roofs and saw a sky black as night. Inside, only the burning beds of coals dimly lit the faces and figures of those near to it. In the darkness, the crowd, like some panting animal, fell silent in dreadful unease.

Fr Laforgue turned to Fr Jerome. "What is happening?" he whispered.

"Come," said the sick priest, as, jacking his crutch under his armpit, he hobbled toward the doorway of the longhouse. In the dim light of the fires, faces moved away, letting them pass. They walked slowly out into the village street and looked up. And as they did, the eclipse moved, the sun gradually reappearing from behind its circle of blackness. "It is an act of God," Fr Jerome said hoarsely. "Our Lord has saved us. Blessed be Thy Name."

An eclipse of the sun, an act of God. Fr Laforgue, looking up as the light returned to the heavens, knew that, indeed, this must be God's hand. But somehow no words of thanks came to his mind, no prayer of gratitude passed his lips. Could this be, like thunder and lightning, an accident of nature, which had happened at this hour? Of course not. But still he felt no sense of miracle. He turned. The Savages were now pouring out of the longhouse, staring up at the sky. Fr Laforgue looked at Fr Jerome. The sick priest's discolored right eye was bright with a strange luminescence.

"Fr Laforgue," he said, "God has given us this grace, this opportunity. Now, we must use it for His glory."

"In what way, Father?"

"You will see," Fr Jerome said. He called out, "Ondesson? Taretandé?"

The leaders came forward, unease plain as speech on their faces.

"You have seen," the sick priest said. "God—our God—has warned you. How dare you try to injure us, who are God's servants? We are going back now to our house to bury our dead. You have seen the hand of God. You must change your ways. If you do not, we cannot help you. That is all I have to say." He turned to Fr Laforgue. "Come, Father, let us go back to the residence."

Fr Laforgue took his arm. Slowly, they moved away, the crutch hitting like a slow drumbeat as the sick priest hauled himself over stony ground. The Savages stood, looking to their leaders. After a few moments, Taretandé made a sign. The villagers began to disperse.

"*Deus qui inter apostolicos sacerdos familium tuum...*" Fr Jerome, his paralyzed bulk looming over the small altar, began to recite aloud the prayer for a priest deceased. As he spoke he looked down at Fr Duval's replacement, who knelt by the freshly covered grave. Soon the men of the village council would return. He knew what he would say to them. This would be his final task: to reap a great harvest of souls.

Fr Laforgue, listening to the Latin, stole a look at the sick man who recited the prayers. He thought of the rotting corpse beneath the ground and in his mind saw the skulls of saints long dead, venerated in sanctuaries as holy relics.

Is this the martyrdom, the glorious end I once desired with all my heart and all my soul? Why have I ceased to pray? What error has come upon me so that today, that eclipse of the sun seemed to me a phenomenon which, were I to believe in it as the hand of God, would have me in the same murk of superstition as the Savages themselves? I should ask Fr Jerome to hear my confession. I should tell him my doubts and ask for absolution. But if I do, this holy man who is close to death will know I am utterly unfit to take his place.

When night came, Fr Laforgue settled the ailing Jerome on his pallet and then, still sickened by the stench in the residence, went outside and stood looking at the Savage dwellings. He heard drumbeats and the cries of sorcerers, trying to drive out the evil spirits which they believed to be lodged in the bodies of the sick. Dogs barked. Above him the sky was clear and cold and filled with stars. The Savages have not yet come to kill us. If they do not come, then this will be my home. When Fr Jerome dies I will be in charge here, my life's work to convert these Savages now dying of a fever against which they have no defense. The Savages will not come to kill me. God did not choose me to be a martyr. He knows I am unworthy of that fate.

• A *biographer and a short story writer,*
noted for his spare prose, Ron Hansen
teaches at the University of California at
Santa Cruz.

RON HANSEN

Mariette in Ecstasy

In the priest's house, four books are on the kitchen table, a dish
towel hides his typewriter, the tea kettle warbles and trills on the
iron stove until Père Marriott hoists it off. "We are having English
tea," he says. "You'll have to take milk with it; that's the English
part." Looking over his shoulder, he says, "You may sit."

She does. She inhales and her faintness passes. She touches
the books and tilts her head to read their spines. Each is in
French: *Annales de médicine universelle, Autobiographie d'une hysté-*
rique possédée, book two of *Esprit des saintes illustres,* and one
volume of *La stigmatisation, l'estase divine, les miracles de Lourdes,*
response aux libres penseurs.

The priest slides a tarnished spoon and frail teacup and saucer
toward Mariette before sighing and falling into a hard wooden
chair. With horror he says, "I have forgotten the sugar!"

"Oh, don't get it for me."

"Sister Dominique has favored us with a bowl of *kiss* pudding.
Have you heard of that, kiss pudding?"

"Coconut sprinkled on top?"

"Exactly! Like snowflakes."

She smiles and sips just a bit of her orange pekoe tea.

"Well," the priest says. "Isn't this pleasant?"

"Yes."

He clinks his spoon around his teacup and then stains his folded napkin tan with it. She can see a freakish reflection of him in the shine of his spoon's silver bowl. Wood in the stove is whistling. Père Marriott finally says, "Your health is fine?"

She smiles. "Except for the holes in my hands and feet."

He blushes and then shades into humorlessness, broodingly turning his teacup with his thumbs. "I have some more questions I'll have to ask you."

Mariette says nothing. She holds the hurt in her hands like a kitten.

"Surely you were expecting that."

"Yes," he says, and grins uneasily, showing grey teeth that are slightly twisted and crossed. "Well, let me begin there, Mariette. You see, I hunted these books in the scriptorium and when I took them out I heard from Sister Marguerite that she's seen you reading these same four books. She quite frankly finds that perplexing. I have an explanation but I would prefer, of course, to hear yours."

"I have had forebodings about it."

"You have had premonitions?"

"I heard his voice."

Père Marriott stares at her for a moment and moves on. "Well, yes. Was there anything, uh, physical?"

"Itching and burning in my hands and feet."

"And then quite suddenly the bleeding?"

"Yes." She thinks of her father bluntly talking of human biology as the dinner plates were cleared. She remembers how his hard white shirt cuffs would often be brownly spotted with some patient's blood.

"You aren't taking your tea, Mariette."

"I haven't been drinking much lately."

"Are you hungry? Would you like some kiss pudding?"

"Everything's fine."

"Excellent," he says, and scratches whiskers under his jaw as he thinks. "Wasn't it surprising that this happened at Christmas?"

"No."

"Explain, please."

"We celebrate the Word being made incarnate then."

"But it is such a joyful day!"

"We give gifts to our family and friends. And these are God's gifts to me."

He hooks his spectacles over his ears and hunts his book stack until he finds one that he handles like a connoisseur, admiring its green leather binding and the gossamer feel of its pages. At last he tilts his nose down and stares over his brass wire rims to ask, "Are you acquainted enough with the books you and I have read, Mariette, to say you have acquired the wounds that have been called the stigmata?"

"Agreeing would make me seem grandiose."

"Even so, you must be quite proud to be in the company of Saint Francis of Assisi, Saint Catherine of Siena, Saint Rita, and so many other holy people."

"Everything is his doing. I have nothing to do with it."

"And yet I still wonder how you feel about it."

She looks just to the right of him in seeking an answer. She holds her stare on a dulled housefly blundering at a frosted window, but she is all inwardness and certainty. "Worried," she says. "Humbled. Embarrassed. I truly don't understand it."

The priest smiles. "We don't have to understand what God is doing for God to be able to do it." Père Marriott deliberately resettles his teacup in the saucer. "You have been given those things which theologians call *gratiae gratis datoe*, or favors freely bestowed by God. We do not earn or warrant them. The Church cannot say that you are *saintly* because of these injuries any more than she would hazard to say that Sister Saint-Pierre, for example, is unholy because she is without them. In history, you see, these wounds have been found in some very unworthy people. And it is often hard to tell whether these things are not just illusions brought on by abnormal sensibilities and neurosis. You see how it follows? Hmm? Have I made myself understood?"

"Yes."

"I have so many questions, though."

"Me too."

"We know, for example, that Christ's crucifixion happened in just one way, and yet history tells us that the five wounds appear differently both in size and location in the hundreds of people who have been given them. You have not been given the crown of thorns, for example, nor the forty lashes. And why is that? Is the human personality one component of the mystery? We don't know. And why are there so many women and so few men? And how is it that the great contemplative orders, the Carthusians, the Trappists, the Benedictines, have practically no examples of the phenomena? The Church and medicine are both silent."

Sister Anne knocks twice at the door while opening it to slap the priest's mail onto a shaker table. She gives Mariette a fraught look and says, "Oh, forgive me," and the old priest gazes without forgiveness until she finally goes.

"And so," he says, "I have another question. You are praying hard, so hard, and you are hearing God inside your head perhaps. We'll say you are in ecstasy. Will you please tell how it is for you at that point?"

Evasively she travels her fingers over four or five water rings that have stained the oaken table. She then stands with her feet flat on the floor and walks without hurt or hindrance to a half-curtained window framing soft white pastures and flesh-pale skies and pinkish trees without hunters in them.

"In prayer I float out of myself. I seek God with a great yearning, like an orphan child pursuing her true mother. I have lost my body; I don't know where I am or even if I am now human or spirit. A sweet power is drawing me, a great and beautiful force that is effortless but insistent. I flush with excitement and a balm of tenderness seems to flow over me. And when I have gotten to a fullness of joy and peace and tranquility, then I know I have been possessed by Jesus and have completely lost myself in him. Oh, what a blissful abandonment it is! Everything in my being tells me to stay there. Every thought I have is of his infinite perfection. Every feeling I have is of his kindness and heavenly love. Every dream I have had is realized in him. Hours may pass, but I have no sense of tiredness or pain or needs of any kind. Exquisite content-ment enthralls me. I have no use for speech except to praise him. I have no desires except to be held there by him forever. I have a vision of him but I cannot see his face or his form, only an infinite light and goodness. I hear his voice in an interior way, his words have sweetness and charm but no sound, and yet they are more felt and permanent in my soul than if I heard Jesus pronounce them. And there are harder times during prayer when I behold my life as if it were a book of hundreds of pages that faithfully recall all my faults and failings. And then such a great sorrow for my sins takes possession of me that it seems to me I would rather die a horrible death than ever sin against God again."

She hesitates and, blushing with embarrassment, turns to the priest as if she's just remembered that he's there. Père Marriott is quiet for a moment and heaves himself up. "Shall I get you more tea?"

She shakes her head.

"Each phrase there, was it your own?"

"Excuse me?"

He does not turn, but tips the tea kettle so discreetly that the hot water twines soundlessly into his cup. "Isn't it possible for me to believe you had formulated that answer in your head before visiting me here? You could have *borrowed*, for example, from the books you have been reading."

"Yes, it is possible for you to believe that."

"And is there another explanation?"

"Christ was my teacher."

Expressionlessly, he carries his teacup back to the kitchen table while saying, "Tell me how it was, praying, just yesterday."

She hears firewood wheezing and thudding apart inside the iron stove. She sees red peppers on his kitchen sill and a knife and fork upright inside a milky glass. "I felt greatly upset at first because of Anne, Mother Céline, but as I began to meditate on the crucifixion and Christ's own trials in this world, I became rapt in thought and I found myself again before Jesus, who was suffering such terrible pain. He was horrible with blood and his breathing was hard, and troubled, but his pain had less to do with that than with his human sense of failure, injustice, and loneliness. An unquenchable desire to join him in his agonies took hold of me then, as if I could have his afflictions by sharing them, and I beseeched Jesus to grant me that grace. And, in his great kindness, he gratified me at once. Kneeling there below his cross, I saw that blood no longer issued from his wounds, but only flashing light as hot as fire. And all of a sudden I felt a keen hurt as those flames touched my hands and feet and heart. I have never felt such pain before, and I have never been so happy. I have no memories of the hours passing, I have only the memories of a kind of pleasure and contentment I haven't ever known, a kind that made me love the world as he does, and hearing his whisper just before dawn that I ought to go to you."

"Christ mentioned my name?"

" 'See Père Marriott,' he said."

"Well, that makes me very happy," the old priest says, and then he half rotates in his chair and takes off his round spectacles.

She hears Sister Anne ringing the tocsin for Vespers but before she asks permission to go, she says, "When the pains started in September, I had no idea what they truly meant. And then I persuaded myself that all Sisters espoused to Christ by their vows would have experienced his wounds. You can't know how stupid and innocent I was! Even yesterday, even after all my reading, I had no true understanding of what was happening to me and at first I hoped to keep it secret, but Christ told me that was impossible in the midst of the priory and with my hands and feet bleeding freely. And now I wonder if I haven't made it all up in some way, or if it's even possible."

Père Marriott slowly puts on his glasses and thinks for half a minute and then smiles up at her as he says, "I don't believe it's possible. I do believe it happened."

• *Nearly thirty years after writing the enormously popular* Black Narcissus, *Rumer Godden was allowed to live at the gate of Stanhope Abbey while researching and writing a long novel on enclosed religious,* This House of Brede. *She also draws on life in two other English abbeys, Talacre and Ryde. "To me and my kind, life is a story and we have to tell it in stories," she said in her autobiography,* A House of Four Rooms, *published in 1989.*

RUMER GODDEN

This House of Brede

Brede Abbey was hushed in a hush deeper even than its normal quiet; though the nuns went about their work and the bells were rung at the appointed time and the chant of voices came, as always, from the church, the hush was there, a hush of waiting. The parlors were closed. "No visiting today," said Sister Renata who answered the door. She and the other extern sisters went softly in and out, but they did not go into the town, where the news had spread. "The Abbess is dying: Lady Abbess of Brede."

This was the community recreation hour but only two figures could be seen at work in the garden, instead of the many, habited in black and white and as alike as penguins, that would usually at this time have been gathered in the park or on the paths or pacing together in the cloisters. The prioress and the senior nuns were keeping vigil in the Abbess's rooms, the others had withdrawn, some to their cells, most to their stalls in choir, to pray while they waited.

The great bell, Mary Major, took over from the bell called Michael; it tolled once every minute, the solemn death toll sounding through the Abbey, across the marshes, and down into the town. "She has gone, then" said the townspeople.

The nuns, as they gathered, had knelt, some sobbing, some white and quiet, round the room and down the corridor as Dom Gervase administered extreme unction, touching eyes, ears, nostrils, lips, hands, and feet with holy oil in the sign of the cross, sealing the five senses away from the world: "By this holy anointing and of this most tender mercy, may the Lord forgive you whatever sins you have committed through your sight" or "hearing" or "sense of smell" or "speech" or "touch." Dom Gervase's voice had faltered as he began, but it had grown firm and clear as he prayed. Then the nuns had heard the words, "Go forth O soul, out of this world in the name of the Father Almighty, who created you . . ." He came to the final prayer, "Dead to this world, may she live to Thee, and the sins she has committed in this life, through human frailty, do Thou in mercy forgive . . ."

The last toll ended. Then, as the nuns rose stiffly from their knees, the voice of the great bell sounded again, beginning the first of the three tolls for Vespers. Silently the nuns filed down to fetch their cowls and go to their station in the cloisters, then, two by two, paced in procession into choir, where the Abbess's shepherd's crook lay across her empty chair, which was already draped in black.

In time a new Abbess was chosen. "Domina Catherina Ismay Abbatissa elect est," intoned the bishop. Dame Catherine had had to step out of her stall as Dame Agnes bowed before her; step out of it forever, though that realization had not come to her then, and go to the wicket, where she had knelt, thankful to kneel, while the Abbot President confirmed her as Abbess in the name of the Holy See, giving her the pectoral cross, the ring, the seal, and the keys of the monastery. The bellringer had slipped up to the bell tribune to set the bells ringing; the doors were unlocked, and the claustral sisters and novitiate trooped in. The new abbess was led to the abbatial chair, its mourning gone now, as the President intoned the *Te Deum* and the nuns took it up. Then, one by one, they had come, each kneeling and putting her hands between the Abbess's, to show fealty, homage, obedience, and to be given the kiss of peace.

The Abbess's rooms were ready, the larger study swept and polished as only Sister Ellen could polish; a fire was burning, fresh flowers had been put in the bracket vase on the wall, clean paper in the blotter. But they are all Mother's, the new Abbess had wanted to cry. How can they be for me? and her own voice had answered, "Not for you. For the Abbess of Brede."

It was not until after dinner—in the strange seat at the high table—giving the knock, the rap with the small wooden mallet that was the Abbess's signal, walking behind the procession to sing the dinner grace in choir, that Abbess Catherine had been able to return to her rooms. Her bed was made up and ready. The Abbess took a step nearer and caught her breath; the pillow and white counterpane were strewn with small picture cards and nosegays. Then, Sister Ellen, coming in with a fresh pile of laundry, found her new Abbess on her knees by the bed, sobbing as if her heart would break. She knelt beside the Abbess, reached up and put her arms around the big strong body, cruelly shaken now. "Don't cry, my Lady," she said. "Don't cry. It will be all right. You will see. It will be all right."

• Born in Southern California of Irish-
American parents, James Costigan was
educated in public and private schools and at
L'Alliance Francaise in Paris. He has written
for the theater as well as films and
television.

JAMES COSTIGAN

Little Moon of Alban

*Dennis, an Irish soldier, is fatally shot by British troops while walking
near a church with his sweetheart, Brigid Mary. "He was the loveliest
thing I ever had, and I gave him gladly to your God, the way he gladly
gave himself," she tells the priest, Fr Curran. "Is this the way a boy like
that is received in God's house?"*

FR CURRAN: Don't speak to me of my God, Brigid Mary Mangan.
He's your God and the God of all of us, and who are you to
question His will?

BRIGID MARY: Question Him? I don't question Him. I might
have so when Da died with half his face blasted off him or
when Colm was burned alive. I'm past questioning now. I deny
Him.

FR CURRAN: God forgive you. Shut your mouth now at once,
and when you've control of yourself again, pray for forgiveness.

BRIGID MARY: I will not shut up. I will say it again and again, in
any place whatever, to anyone who will listen. I deny Him!

FR CURRAN: Go out from this holy place then.

BRIGID MARY (*stamping out votive candles with the palms of her
hands*): There is no God! There is only fire! Fire!

(Fr Curran, despairing of subduing her, strikes her violently in the face once, twice, three times, shocking them both terribly. He sinks to his knees while Brigid Mary turns up the palms of her hands like a little girl showing cleanliness, but they are sooted and badly burned. Fr Curran takes them gently in his own.)

BRIGID MARY: I hurt myself but help me, Father.

The light fades. Out of the void comes the sound of women's voices, singing the Salve Regina.

VOICES: Salve Regina, mater misericordia; vita dulcedo et spes nostra salve.

Light comes up on a small procession of women moving across the stage from back to front. All wear the habit of the Daughters of Charity of St Vincent de Paul, blue-grey in color. They advance like a cordon of earthbound birds, their great winged white headdresses undulating gracefully as they walk . . . then the light comes up on a small, barren hospital room.

FR CURRAN: How are your hands?

BRIGID MARY: Sister took the bandages off this morning. The blisters are all healed.

FR CURRAN: They look like new. Why are you sitting here in the dark?

BRIGID MARY: I didn't notice the day go. Is it night again? So soon?

FR CURRAN: It is. A fine one with a slip of a moon.

BRIGID MARY: Little moon, little moon of Alban.

FR CURRAN: What?

BRIGID MARY: I was thinking of some words from a play that Dennis and I were reading together once. *Dierdre of the Sorrows.* Her young man is killed, and she is left standing beside his open grave and she says, "I see the trees naked and bare, and the moon shining. Little moon, little moon of Alban, it's lonesome you'll be this night, and tomorrow night, and long nights after, and you pacing the woods beyond Glen Laoi, looking every place for Dierdre and Naisi . . ."

FR CURRAN: Brigid Mary, your mother, Shelagh, is here. She wants to see you.

BRIGID MARY: She wants to take me home. I won't go. I can't go.

FR CURRAN: Hear what she has to say. Talk to her.

BRIGID MARY: What's the good? We've talked every day since I made up my mind to stay here with the Sisters.

SHELAGH: I've come to fetch you home.

BRIGID MARY: I can't. . . . You don't know what it was like the night Father brought me here. If I hadn't burnt my hands, if he hadn't brought me here to let the Sisters care for them, if he'd let me go my way, I swear to you I would have thrown myself into the river. I would have died somehow that night. I would have found the men who shot Dennis and tormented them into killing me, too. When the Sisters saw what a state I was in, they knew it was more than my poor hands wanted tending, and they took me in. Not half an hour before, I had renounced God, and here He was, taking me back and nursing me where I had wounded Him. I have to stay here, Mama. It's what I have to do.

SHELAGH: Is that what they mean by a "calling," Father? If I burn me two hands and a nun treats them, do I become a nun? Is that all there is to it?

FR CURRAN: No, and I don't think it was that way with Brigid Mary.

SHELAGH: I always prayed that one of my children might enter the church. But only if God himself had given a sign. Wasn't I always remembering me own brother, dear little Bub, who joined the Dominicans just to please our mother and broke his heart trying to measure up? I had a vision of him once floating face down in the cold sea off Drougheda, all white and bloated and nothing on him but his stiff collar, and that strangling him. "There'll be no priests or Sisters in this house," I says to Matt that very night. "Not if the persuasion hasn't come from above," says I, and I've stuck to that. Am I right, Father?

FR CURRAN: My dear, if Brigid Mary wants to join these Sisters here, it's between her and God. You and me don't enter into it.

SHELAGH: Did God speak to you? With this holy man and your mother as witnesses, tell the truth now. Did God speak to you?

BRIGID MARY: No.

SHELAGH: There!

BRIGID MARY: But I spoke to Him.

SHELAGH: You did what?

BRIGID MARY: It was as if I spoke to Him and He listened. If I thought He had called to me, I'd be entering a convent and spending my life in a quiet place where nothing could interfere between His voice and me. But I called to *Him*, Father, and that's the next best thing, isn't it?

FR CURRAN: I suppose it is.

BRIGID MARY: That's why I want to be one of the Daughters of Charity here, working with the sick and the poor the way they do, working with children. Because they're not nuns, but they are Sisters who do God's work, and my life is a call, not a calling.

SHELAGH: There's no reasoning with her. She is lonely for the grave and has mistaken it for a little private cell. She'll kill herself trying to be worthy, just as poor Bub did, and that'll be an end to her confusion.

BRIGID MARY: Mama—

SHELAGH: Do what you will, and God help you.

BRIGID MARY: Give me your blessing, Mama.

SHELAGH: I can't.

BRIGID MARY: Please.

SHELAGH: No, by all that's holy, I can't. I'm your mother, and I know you. How can I give you over to live and work among these dedicated Sisters? What good will you be to them at all, and half your heart buried in Glasnevin Cemetery?

BRIGID MARY: Mama, don't.

SHELAGH: Grief is your persuasion. Fear is holding you here.

BRIGID MARY: No!

SHELAGH: Come on away out of this, then.

BRIGID MARY: I've told you and told you—there's nothing for me out there.

SHELAGH: That's no reason. Nobody comes this way because

there's nothing out there. Only because, to them, everything is here. They walk through these doors serenely, with a great pride to them. They're not running. They are not running away from life, from love, from a man who might be holding you in his two arms one minute and lying dead the next.

(The Sister Servant [superior] enters.)

SISTER SERVANT: Brigid Mary, the new postulants are gathering for prayers and meditation. I thought you might want to join them. It's time you began.

As the light fades, chapel bells begin to ring. The light comes up on a corridor in the Chapter House [convent]. Several young women, wearing the seminary bonnet and shawl, move along the corridor, all carrying prayerbooks. As the last of them passes, Brigid Mary, similarly dressed, appears at the far end of the corridor but moves over to a corner by herself.

SISTER SERVANT: Will you not come and pray with the others?

BRIGID MARY: I would, Sister, but they always seem to be finished before I've properly begun.

SISTER SERVANT: I see. You are creating a private atmosphere of austerity for yourself, is that it? You are too hard on Brigid Mary Mangan.

BRIGID MARY: Too hard?

SISTER SERVANT: We don't make our own terms of expiation. We have priests for that. It's through them we communicate our confession and our penance to the Heavenly Father. None of us has the right to sit in judgment on herself.

BRIGID MARY: No, but we have to question ourselves, don't we, Sister? We have to be *sure* of ourselves.

SISTER SERVANT: Don't you remember what St Vincent de Paul said to the first Daughters of Charity there in Paris? "Just think," he said, "when God chose you there were plenty of other people in the world. He had his pick, and yet He chose *you*."

BRIGID MARY: Chose me?

SISTER SERVANT: You think you chose God, do you? That's all

right. We mustn't take St Vincent too literally, must we? It's good
to remember that he was speaking French, after all, and it's a
devious, subtle language.

BRIGID MARY: But there must be some sort of sign, mustn't
there, Sister?

SISTER SERVANT: St Vincent says the fact that we're here is sign
enough. What did you think it would be, child?

*The Sister Servant goes, leaving Brigid Mary staring after her. The
light on the corridor fades. Brigid Mary moves downstage into a pool of
light.*

BRIGID MARY: A year. A whole year before I shall put on my
blue habit and my white cornette and leave this town forever,
this town where every street-name is a memory and every memory
a grief. . . . In early summer, children play in the bombed-out
houses. . . . Oh, God, watch over little children! . . . Hundreds are
being evacuated to the country, and they are taking my heart and
my prayers with them in their little satchels and kerchiefs. If I am
worthy when this year is up, then I shall be sent after them, to
care for them, to heal them where they are hurt in body and mind.
I shall follow them like a shepherd, like Jesus tending his lambs . . .
knowing He has chosen me for that work.

The scene shifts to a corridor.

SISTER SERVANT: Sister Brigid Mary—how does it sound to you?

BRIGID MARY: I made a long list of names I might have taken,
and none of them seemed to be me. They were all lovely but they
were somebody else. So I kept my own. It's the only familiar thing
I've kept, and I wondered was I right to do it, but then you said it
just now and it sounded so natural. I turned without thinking.
Well, Sister?

SISTER SERVANT: Your sleeves, Sister. Turn them back to make a
cuff. Like mine, you see? That's better. Yes.

BRIGID MARY: You're my looking glass, Sister. I'm trying to see
myself in you. I've no other way of knowing if I look all right.

SISTER SERVANT: You look beautiful.

BRIGID MARY: Ah, no, I was never even pretty.

SISTER SERVANT: You're beautiful now. God thinks so.

BRIGID MARY: You think He's pleased? He's brought me along so patiently, and now here I am. Oh, He must have wanted me this way, mustn't He, Sister? He must have remembered that I have a green finger with children, and said to Himself, "This girl will be all right when she's settled into a country orphanage somewhere, somewhere away from the fighting and killing, a place where—"

SISTER SERVANT: I know you'd your heart set on being sent to Longford or Roscommon where the children are. But you must prepare yourself for a disappointment. The fact is that during your training here you've shown a special aptitude for hospital work.

BRIGID MARY: I'm not to go to the children, is that it? I'm being sent to the hospital instead.

SISTER SERVANT: I'm sorry.

BRIGID MARY: It doesn't matter.

SISTER SERVANT: I had no choice, you see. As many Sisters as are proficient nurses are needed at once in the hospital there in Adelaide Road. If I'd any option to exempt a Sister from this duty, believe me, child, I'd send you elsewhere, anywhere. They're desperate for nurses. We told them the Daughters of Charity work mainly among the poor, and the English doctor-in-charge there says to her, "Sister, these wounded boys are very poor. An Englishman on Irish soil is without friends, and that is a great poverty."

BRIGID MARY: Did you think I wouldn't go, Sister?

SISTER SERVANT: Oh, I know you'll go wherever you're stationed. I was only thinking, because of the losses you endured in the world, if I'd had the chance to ask only one exemption—

BRIGID MARY: Please don't, Sister. You shame me. I know you're saying that out of kindness. But I'm a Daughter of Charity now.

The scene shifts to the hospital room of Kenneth, a wounded British soldier.

KENNETH: How is it you mentioned you're not a nun? You look like a nun. So very sanctimonious.

BRIGID MARY: Now—

KENNETH: I didn't mean that. I mean pious. All nuns look very pious and mysterious.

BRIGID MARY: Mysterious? Go on!

KENNETH: They are to me. I don't believe in anything they represent and yet I never fail to leap up and offer one my seat in a tram or a bus. Why is that? It must be the medieval costume. You do *dress* like a nun.

BRIGID MARY: Yes, but St Vincent de Paul didn't want his daughters to be nuns, because when you say "nun" you're talking about a cloister; but we have to go everywhere. St Vincent says, "Your convents are the houses of the sick. Your cell is a hired room. Your chapel, the parish church. Your cloister, the streets of the city. Your enclosure, obedience. Your grille, the fear of God. Your veil, holy modesty."

KENNETH: It sounds rather like punitive duty in the Army. You do the dirty work.

BRIGID MARY: Our work is to look after the material and the spiritual needs of the poor.

KENNETH: Ah, but I'm rich, you see. I have an enormous annuity. I'm very rich.

BRIGID MARY: You're poor in spirit, though, aren't you, Lieutenant?

KENNETH: Am I? I believe that's a stock phrase you have for people who don't think the way you do.

BRIGID MARY: St Vincent tells us to humble ourselves and to ask God incessantly for the ability to pray.

KENNETH: How monotonous for God.

The night passes and Sister Brigid Mary returns to relieve Sister Barbara.

KENNETH: I was asking her about the Daughters of Charity. She says you renew your vows every year and that every 25th of March you're free to leave.

BRIGID MARY: On Lady Day, that's right. But very few ever leave.

KENNETH: The point is, you can do so if you wish, if you don't feel you belong here.

BRIGID MARY: Yes. But it was through you that *I* heard Him for the first time. I'd been listening with my ears only for such a long while. And then yourself came, and you talking such a great storm of words till I'd no ears left in the night when you were sleeping under threat of death, and I was alone with Him, praying that you'd be spared. I think now that must have been the first time *I* ever listened with my heart. Oh, what things I heard then! No words. Just things. For the first time I understood what it meant to be doing God's work out of love and not out of fear. In the beginning I was only a Sister by sufferance. Every day I thought, today God will give me the sack. And now He's given me a promotion instead. He's made me a Sister in truth. I can never forsake Him now.

• Based on the life of a Belgian nurse befriended by Kathryn Hulme after World War II, The Nun's Story *quickly became a best-seller and the most popular book ever circulated by* Reader's Digest. *As a film it featured Audrey Hepburn. A few years earlier, in 1953, Miss Hulme won the Atlantic Award for Nonfiction for* The Wild Place, *about the postwar homeless in Germany.*

KATHRYN HULME

The Nun's Story

The changing colors of the altar hangings from the violet of Advent, through the whites and gold of Christmas and on to the purples of Lent, told of the passing year.

Or, there were the four letters she was permitted to write annually to her family, of four pages each and not a sentence more except with special permission which she seldom sought; instead, she shrunk her bold square handwriting down to the spidery lace that gave more lines to the page and saw herself finally writing just like all the other missionary Sisters.

There was the continuous drop on Father Andre's leg for three months after his accident and then bi-monthly X-rays of slowly mending tissues which always gave her a struggle with pride. And, every so often, Mother Mathilde reported that she had written to the Mother House for the nursing reinforcement that never came.

Afterwards, when Sister Luke looked back on her first Congo

year, she saw but one really important experience in it. It was
nothing she could report to her family as a major impression. You
had to be a nun to see it that way. God caught up with her and
gave her one more chance to recite her vows without reservation.
Then, when she was safely in His pocket, He let her see with
shattering clarity how little humility she had. She repeated her
vows on what she hoped and prayed was her deathbed, struck
down with a dysentery that left no desire to live or even the
memory of what it had been like to be alive without the agonizing
pain that tore the will to shreds.

When she discovered her condition, she hid it as long as she
could. It was humiliation, a loss of a working hand in the
community, a waste of God's time through her own carelessness,
she believed. She traced her malady to tropical fruits which had
possibly been stung by the fruit fly.

Twice weekly when she went to the native hospital to take
lumbar punctures, a serving boy showed his ardor by waiting for
her at the clinic door with a bowl of iced fruit, usually mangos he
had traded in the native market. It was his way of saying, I like
you. The chilly golden flesh of the mangos was delicious to eat in
the humid forenoons when you had a dozen lumbar punctures lined
up and the sensitive tests of spinal fluids to make afterwards, in
quest of the trypanosomes of sleeping sickness.

The dysentery was the fulminant type, quick and acute. The
day she collapsed in surgery seemed to be her last. The doctor
raged at her as she was placed on a stretcher.

They carried her to the convent infirmary. In a haze of pain
and exhaustion she swallowed what the doctor ordered and felt the
needle-prick of his opium injections. The black face of Emil, the
doctor's yellow face, and the delicate, tanned ovals of Mother
Mathilde's and Sister Aurelie's hung alternately over her until late
in the night, and she guessed she must be passing the bright-red
gelatinous mucus of the last stage when she heard Mother Mathilde tell the doctor she would summon the priest and nuns.

She was floating above the bed, looking down on a young nun
dying there, when she heard the Sisters at 3 o'clock in the

morning coming along the path from dormitory to infirmary, singing the *Miserere* softly in the cricket-shell African night. She saw all twenty Sisters with lighted candles in their hands and old Father Stephen at the end of the procession carrying the Viaticum, with Mother Mathilde and her senior nun beside him with the holy oils. You die so beautifully when you are a nun, she thought. She looked down again upon the bed where the dying one lay, so young, so heroic, so humbly waiting with folded hands for a bit of parchment to be placed between them—her vows signed on the altar of the Mother House years ago in Belgium.

She listened to the *Miserere* plead that she would have strength to ask God for His mercy, confess her iniquities, and offer up to Him a contrite and humbled heart. Coming toward the dying, the Sisters sang their hopes for her. Going away, they would sing the *Te Deum* to thank God for accepting her nothingness. All this for me, she thought. And even more. Next day a cable would inform the Mother House of her death and shortly after, every convent in the entire congregation would make the Stations of the Cross in her name. She saw the processionals winding through all the European houses, on to the Orient and back again through India and the Congo . . . ah, those beautiful processionals that had always caught her by the throat, even when, like these oncoming Sisters, she had been routed from sleep at some unearthly hour to wind around a dying nun a shroud of heavenly song.

There was a smile on her lips when Father Stephen entered her room, raised the Viaticum, and intoned the opening phrase of extreme unction.

"Peace to this house," he sang in a rich baritone.

"And to all who live herein," responded her Sisters, holding their candles before their faces.

But she recovered. She knew why, even before she returned to the community to be congratulated by her Sisters for her readiness to die. One by one during the weeks she lay in the hospital, her conscience turned up the humiliating truths of her illness. Her entire preparation to die had been a fraud, an indulgence in heroism and self-pity. The smile the Sisters had seen and called courageous had been for gratification at the thought of a thousand nuns circling the globe in a memorial procession in her name. Had there been a single moment, even in that most solemn ceremony of last rites, when her heart had been truly humbled and every thought bent directly toward God?

Her self-examination grew more relentless as she gained strength. She made it as meticulously as she prepared slides for the microscope, looked down the tube, and named what she saw. You walk, you talk, you even write like a nun. But you are not a nun, not yet. The mold has shaped you to look like one, but inside the deceptive shell still flourishes pride and vainglory, worldliness and self-love.

On a scorching afternoon when the winged ants flew thickly around the recreation kiosk, she returned to the community. From the sickbed she brought one fixed idea—that God would pursue her with humiliations until she learned humility. Her first hour with her Sisters confirmed the belief. She shrunk with shame when they congratulated her on her courage before death. When she could stand that praise no longer, she said, "It wasn't courage." She hunted for something other than her own truth to say. "It was more of a . . . a snobbism."

The nuns knew what she meant. Sometimes, the more lowly and humble you made yourself, the more superior you felt. Some of the nuns were shocked by her frankness, others admired it. Mother Mathilde tapped twice on the arm of her chair to indicate that she would take over the talk.

"Sister Luke didn't die," she said quietly, "because her mission is not yet accomplished. Moreover, my Sisters, it was not she who was tested, but us, the community." She nodded emphatically. "Ah yes, God was only testing us to see if we were willing to give up a number." Her smile embraced the circle and reminded them that they were all only numbers. "One number less in our understaffed community would have been a heavy cross for us to bear."

Not one Sister less, not one nun with a known name and background less . . . just one number less, Sister Luke thought. She looked up at her Superior, who never forgot first principles of the religious life. Be nothing before you can be something. She saw some of her Sisters squirming inwardly under the anonymity that Mother Mathilde had thrust upon them. But upon me mostly, she thought.

She trained her dressing boys soon after she returned to work and made Emil her deputy. Both innovations brought the spotlight of singularity upon her.

The chief in charge of nursing in the hospital had always had a nun as deputy, as she had been given Sister Aurelie. But why a nun? Why not, she asked herself, old Emil, who has seen generations of us pass through the hospital and knows as much about nursing as any of us?

"I'd like to make him my deputy," she informed Mother Mathilde. "Then we can free Sister Aurelie for total time in the maternity pavilion. Were Emil my deputy, moreover, all punishment of the staff would be dealt out by him instead of by the nuns, and I think that would be good."

Mother Mathilde thought for a moment, seeming to weigh the intention rather than the suggestions. Sister Luke felt the probe of her bright eyes. Desire for change, merely for the sake of doing something different, was one of the big temptations of every nun. It could catch you on even such little things as having to fold your habit in exactly the same way, day after day, year after year, for no other reason than that the Rule said thus and thus and not so and so. And your occasional rebellions, boiling up with the force of almost a physical passion and as difficult to overcome, reminded you that obedience was no mouselike virtue, easily captured and kept. Sister Luke knew that all this had passed through her Superior's mind before she gave her consent.

"Very well," she said at last. "And I myself will inform the doctor, who could have no objections, as far as I can see."

Sister Luke returned to the hospital to hand over to Emil a responsibility nearly equal to her own. She called together all her registered male nurses and technicians, most of whom had had four years of study and were fluent in French, and all her messengers, cleaning boys, and kitchen staff. She told them that from that day forward, Emil was to be their Capita. Knowing how they loved the idea of hierarchy and understood it through their own tribal traditions, she explained that she was setting up a line of authority. A ripple of approval passed through the room.

Emil became her shadow. He told her much of tribal life. And he asked her questions, including his puzzlement about why the Sisters didn't have husbands.

When she tried to explain, she discovered how incomprehensible to the mentality of the bush was the idea of chastity. The concept of a mystic marriage was impossible to explain without getting into the subject of polygamy. Eventually, Sister Luke solved the dilemma by telling Emil that indeed she had a husband who was in Heaven and that she had made him a promise never to marry anyone else. Emil understood promise. He understood widow. Grave with sympathy, he nodded and never spoke of it again.

Emil helped her to work out her plan to give specialized training to some of her male nurses. Observation had taught her that the Congolese was an excellent routine worker. Once shown how to do a thing, he would follow the original teaching without a hair's deviation. And he carefully trained his men so that within a fortnight she had a production-line system for changing dressings which enabled her to attend to twenty-five post-operatives in an hour and have a full report on each ready for the doctor when he made his rounds. When he saw the dressing boys in action, Dr Fortunati looked from them to her with something of the same expression he had when he inspected her work in saving Father Andre's crushed leg. "So you're a teacher, too, Sister Luke!"

Perhaps if he had not bragged to other doctors of how efficiently things were running in *his* hospital and how they ought to have a nun to show them how to utilize the native manpower in their own medical center, there would have been no spotlight. The colony was a small place for gossip. The Apostolic Delegate of the province telephoned to Mother Mathilde to inform her that one of her nuns had apparently gone out of the mold and was being named by name in public places.

You could be named as a white Sister, or a grey or a blue

Sister, as a Dominican, a Franciscan, a Benedictine, or an Ursuline—if the public knew enough to read coif and habit and place you in the congregation to which you belonged. You could be called a teaching Sister, or a nursing Sister, or an evangelizing or a visiting Sister. But outside your own walls, your own sphere of work and co-workers black and white, you were not supposed to be called by your name in Christ. There was nothing written on it; it simply was not done. And if it was, it meant that you had somehow singularized yourself.

Sister Luke knew when Mother Mathilde came to the men's pavilion to watch her dressing boys in action that it was for a reason other than routine inspection. A shadow lay beneath her never-failing smile, imperceptible to any but the perceiving eyes of a nun. The boys thought she had come to admire them and performed beautifully.

Sister Luke lifted the gauze and inspected the clamps on a large abdominal incision. Ordinarily she would have told the boys why they were not yet ready for removal, but she dared not trust her voice. It would not be the sure steady one they knew. Like her heart, it would tremble with the awareness she had plucked from the air when she stood by Mother Mathilde. She had erred, she had failed her Superior somehow. It meant nothing that Mother Mathilde's voice and manner betrayed no more than appreciative interest in a nursing job well done, for no nun ever rebuked another in the presence of others.

If I have failed her, Sister Luke thought, O God, let it be anyone else... the doctor, a patient, any or all of my Sisters, but not her... not her. She called for a clean collodion gauze and laid it on the wound and stepped back.

"I must go now, Monsieur," said Mother Mathilde to Emil. "I leave you indeed in capable hands."

As was customary, Sister Luke accompanied her to the door of the pavilion. The Superior paused in an alcove apart from the traffic of the corridor.

"Your only fault, Sister," she said softly, "was in failing to tell me about this in advance. I see now that you are not responsible for a certain acclaim this work has brought. It would have been noted eventually no matter which Sister inspired it. But earlier, when our Delegate telephoned me to ask me why one of my nuns sought to singularize herself, I had no answer. But I have my answer now, Sister. I shall telephone to our Delegate, perhaps even invite him to come see how we make both ends meet, lacking sufficient nursing Sisters." Her parting smile made it all seem a very small matter.

But it was not a small matter, not when you were a nun. Though but a sin of omission, the most forgivable, you nevertheless had to connect it to all the others that had gone before. You had to put it into the context of your religious life.

The more failings she put into the context, the more depressed she became. The doctor was the first to see a change in her. One morning he detained her in surgery. He showed her the final x-ray of Father Andre's leg and gave her a photo print of it for a keepsake. "To remind you always," he said, "that you are an excellent nurse." He watched her slip the photo without comment into her pocket, then he said, "But you know something, Sister? You're much too stark and disciplined a person. Something in your life here has made you so. I remember how you were when you first came out to the colony. Recently, I've watched you tighten, fold in upon yourself, and I cannot think why. What is it, Sister?"

Caught off guard, she flushed. That this irreligious layman had guessed her inner struggle nearly brought tears. She turned quickly and left the surgery, but his sharp face grown suddenly sympathetic was difficult to banish from her thoughts. And the way he had talked to her—as if she were a human being in the world, beset like any other with troubles that a friend might be able to understand and help to iron out. She knew that if she were the kind of docile nun who thought every emotion worth reporting to the Superior, she would go to Mother Mathilde and tell of her reactions to the doctor's personal remarks. She stood for a moment undecided. She heard very distinctly the voice of the Mistress of Novices saying, "Every failure to a Superior, no matter how small or how innocently committed, is a tug at your sleeve from the world, trying to pull you back to it."

But she was never to know if she would have gone that day. Duty came toward her down the hospital corridor in the form of Father Vermeuhlen, the famous priest of the leper colony, and Etienne, the town's coiffeur. Etienne was there to dress the banker's wife and Father Vermeuhlen had come for his annual precautionary check. The saint and the sinner, she thought as she watched them approach.

SHORT STORIES

• *Although he was born in Buffalo, Paul*
Horgan spent much of his life in the
Southwest, graduating from the New Mexico
Military Institute at Roswell and returning
there some years later to serve as librarian.
He won the 1933 Harper Prize for his novel
The Fault of Angels.

PAUL HORGAN

The Surgeon and the Nun

When I was a young doctor I heard of a new section of country opening up down toward Texas, and thinks I, I'll just go and see about it. The hottest day I ever spent, yes, and the next night, and the next day, too, as you'll see.

The railroad spur had been pushing down south through the Pecos Valley, a few miles a week, and it was in July that I got on the train and bought a ticket for Eddy, the town I was thinking about trying for my practice.

Two seats across the aisle from me was a Sister of Mercy, sitting there in her black robes, skirts, and sleeves, and heavy starch, and I wondered at the time, how on earth can she stand it? The car was an oven. She sat there looking out the window, calm and strengthened by her philosophy. It seemed to me she had expressive hands; I recalled the Sisters in the hospital in Chicago, and how they had learned to say so much and do so much with their skilled hands. When my traveling nun picked up a newspaper and fanned herself slowly, it was more as if she did it in grace than to get cool.

She was in her early thirties, I thought, plump, placid, and full of a wise delicacy and yes, independence, with something of the unearthly knowingness in her steady gaze that I used to see in the Art Institute—those portraits of ladies of the fifteenth century, who look at you sideways, with their eyebrows up.

She wore glasses, very bright, with gold bars to them.

The train came to a long halt and I thought I couldn't stand it. When we moved, there was at least a stir of air, hot and dusty, but at that, we felt as if we were getting some place, even though slowly. We stopped, and the cars creaked in the heat, and I felt thick in the head. I put my face out the window and saw that we had been delayed by a work gang up ahead. They were Mexican laborers. Aside from them, and their brown crawlings up and down the little roadbed embankment, there was nothing, no movement, no life, no comfort, for miles. A few railroad sheds painted dusty red stood by the trackside.

I sat for ten minutes, nothing happened. I couldn't even hear the sounds of work, ringing pickaxes or what not; I felt indignant. This was no way to maintain a public conveyance!

It was around one o'clock in the afternoon.

Mind you, this was 1905; it isn't a wilderness any more out there. Oh, it was then. Every time I looked out at the white horizon my heart sank, I can tell you. Why had I ever left Chicago?

Then I wondered where the Sister was traveling to.

It was strange how comforting she was, all of a sudden. I had a flicker of literary amusement out of the Chaucerian flavor of her presence—a nun, traveling, alone, bringing her world with her no matter where she might be, or in what circumstance; sober, secure, indifferent to anything but the green branches of her soul; benign about the blistering heat and the maddening delay; and withal, an object of some archaic beauty, in her medieval habit, her sidelong eyes, her plump and frondy little hands. I almost spoke to her several times, in that long wait of the train; but she was so classic in her repose that I finally decided not to. I got up instead and went down to the platform of the car, which was floury with dust all over its iron floor and coupling chains, and jumped down to the

ground. How immense the sky was, and the sandy plains that
shuddered with the heat for miles and miles! And how small and
oddly desirable the train looked!

It was all silent until I began to hear the noises that framed the
midsummer midday silence . . . bugs droning, the engine breathing
up ahead, a whining hum in the telegraph wires strung along
by the track, and then from the laborers a kind of subdued chorus.

I went to see what they were all huddled about each other for.
There wasn't a tree for fifty miles in any direction.

In the heat-reflecting shade of one of the grape-red sheds the
men were standing around and looking at one of their number who
was lying on the ground with his back up on the lowest boards.

The men were mostly little, brown as horses, swearing and
smelling like leather, and in charge of them was a big American I
saw squatting down by the recumbent Mexican.

"Come on, come on," he was saying, when I came up.

"What's the matter?" I asked.

The foreman looked up at me. He had his straw hat off, and
his forehead and brows were shad-belly white where the sunburn
hadn't reached. The rest of his face was apple colored, and shiny.
He had little eyes, squinted, and the skin around them was white,
too. His lips were chapped and burnt powdery white.

"Says he's sick."

The Mexicans nodded and murmured.

"Well, I'm a doctor, maybe I can tell."

The foreman snorted.

"They all do it. Nothin' matter with him. He's just play-
actin'. Come on, Pancho, you get, by God, t'hell up.

He shoved his huge dusty shoe against the little Mexican's
side. The Mexican drooled a weak cry. The other laborers made
operatic noises in chorus. They were clearly afraid of the foreman.

"Now hold on," I said to him. "Let me look him over,
anyway."

I got down on the prickly ground.

It took a minute or less to find out. The little cramped-up
Mexican had an acute attack of appendicitis, and he was hot and

sick and when I touched his side, he wept like a dog and clattered on his tongue without words.

"This man is just about ready to pop off," I told the foreman. "He's got acute appendicitis. He'll die unless he can be operated on."

The heat; the shimmering land; something to do; all changed me into feeling cool and serious, quite suddenly.

"I can perform an emergency operation, somehow, though it may be too late. Anyway, it can't do more'n kill him, and he'll die if I don't operate, that's sure!"

"Oh, no. Oh-ho, ho, no, you don't," said the foreman, standing up and drawling. He was obviously a hind, full of some secret foremanship, some plainsman's charm against the evil eye, or whatever he regarded civilization as. "I ain't got no authority for anythin' like that on my section gang! And ennyhow, they all take on like that when they're tarred of workin'!"

Oh, it was the same old thing.

The blasted foreman infuriated me. And I can swear when I have to. Well, I set to and gave him such a dressing down as you never heard.

The foreman talked to the men... there must have been about three dozen of them.

He may have been a fool but he was a crafty one.

He was talking in Mexican and telling them what I wanted to do to Pancho, their brother and friend. He pantomimed surgery— knife in fist and slash and finger-scissors and then grab at belly, and then tongue out, and eyes rolled out of sight, and slump, and dead man: all this very intently, like a child doing a child's powerful ritual of play.

"Oh, yo, yo, yo," went all the Mexicans, and shook their fists at me, and showed their white teeth in rage. No sir, there'd be no cutting on Pancho!

I went back to the train and had more on my mind now than chivalry and Chaucer and Clouet.

She was still sitting there in her heavy starch and her yards and yards of black serge. Her face was pink with the heat and her glasses a little moist. But she was like a calm and shady lake in the blistering wilderness, and her hands rested like ferns on the itchy plush of the seat which gave off a miniature dust storm of stifling scent whenever anything moved on it.

When I stopped in the aisle beside her, she looked up sideways. Of course, she didn't mean to, but looked sly and humorous, and her glasses flashed.

"Excuse me, Sister," I said. "Have you ever had any hospital experience?"

"Is someone ill?"

Her voice was oddly doleful, but not because she was; no, it had the faintest trace of a German tone, and her words an echo of German accent, that soft, trolling charm that used to be the language of the old Germany, a comfortable sweetness that is gone now.

"There's a Mexican laborer out there who's doubled up with appendicitis. I am a surgeon, by the way."

"Yes, for a long time I was dietitian at Mount Mercy Hospital, that's in Cleveland?"

"Well, you see what I think I ought to do."

"So, you should operate?"

"It's the only thing'd save him, and maybe that'll be too late."

"Should we take him in the train and take care of him so? And operate when we reach town?"

Yes, you must see how placid she was, how instantly dedicated to the needs of the present, at the same time. She at once talked of what "we" had to do. She owned responsibility for everything that came into her life. I was young then, and I'm an old man now, but I still get the same kind of pride in doctors and those in holy orders when they're faced with something that has to be done for somebody else. The human value, mind you.

"I don't think they'll let us touch him. They're all Mexicans, and scared to death of surgery. You should've heard them out there a minute ago."

"Yes, I hear them now."

"What I think we'd better do is get to work right here. The

poor wretch wouldn't last the ride to Eddy, God knows how long the train'd take."

"But *where*, doctor!"

"Well, maybe one of those sheds."

"So, and the train would wait?"

I went and asked the conductor up in the next car. He said no, the train wouldn't wait, provided they ever got a chance to go.

"We'd have to take a chance on the train," I told Sister. "Also, those men out there are not very nice about it. Maybe if you came out?"

At that she did hesitate a little; just a moment; probably the fraction it takes a celibate lady to adjust her apprehensions.

"It would have been more convenient," I said, "if I'd never got off the train. That groaning little animal would die, and when the train went, we'd be on it; but we cannot play innocent now. The Mexican means nothing to me. Life is not that personal to a doctor. But if there's a chance to save it, you have to do it, I suppose."

Her response to this was splendid. She flushed and gave me a terrific look, full of rebuke and annoyance at my flippancy. She gathered her great serge folds up in handfuls and went down the car walking angrily. I followed her and together we went over to the shed. The sunlight made her weep a little blink.

The men were by now sweating with righteous fury. Their fascinating language clattered and threatened. Pancho was an unpleasant sight, sick and uncontrolled. The heat was unnerving. They saw me first and made a chorus. Then they saw Sister and shut up in awe, and pulled their greasy hats off.

She knelt down by Pancho and examined him superficially and the flow of her figure, the fine robes kneeling in the dust full of ants, was like some vision to the Mexicans, in all the familiar terms of their Church. To me, it gave one of my infrequent glimpses into the nature of religious feeling.

She got up.

She turned to the foreman, and crossed her palms together. She was majestic and ageless, like any true authority. "Doctor says there must be an operation on this man. He is very sick. I am ready to help."

"Well, lady," said the foreman, "you just *try* an' cut on that Messican and see what happens!"

He ducked his head toward the laborers to explain this.

She turned to the men. Calmly, she fumbled for her long rosary and held up the large crucifix that hung at its end. The men murmured and crossed themselves.

"Tell them what you have to do," she said to me coldly. She was still angry at the way I'd spoken in the train.

"All right, foreman, translate for me. Sister is going to assist me at an appendectomy. We'll move the man into the larger shed over there. I'd be afraid to take him to town, there isn't time. No, listen, this is better. What I *will* do: we could move him into the train, and operate while the train was standing still, and then let the train go ahead after the operation is over. That way, we'd get him to town for proper care!"

The foreman translated and pantomimed.

A threatening cry went up.

"They say you can't take Pancho off and cut on 'im on the train. They want him here."

Everybody looked at Pancho. He was like a little monkey with eyes screwed shut and leaking tears.

The little corpus of man never loses its mystery, even to a doctor, I suppose. What it is, we are; what we are, must serve it; in anyone.

"Very well, we'll operate here. Sister, are you willing to help me? It'll mean staying here till tomorrow's train."

"Ja, doctor, of course."

I turned to the foreman.

"Tell them."

He shrugged and began to address them again.

They answered him, and he slapped his knee and h'yucked a kind of hound-dog laugh in his throat and said to us, "Well, if you go ahaid, these Messicans here say they'll sure 'nough kill you if you kill Pancho!"

Yes, it was worse than I could have expected.

This was like being turned loose among savages.

You might have thought the searing heat of that light steel sky had got everybody into fanciful ways.

"Why, that's ridiculous!" I said to him. "He's nearly dead now! Nobody can guarantee an operation, but I can certainly guarantee that the man will die unless I take this one chance!"

"Well, I dunno. See? That's what they *said . . .*"

He waved at the Mexicans.

They were tough and growling.

Sister was waiting. Her face was still as wax.

"Can't you *explain*," I said.

"Man, you never can 'splain *nothin'* to this crew! You better take the church lady there, and just get back on that train, that's what you better do!"

Well, there it was.

"You go to hell!" I said.

I looked at Sister. She nodded indignantly at me, and then smiled, sideways, that same sly look between her cheek and her lens, which she never meant that way; but from years of convent discretion she had come to perceive things obliquely and tell of them in whispers with many sibilants.

"Come on, we'll move him. Get him some help there."

The Mexicans wouldn't budge. They stood in the way.

"Give me your pistol!"

The foreman handed it over. We soon got Pancho moved.

Sister helped me to carry him.

She was strong. I think she must have been a farm girl from one of the German communities of the Middle West somewhere. She knew how to work, the way to lift, where her hands would do the most good. Her heavy thick robes dragged in the dust. We went into the tool shed and it was like strolling into a furnace.

I hurried back to the train and got my bags and then went back again for hers. I never figured out how she could travel with so little and be so clean and comfortable. She had a box of food. It was conventional in its odors: bananas, waxed paper, oranges, something spicy. Aside from that she had a little canvas bag with web straps binding it. I wondered what, with so little allowed her, she had chosen out of all the desirable objects of the world to have with her and to own.

My instrument case had everything we needed, even to two bottles of chloroform.

I got back into the dusty red shed by flashing the foreman's pistol at the mob. Inside I gave it back to him through the window with orders to keep control over the peasants.

What they promised to do to me if Pancho died began to mean something, when I saw those faces, like clever dogs, like smooth-skinned apes, like long-whiskered mice. I thought of having the engineer telegraph to some town and get help, soldiers, or something, but that was nervously romantic.

It was dark in the shed, for there was only one window. The heat was almost smoky there, it was so dim. There was a dirt floor. We turned down two big tool cases on their sides and laid them together. They were not quite waist high. It was our operating table.

When we actually got started, then I saw how foolish it was to try it, without any hospital facilities. But I remembered again that it was this chance or death for the little Mexican. Beyond that, it was something of an ethical challenge. Yes, we went ahead. It was an early afternoon. The sky was so still and changeless that it seemed to suspend life in a bowl of heat.

Faces clouded up at the window, to see; to threaten; to enjoy. We shook them away with the pistol. The foreman was standing in the doorway. Beyond him we had glimpses of the slow dancing silvery heat on the scratchy earth, and the diamond belt of light among the rails of the track.

The camp cook boiled a kettle of water.

Sister turned her back and produced some white rags from her petticoats.

She turned her heavy sleeves back and pinned her veils aside.

The invalid now decided to notice what was going on and he tried to sit up and began to scream.

Sister flicked me a glance and at once began to govern him with the touch of her hands, and a flow of comforting melody in *Deutsch* noises. I got a syringe ready with morphine. And the mob appeared at the door, yelling and kicking up the stifling dust which drifted in and tasted bitter in the nose.

I shot the morphine and turned around.

I began to swear.

That's all I recall; not *what* I said. But I said plenty. Pancho yelled back at his friends who would rescue him. It was like a cat concert for a minute or so.

Then the morphine heavied the little man down again, and he fell silent.

Then I shut up, and got busy with the chloroform. Sister said she could handle that. It was suddenly very quiet.

My instruments were ready and we had his filthy rags off Pancho. Sister had an instinctive adroitness, though she had never had surgical experience. Yet her hospital service had given her a long awareness of the sometimes trying terms of healing. In fascinated silence we did what had to be done before the operation actually started.

There was a locust, or a cicada, some singing bug outside somewhere, just to make the day sound hotter.

The silence cracked.

"He is dead!" they cried outside.

A face looked in at the window.

Now the threats began again.

I said to the foreman, "Damn you, get hold of that crowd and make them shut up! You tell them he isn't dead! You tell them—"

I began to talk his language again, very fancy and fast. It worked on him. I never cussed so hard in my life. Then I turned back and I took up my knife.

There's a lot of dramatic nonsense in real life; for example: my hand was trembling like a wet dog, with that knife; and I came down near the incisionary area, and just before I made the first cut, steady? That hand got as steady as a stone!

I looked at Sister in that slice of a second, and she was biting her lips and staring hard at the knife. The sweat stood on her face and her face was bright red. Her light eyebrows were puckered. But she was ready.

In another second things were going fast.

There was hazard, too, of my youth, my inexperience as a surgeon. There was my responsibility for Sister, in case any trouble might start.

The patient would almost swallow his tongue making a noise like a hot sleeping baby.

So I'd swear.

Sister said nothing.

She obeyed my instructions. Her face was pale, from so many things that she wasn't used to—the odors, the wound, manipulation of life with such means as knives and skill, the strain of seeing Pancho weaken gradually; she was glassy with perspiration. Her starched linen was melted. There was some intuitive machinery working between us. Aside from having to point occasionally at what I needed, things she didn't know the name of, but I've never had a more able assistant at an operation in all my long life of practice.

I think it was because both she and I, in our professions, somehow belonged to a system of life which knew men and women at their most vulnerable, at times when they came face to face with the mysteries of the body and the soul, and could look no further, and needed help then.

Anyway, she showed no surprise. She showed none even at my skill, and I will admit that I looked at her now and then to see what she thought of my performance. For if I do say it myself, it was good.

She looked up only once, with a curious expression, and I thought it was like that of one of the early saints, in the paintings, her eyes filmed with some light of awareness and yet readiness, the hour before martyrdom; and this was when we heard the train start to go.

She looked rueful and forlorn, yet firm.

The engine let go with steam and then hooted with the exhaust, and the wheels ground along the hot tracks.

If I had a moment of despair, it was then; the same wavy feeling I'd had when the train had stopped a couple of hours before.

The train receded in sound.

It died away in the plainy distance.

Shortly after there was a rush of voices and cries and steps toward the shack.

It was the laborers again, many of whom had been put back to work on the track ahead of the engine, in order to let the train proceed. Now they were done. Now they were crazy with menace.

It was about four o'clock, I suppose.

Fortunately, I was just finishing up. The door screeched on its shaken hinges and latch. I heard the foreman shouting at the men.

Then there was a shot.

"Most Sacred Heart!" said the Sister, on her breath, softly. It was a prayer, of course.

Then the door opened, and the foreman came in and closed it and leaned back on it.

He said they sent him in to see if Pancho was still living. I told him he was. He said he had to see. I said he was a blankety-blank meddling and low-down blank to come bothering me now; but that I was just done, and if he had to smell around he could come.

I showed him the pulse in the little old Mexican's neck, beating fast, and made him listen to the running rapid breath, like a dog's.

Then he looked around.

He was sickened, first, I suppose; then he got mad. The place *was* dreadful. There were unpleasant evidences of surgery around, and the heat was absolutely weakening, and the air was stifling with a clash of odors. Sister had gone to sit on a box in the corner, watching. She, too, must have looked like a challenge, an alien force, to him.

He grew infuriated again at the mysterious evidences of civilization.

He began to wave his gun and shout that next time, by God, he'd fire on us, and not on them Messicans out yander. He declared that he, too, was agin cuttin' on anybody. He was bewildered and sick to his stomach and suffering most of all from a fool's bafflement.

He bent down and tried to grab back the meager sheeting and the dressing on Pancho's abdomen. He was filthy beyond words. I butted him with my shoulder (to keep my hands away and reasonably clean) and he backed up and stood glaring and his mouth, which was heavy and thick, sagged and contracted in turn, like loose rubber.

Sister came forward and without comment knelt down by the wretched operating table which might yet be, for all I knew, a bier, and began to pray, in a rich whisper, full of hisses and soft impacts of r's upon her palate, and this act of hers brought some extraordinary power into the room; it was her own faith, of course; her own dedication to a simple alignment of life along two channels, one leading to good, the other to evil.

I was beginning to feel very tired.

I had the weakness after strain and the almost querulous relief at triumph over hazard.

I'd been thinking of her all along as a woman, in spite of her ascetic garb, for that was natural to me then. Now for the first time, listening to her pray, I was much touched, and saw that she was like a doctor who thinks enough of his own medicine to take some when he needs a lift.

The foreman felt it all too, and what it did to him was to make him shamble sullenly out of the shed to join the enemy.

We watched all night.

It got hardly any cooler.

Late at night Sister opened her lunch box with little delicate movements and intentions of sociability, and we made a little meal.

I had a sense of what, together, we had accomplished, and

over and over I tried to feel her response to this. But none came. We talked rather freely of what we still had to do, and whether we thought the Mexicans *meant* it, and whether the train crew knew what was going on, and if they'd report it when they reached Eddy.

We had an oil lamp that the foreman gave us.

When I'd get drowsy, my lids would drop and it seemed to me that the flame of the wick was going swiftly down and out; then I'd jerk awake and the flame would be going on steadily, adding yet another rich and melancholy odor to our little surgery.

I made Sister go to sleep, on her corner box, sitting with her back against the wall.

She slept in state, her hands folded, her body inarticulated under the volume of her robes, which in the dim lamplight looked like wonderful masses carved from some dark German wood by trolls of the Bavarian forests . . . so fancifully ran my mind through that vigil.

Early that day Pancho became conscious. We talked to him and he answered. When he identified the Sister by her habit, he tried to cross himself, and she smiled and crowed at him and made the sign of the cross over him herself.

I examined him carefully, and he was all right. He had stood the shock amazingly well. It was too early for infection to show to any degree, but I began to have a certain optimism, a settling of the heart. It had come off. I began to think the day was cooler. You know: the sweetness over everything that seems to follow a feeling of honest satisfaction.

Then the crowd got busy again.

They saw Pancho through the window, his eyes open, his lips moving, smiling faintly, and staring at Sister with a child's wonder toward some manifest loveliness, hitherto known only in dream and legend.

In a second they were around at the door, and pushing in, babbling like children, crying his name aloud, and eager to get at him and kiss him and gabble and marvel and felicitate.

The foreman's mood was opposite to theirs. We had the unpleasant impression that he felt cheated of a diverting spectacle.

The train finally arrived, and as it first slowed, standing down the tracks in the wavering heat, it looked like a machine of rescue.

We reached Eddy in the evening. It was about time to say good-bye to Sister for she was taking a stagecoach on down into Texas somewhere and I was going to stay a few days and see my patient out of the woods.

So we said good-bye in the lobby of the wooden hotel there, where she was going to spend the night.

Nobody knew what a good job I had done except Sister, and after we shook hands, and I thanked her for her wonderful help, I waited a moment, just a little moment.

She knew I was nervous and tired, and it was vanity of course, but I needed the little lift she could give me.

But she didn't say anything, while I waited, and then as I started to turn off and go, she did speak.

"I will pray for you, doctor."

"What?"

"That you may overcome your habit of profanity."

She bowed and smiled in genuine kindliness, and made her way to the stairs and disappeared.

Duty is an ideal and it has several interpretations, and these are likely to be closely involved with the character that makes them.

You might say that Sister and I represent life eternal and life temporal.

I never saw her again, of course, but if she's still alive, I have no doubt that she's one of the happiest people in the world.

- *Educated by nuns, brothers, and priests*
from grammar school through college,
Richard Coleman had no trouble recreating
the atmosphere of the parochial school of
yesteryear. He was born in 1907 in
Washington, D.C., later lived in Charleston,
South Carolina, and was known here and
abroad as both novelist and short story
writer.

RICHARD COLEMAN

Fight for Sister Joe

Sister Joseph reached into her great bottomless pocket and took out her signal, a wooden prayer book, that gave a loud clack when its two halves were snapped shut. The class folded their tracings of the map of Arkansas, signed their names on the upper left-hand corner, handed in the papers to the boys in the front. When the eight papers of each row were in the hands of the boys in the first seats, Johnny Briley slid from his seat by the door, collected the sets of tracings, and took them up to Sister Joseph, bowing almost imperceptibly as he handed them to her.

The little wooden signal that was made to look just like a prayer book snapped again. "JesusMaryandJosephhelpmenottowaste-amomentofthishour." The class droned the prayer, running the words together in a meaningless jumble. At the first word, the name of Jesus, heads jerked forward in a bow of automatic reverence.

"You will please to take your arithmetic books and work the fifth, eighth, and tenth problems in short division on page 29."

Up shot Benny Cavanaugh's hand when Sister Joseph had barely finished the sentence. Eddie watched the hand covered with rusty brown freckles waggle back and forth insistently, and wondered why Sister Joe did not box his ears for him some day when he demanded importantly that she repeat what she had just said. "Yes, Benedict?" said Sister Joseph patiently.

"Please, Sister, I didn't get the page."

"Page 29, Benedict. How did you ever happen to get the numbers of the problems?"

The class tittered and Benny sat down swiftly and wrote page 29 on his pad and the numbers of the problems. There was a slipping of pages and the struggles against problems fifth, eighth, and tenth began. The room was still but you could almost hear the creakings and strainings of minds that were still a little stiff because they were rather new. Eddie chewed on the red rubber eraser on his pencil. It broke away and he chewed it meditatively as he wondered how many times 7 went into 37. Should be even with a 7 on the end of it. The eraser crumbled in his mouth. He chewed the dry little bits of rubber thoughtfully until he saw Sister Joseph's eyes upon him. In sudden fright he swallowed hard. Sister Joseph would make the seat of his pants smoke from a ruler if she thought he had chewing gum in his mouth. He worked frantically, writing 7 and 37 all over his paper. He knew she was still watching him. When he dared to look up again, she was reaching into the voluminous pocket for her little red demerit book. Eddie thought it must be wonderful to have two pockets as big as Sister Joseph had. She carried almost as much stuff as the little fellows in her class.

You could never be sure of what she would take out of one of those pockets next. Eddie had seen the little tin capsules that held tiny lead statues of the Blessed Mother, St Joseph, and St Benedict. The little statues had tiny crooked faces. The small dot that was the face of the infant Christ Child who was in the Blessed Virgin's arms was perfectly blank except for a slight projection in the lead that was meant to be a nose.

There was always a clean, large grey-checked workman's handkerchief in one of the pockets, the wooden prayer book that was a signal, a little pencil sharpener that Eddie himself had bought for her from the ten-cent store at Christmas and which Reverend Mother had allowed her to keep as her own. There was a pearl-handled penknife, a pen wiper which she had made herself and in which she was always putting clean bits of old cloth. She carried a copy of *The Following of Christ*, a pocket dictionary, and a big shiny Ingersoll watch. There was room too for a telescoping drinking cup with a lid. From the left side of her old shiny leather cincture was hung, by a piece of black tape, a pair of scissors in a sheath. She had a box of Smith Brothers cough drops for any boy who was lucky enough to strangle sufficiently to need one. Once she had taken from her pocket a little bag of gum drops and given them to Eddie when he had washed down the blackboard and beat the erasers until his hair was white with chalk dust and his hands felt dry and hard. When a boy gave Sister Joseph an apple, orange, or pear, she thanked him and dropped it into one of the great pockets where it was lost. There was no bulge, no curving outline of the apple lying among all the other treasures.

Eddie watched Sister Joe write his name in the demerit book for eating in class. It was tough to have to write ejaculations a hundred times for eating a dried-up eraser, but there wouldn't be any use telling that it wasn't candy or anything good. Eraser or not, he had eaten it. For almost an hour after school he would have to scrawl, "Mother of Christ teach me to obey."

Eddie remembered the nuns who had been his first three teachers. When he had been brought to the convent as an orphan to be kept until his elementary education was complete and then returned to his guardian, he was ready for the kindergarten, or what was known at St Bonaventure's as the Chart Class. Sister Rabona, tall and lean, had pointed out the meanings of the pictures, fables, and figures on the charts which lined the room. In her less rigid moments she called the Chart Class the Rubbish Class because she said it was made up of hopeless odds and ends. The only time the little boys did not tremble when she looked at them was when she called them the Rubbish Class. She expected so much of babies who were first learning to tell red from green, A from R, and a 5 from a 2. Her discipline was as strict as if she had had a roomful of callous adolescents fit for the reform school. A boy in the Rubbish Class waited until his mouth felt like he'd eaten too many persimmons before he would ask for a glass of water from the big enamel pitcher on the window sill. Sister Rabona believed that as the twig was bent so grew the tree, and the best time to start bending the twig in the right direction was in the Rubbish Class.

Eddie was a skinny little Irishman. Sisters Rabona, Theresa, and Veronica had put the fear of the Lord into him. When he came to the third grade he wondered what Sister Joseph would be like. He had watched her in the play yard. Once he had actually seen her pick up a ball that had rolled at her feet while she was saying her breviary and throw it back deftly and surely to a delighted group of little boys. They said she was "regular." Didn't everybody call her Sister Joe? Not to her face, of course. A mortal sin would not have been eyed less askance than such a thing as calling one of God's religious by a nickname. But to all the boys who passed through the third grade she was Sister Joe. Somehow she seemed like one of them, and yet she never lost that inspiring distance that lay between her and any layman and was greater still between her and those worthless little hooligan boys.

Eddie loved Sister Joe with all the love in his small Irish heart. She was Irish, too. When you asked her (with a great show of respect, of course) where she was from, she invariably answered, "From County Kerry, God Help Us." Eddie, like the other boys, thought that the "God Help Us" was part of the name. Benny Cavanaugh told his mother one day that Sister Joseph was from a funny place in the old country called County Kerry-God-Help-Us, and did not know why his mother was always repeating the story.

To Eddie, Sister Joe was more than regular. She was wonderful. Hadn't she whittled out her signal to look just like a prayer book with her own pearl-handled knife? Lying on the desk it looked so much like a prayer book that even Father O'Rourke had been fooled by it. Sister Joe had whittled it perfect, then she'd made thin little grooves at the end to look like pages, skillfully hiding the hinges in the wood, painting the ends white and the back black. She had even painted "Prayer Book" on the front in gilt.

Because Eddie was an orphan and didn't have a loud, cheery Irish home to go to, but had to live in a little room in the convent, Sister Joe had helped him make a pencil box. When it was through she asked him what kind of picture he wanted painted on the lid; he asked her to help him decide. She didn't think of a thing religious and had ended up by painting five lively little monkeys clinging by long arms or curling tails to a green limb.

She wasn't less religious than the other nuns. Anybody could see that. When Eddie watched the procession of nuns going into the chapel for vespers he looked for plump, stubby little Sister Joe. Her face was bright and holy when the spatter of light from the altar candles fell on her. Eddie's heart bumped with love as he saw her take her place beside tall, lean Sister Rabona and steamboat Sister Veronica.

After problems fifth, eighth, and tenth had been worked to yield some twenty answers from thirty boys, the bell rang for mid-morning recess. The prayer book clacked, the boys slid up from benches, filed out decorously, alert after having been drugged with arithmetic. At the door they broke into a wild screaming mass. "Comanches," muttered Sister Joe in the doorway. "A tribe of wild Comanches." She went to get her glass of cold milk and piece of bread with jam.

Sitting at the refectory table by herself, she was dreaming of her girlhood in County Kerry-God-Help-Us, the new vestments she and Sister Juliana were making as a surprise for Father O'Rourke for his ordination anniversary, and the new Mass by Bach that she was trying to learn on the chapel organ, and hoping that she would remember to tell Sister Wardrobe that she was one coif short last week in the laundry.

The Comanches seemed wilder than ever as their piercing screams came through the high latticed windows. She put down her glass of milk and listened carefully. Instinctively she felt a little thrill of excitement when she realized that there was a fight going on. From the sound of it, a good fight. She ate her last bit of bread hurriedly, drank the milk lest it be wasted, and hurried down the corridor, her giant rosary whipping about her wide skirts in which her short strong legs were hidden. The rattling of a rosary was a sound for which all ears had learned to listen. Bedlam became a place of utter quiet and repose when the word went up because some ear had caught the warning sound. The fight put the boys off guard. Sister Joe's rosary was swinging wildly and rattling loud, but no one heard.

She stopped at the door to take in all the details so that punishment would go to every boy that deserved it. She caught her breath sharply when she saw what was going on inside the ring of howling boys. Rick Mulhall, a big boy in the fifth grade, was beating her own Eddie unmercifully. All the boys fought when the time came, but Eddie just put up his poor skinny arms in an effort to save himself. No one had ever seen him take his arms down long enough to strike out once against another boy. He wasn't yellow exactly. He could take it. But that was his trouble. Always, Eddie stood up and took it.

Sister Joe loved Eddie, not just because he had no good Irish mother as he should have had, but because there was something about him that stirred her love as well as her sympathy. She tried to hide her love from the community and the boys. And from Eddie himself. She was positive her secret was her own. Silently she moved toward the flowing ring of children. Benny Cavanaugh looked toward the door at that minute and gave the word. The ring broke, spread in all directions. Rick Mulhall hurriedly started a game of hit-the-stick. Eddie stood there, thankful for whatever had ended his beating. He didn't cry but whimpered a little because no one was watching him now. He rubbed his arm across his face, then saw the soft-looking, high-topped shoes peeping from beneath a black robe on the gravel in front of him. Was it Sister Theresa who would box him harder than Rick had? Or was it Sister Veronica who would make his heart stand still by her freezing look? He took his arm slowly away from his face and looked up. He didn't have to look up as far as he would have had it been Sister Rabona.

"Would you like a glass of milk and a bit of bread and jam, Eddie?" said Sister Joe slowly. He followed her, carefully spitting onto his handkerchief and wiping his grimy face. She washed his face herself in the refectory sink. He ate the soft fresh bread that Sister Philomene had baked that morning, and sort of breathed in the tart lumps of jam. He closed his eyes while he drank the cold, sweet milk. When he opened them he sighed a little at Sister Joe's back over by the china shelf.

After the lunch-hour recess, Sister Joe rapped Benny Cava-naugh on the head with her wooden prayer book because he didn't know the Feast Days, and it made such a loud crack that Eddie thought she must have split the soft wood. Benny rubbed his head gingerly. He knew he had not got that lick because he could think of only the Ascension, Christmas, and Circumcision. And that he had got off light. Sister Joe had given him the ruler across the knuckles because he had given Rick Mulhall the signal when he should have helped his own classmate. Sister Joe was a staunch third-grader herself and wanted all her boys to be. She didn't hate a fight as much as she made out, but she hated to see a third-grader get the worst of it.

After school Eddie waited to be told that he would have to stay and write a hundred ejaculations for eating the eraser. As the boys marched out he felt her hand on his shoulder and he stepped out of line.

Sister Joe wasn't thinking of ejaculations. She hesitated before she started to talk when they were alone. She wanted to reach him, to talk to him the way his father would have talked to him if he had not been dead. At last she said, "You're an Irishman, Eddie. There are some things an Irishman just doesn't do. When he sees he's in for a fight, he puts up his fists and goes at it as fiercely and proudly as if he were fighting for the old sod itself. I don't want you to be a bully, a boy who starts fights, but I do want you to be man enough to finish one when a fight is forced on you.

"All this is our secret, Eddie. No one else is to know about it

but you and me. Your dear father's dead, God rest his soul, but if
he were living, he'd teach you the way I'm going to teach you. I'm
going to be your mother *and your father*. That's our secret. In class
I'm just your teacher, and you're just a pupil, but in everything else
you'll find me on your side, if you're right.

"The first thing I've got to teach you is this." She doubled her
rosary up into the worn leather cincture so that it would not get in
the way. She rolled back her great sleeves, planted her small feet
firmly on the ground, and held her fists under his nose. When
Eddie got over his amazement, he laughed as Sister Joe danced
about in the soft old high-topped shoes, thrusting and parrying,
urging him to put his hands up and fight. Every day after school
they practiced. The plump, stubby little nun with her full black
skirts swishing about her, and the little boy standing up to her with
thin little arms fighting for an opening.

At every recess she gave him milk and bread, with butter and
sugar, or preserves, and every day she taught him that an Irishman
doesn't stand and take it, but fights back proudly and righteously
as a man should. She made a punching bag out of an old gingham
apron that belonged to Sister Wardrobe and that had been filled
with sand. He could hit it hard. She hit him, but he seldom hit
her. She was too quick for him. At first he was overcome at the
thought of having struck a nun, but Sister Joe laughed and urged
him on by a smart clip to the cheek.

He watched fights in the yard and learned from them too. It
was over a month before a fight of his own was thrust upon him.
Terry McGovern of the fourth grade decided it was time for Eddie
to have another licking. Once he had started the fight, Terry
couldn't very well back out, but he soon wished he could. The
boys crowded around, screaming encouragement to Eddie when
they saw the smaller boy putting up a real fight. Sister Joe had
listened for a fight every day. She peeped from behind the ferns in
the music room to see if it was Eddie this time. When she saw it
was, she rolled up her sleeves and watched excitedly. Eddie took a
lot of punishment, but he put Terry onto his knees and beat him
properly. He looked at the music room window and caught a

glimpse of a bobbing white coif, and a plump face encircled with white and black. His heart beat wildly. She had seen him. He hated to stop. He couldn't hit Terry now that he had said "nuff" and was down. He looked around threateningly. He saw Rick Mulhall in the ring and pushed aside the boys near him. His thin little arm shot out in one clean, hard blow that brought the blood running out of Rick's nose. The big boy was so surprised and the blow had stung him so that he didn't even put up his hands to strike back. Eddie waited until it was plain that Rick had no fight in him and then ran headlong to the door of the convent. Sister Joe met him in the corridor from the music room. She snatched him up to her and his forehead felt the cool, hard, immaculately white coif, his cheek felt the rough, heavy black habit and beneath the soft sweet bosom. He held tight and his heart ached with love.

RICHARD SULLIVAN

Jubilee at Baysweep

In the early part of her life Sister Calasancta's greatest worry was
that she would be taken away from Baysweep.

Ordinarily the nuns were moved every three or four years, so
that they would not become too deeply attached to any one place.
The Mother General at the Mound was very strict about this
moving; she said that it was periodically good for schools to have
fresh blood and for nuns to have a change of scenery. But Sister
Calasancta, by some blessed exception, had never been moved
since first she came to Baysweep.

She had been sent to St James a young nun and she had been
left there to grow old. She had never even been moved from one
classroom to another in the vine-covered grey stone school; she
still taught third grade. After she had been in Baysweep twenty-
five years she was teaching children whose parents she had taught,
the children of boys and girls who had sat before her and whispered and raised their hands a quarter of a century before.

Sometimes there would be a face, a gesture, a voice she could
remember: the turn of a head or the color of hair. And often the
sense of this continuity, the thought of this beautiful existence of

243

hers in the middle of flowering life, touched her poignantly and with an inexplicable suddenness made her want to cry.

Baysweep was very dear to her. She could not help feeling herself a part of life in a place where she had helped a generation to grow up and where she herself had passed slowly into age; she loved the town with all the warmth and quiet strength of her heart. The thought of leaving Baysweep frightened her.

When she had first come there, a young nun fresh from the Mound, she was twenty-three years old. She had just taken the veil a few months before, in the spring. She was timid and very eager; Baysweep was her first place, St James her first school. She remembered Sister Eugenie, who was at that time superior at St James. They had traveled together from the Mound on a crowded train, the old nun and the young. At Baysweep, late in the afternoon, a hack had met them at the station. She remembered how poised and serene Sister Eugenie had been; how competently she had managed the transfer of luggage; to Sister Eugenie traveling was no longer a novelty.

But to the young nun the excitement of that whole long day was almost unbearably keen; she could never afterward forget her first breathless anxiety. The hack had swung and squeaked along the soft dirt street; and to Sister Calasancta, staring expectant and yet half frightened through the window, there had come a long confused impression of great drooping green boughs, through which sunlight splattered on the cool dusty road; white picket fences, long lawns, women in sunbonnets, wooden sidewalks, and children playing with their soft bright laughter on the corners.

"Look," Sister Eugenie had said, laying her hand on Sister Calasancta's arm. And through the trees they had both seen a church steeple rising high and dark and solid against the twilight sky. "St James," said the old nun. "The school is next door, and then the convent." A moment later the Angelus had begun to strike; Sister Calasancta remembered it very clear and silvery toned in the still air. The two nuns had bowed their heads.

It was at that moment that Baysweep took possession of Sister Calasancta's open and receptive heart. At that moment of soft twilight and church bells, as she bumped along in that jerky old hack, there rose the fear that was ever afterward to grow stronger. From that moment she began to dread the day when she would have to leave Baysweep.

And there was always the danger, the lurking chance, that she would be moved to another place. Once, in the spring of her fourth or fifth year, she had been told that next fall she would be sent with others to a new school up north; the word was unofficial, yet it filled her with an uneasy nervousness for many days. That spring two of the sisters at Baysweep died of scarlet fever, and the convent was in quarantine all summer; the only changes made that fall were the two nuns who came as replacements. But the incident made Sister Calasancta fearfully aware of how dear the place had already become to her. First the dread of her own removal, and then the sudden terrifying death of her two sisters made her conscious as if for the first time of the urgent sweetness of life here, of the joy of being with children, of the worn beauty of her bare old classroom, with its great oak tree spreading outside the windows.

Then when she realized that she loved the town a sort of scrupulous shame came over her; because she knew that it was not right for a nun to become too warmly attached to the things of this world. She felt guilty loving Baysweep, and for many years afterward she kept trying to put down the love. Yet each fall, after a summer in the mother-house at the Mound, she returned with a humble gratefulness that for another year at least she would remain.

Each winter she hid her fear with work. But in spring, when the new assignments were made, the worry was upon her again. And each year after the suspense of waiting and then the relief, she could not understand how she had again escaped; she could not see how she deserved remaining. The fortune seemed too good to last; and the succession of years without change, far from soothing her fear, only sharpened it: because time was passing and she knew that some day after all she would inevitably be ordered away to a new place. And so her worry gradually took on the silent pressure of delay.

246 • Richard Sullivan

There were other worries, too. A nun's life was not as simple and peaceful as it seemed to the children in the school. When little girls told Sister Calasancta that when they grew up they were going to be sisters she always smiled and told them to wait till they were old enough—God would take care of that. Now it seemed simple to them. But it would seem harder when they had to get up every day for 7 o'clock Mass, and then whisk away, rosaries clicking, to a hurried breakfast so that they could get back on time to the children's Mass at eight; and then school all morning; and dinner, with one of the sisters reading; and school again till four.

Then there were walks to take, shopping to do, quiet calls to be paid upon the sick, exciting calls upon the parents of the nice children, timid calls upon the parents of the wayward or dull. It was all work, and if a woman did not feel well it made no difference—there was always the work to do anyhow. At night after supper there were the papers to correct and the next day's lessons to prepare. A half-hour of recreation—during which one might read or talk—and then bed at ten.

The days went fast—for Sister Calasancta the years went fast—and it was a blessed life in the dear and familiar place. But there were trials in it, as in all life. Ten women, nuns or no, cannot live together a school year through without occasional peeves and flurries; and although Sister Calasancta was gentle by disposition she occasionally had her flurries too.

There was the time when Sister Lillian, the young nun, had been called to account by the superior for an unbecoming worldliness. It was known that Sister Lillian had led her children in a ring-around-the-rosy dance one day in spring when an organ-grinder had passed by the school. To Sister Calasancta—who a few years before might have done the same thing herself—this indiscretion seemed a matter of simple innocence rather than of cold-blooded boldness; and besides—what was most important—the children had liked it. She defended Sister Lillian stoutly against the superior's accusations, and in a few minutes there were some high and rather cutting words, and then for several days a strained coolness in the convent, until the affair was forgotten in the press of spring work.

But her most serious quarrel came years afterward, when Sister Nicholas was superior. At that time there was an Irish nun, Sister Carmen, in the convent: a red-cheeked dark-eyed woman with a snapping tongue. Sister Calasancta could not like her very well, because with her quick wit she was impatient with the children and made fun of them to their faces. To Sister Calasancta the children somehow represented Baysweep, with all its years of quiet laborious familiar living; they were therefore dear and to be loved. It was like an affront to her own affection that anyone should ridicule them. She bore with Sister Carmen's comments for a long time, but one night in the study room when all the nuns were grouped silently around the long community table she suddenly could stand the gnawing pressure no longer. Aware that she was causing a minor sensation, she jumped up from her seat and announced sharply that it was not fitting for a sister to mumble over her examination papers as Sister Carmen was now mumbling. She was very angry, and then all at once she saw that everyone was looking at her.

"Sister!"

"Sister—!"

Little shocked gasps went around the table. The heavy sagging face of Sister Nicholas seemed caught in a twitch of surprise as she exclaimed in remonstration. All the nuns seemed surprised; even Sister Carmen herself; their faces were all turned to her, questioningly; their eyes were piercing her. Standing before them, Sister Calasancta swayed a little. Now all at once she felt terribly sorry. She began to sob bitterly; she was ashamed; she swayed, and fell forward on the table.

A moment later she was upstairs, undressed, in her bed between the cool sheets. Sister Kevin was leaning over her smiling sweetly. "Are you better now, dear? What a fright you gave us! You fainted on the study table." Behind Sister Kevin the other nuns were clustered, a swaying black and white mass in the dim light of the dormitory. Sister Carmen came forward, bent over, and seized her hand. "Ah, I'm sorry, Sister. I didn't know," she whispered. "I'm so sorry." Sister Calasancta felt very weak and peaceful. Sister Nicholas, with her big heavy smile, was nodding to her indulgently. Watching Sister Nicholas nod she fell asleep.

In the morning everyone was so kind and considerate that Sister Calasancta felt more ashamed than ever. They all seemed worried about her health. Sister Kevin said, "We must be careful, Sister. We're not as young as we used to be."

"Not as young?" thought Sister Calasancta with a strange cloudy feeling in her mind. "Nonsense, Sister!" she said gaily. And aware of the need for changing the subject she quickly began to explain that she would never have talked the way she did the night before had she not stupidly—and to her own great fault—supposed that there was contempt in Sister Carmen's mutterings.

Sister Kevin was smiling at her, "You love Baysweep so much, Sister!"

"But I have never known any other place," said Sister Calasancta. "You others, you travel about. Already, Sister, you have been in—how many places?"

"Six."

"Six! And you are younger than I am!"

"You will be superior here next," said Sister Kevin in a whisper.

"No," said Sister Calasancta, rather sadly. She too whispered, almost to herself: "That is not for me. I would not make a good superior!"

After that, aware of age, she feared more than ever the approaching spring. But each fall brought her back to Baysweep again, to the old convent and the old school. There had been three Mother Generals at the Mound since first she had been sent to St James, but one after another all three had happily forgotten her. But in their forgetfulness there was ever the chance of a sudden remembering, and Sister Calasancta's contentment was always uneasy. She tried perpetually to bury the uneasiness in work.

There was much to do. And now she found the work harder.

She had not the resiliency and strength she once had, and she had heard of rumors about the parish that her eyesight was failing and that she could no longer keep order in the classroom. The rumors hurt her and then angered her a little, made her stubborn. She was not really worried about her eyes; it was her hearing she feared for; she knew that her ears were failing. Of course she did not confess the deafness to anyone; with a sort of resentful pride she kept it to herself. But the thought that she might not be fulfilling her duties capably made her take to walking up and down and up and down the rows of desks in her room, to be near the children when they repeated their lessons. And the strain of always listening made her very nervous and very strict. She kept more children after school than she ever had before; it was easier for her to teach them now in smaller groups.

She had a group after hours the day of the great tragedy of old St James. It was a Friday afternoon in May. There was to be an eighth-grade baseball game in the schoolyard, and most of the children were already outside. Sister Calasancta was trying to fix the boundaries of South America into the athletic little brains of half a dozen boys; she knew where their real thoughts were, and herself was already despairing; there were three little girls washing the blackboards. When the fire bell rang it interrupted Sister Calasancta in the words, "Pacific Ocean." "Pacif—," she said, and halted.

She knew at once that this was no fire drill; fire drills came in school hours and the sisters were warned beforehand. She felt that she should be frightened, but she opened the classroom door coolly and looked out. The hall was white with smoke. She bundled the children along ahead of her, down the stairs quickly to the first-floor hall. Here the smoke was thicker, more active; it was dry and rolling. The children ran out the door. Passing the little office, Sister Calasancta, stumbling now and coughing, hesitated and then turned hastily in. The large statue of the Blessed Virgin stood calm in its niche in the wall, and on the table were the files of records and the two large black books of the school lying open as Sister Lorenza had left them a few minutes before—a penholder marking her place. With a sweep of her arms Sister Calasancta gathered in the files and the books and ran. She was sorry to leave the statue, but she thought she would return for it. When she was outside she started back, but the firemen, just arriving, stopped her.

Sister Calasancta felt sad about the statue, remotely sad, as if she had neglected something important which she could no longer do. But as Sister Lorenza said, it had been in St James since 1860 when the building was built, and it was somehow fitting that it perish with the old school.

The nuns were all very quiet that night as the ashes of the old school smoldered redly, and Sister Calasancta, now the oldest of all in Baysweep, sat more still and silent than any. The others speculated in hushed voices as to the cause of the fire. To Sister Calasancta the cause did not matter. A flying spark from a chimney would have been enough to set off the dry old shell. It was gone—that was the thing—and with it half her heart. She felt that her time had come too now; a hopeless intuition told her that the passing of the old school marked her passing; she would never return to Baysweep.

A few days after the fire she fell sick; only a spring cold, she said, but she was on her back for ten days. A new Mother General—the fourth—unexpectedly visited the convent at Baysweep while she lay abed. In June, just before the assignments for the next year were made, a whisper went through the school and thence through the parish that Sister Calasancta was going to be moved. Sister Calasancta, on her feet again, met the rumor with a sort of dull dismay; it hurt her deeply, but hardly as she had expected; she could not respond to it. She was still weak from her illness, and very tired; the bitter thought that she was old and no longer useful was easier for her to comprehend than the unimaginable prospect of leaving Baysweep.

There was much excitement that year with graduation to be held in the church for want of a school building, and many new arrangements to make. But she went through all the excitement in a sort of heavy listlessness, not knowing or caring what happened, only repeating over and over again to her sisters a story which she herself did not believe—that after all she was tired and getting old and maybe the change would be good for her.

This despondent mood was so unusual for her that the other nuns began to worry. But then of itself a strange thing happened which suddenly brought Sister Calasancta completely out of her despair. Affection of any sort could always move her, and on the day of graduation a great tribute of affection was paid her. A petition signed by two hundred mothers and fathers of St James parish was sent up that morning to the Mound, to the Mother General, requesting her kindly to send Sister Calasancta back to Baysweep next year. When Sister Calasancta heard of the petition she began to cry. There was only one meaning; they wanted her here. It had never seemed so blessed, so unutterably sweet, to be wanted. They loved her; the thought made her humble and grateful.

The petition went on to say that her forty-odd years of life in Baysweep had eminently fitted her for advisory work on the proposed new school, but that was all fiddlesticks—the thing was they wanted her. That night during the graduation ceremonies she kept wiping her eyes, feeling again all the old warm tenderness, the love, the loyalty, the beauty of life in a familiar place. She felt at home here; they needed her here. She knew that a nun should not be attached to the things of the world, but here in Baysweep they needed her.

The burning light of the candles on the altar, the resonant words of the graduation sermon, the procession of little boys and girls to and from the Communion rail to get their diplomas, all blurred in her mind into one constant throbbing happy thought: they needed her here. The fear that the Mother General might ignore the petition entered her mind, but it was lost at once in her firm glowing trust; she knew that Baysweep and herself were providentially united in love forever.

And the following fall she returned, slightly stooped, slightly wrinkled now, but alive with eagerness. Most of that year the nuns in Baysweep taught school in two old vacant private houses on

Congress Street. An immense excavation had been started on the site of the old school; and for the first few months there were many intent discussions, much studying and restudying of blueprints, many conferences and many conversations. And all the time, slowly, the walls of the new school were rising, tan brick, a huge imposing structure.

It was ready in spring, and they moved in just in time to have graduation in the new auditorium. But it took Sister Calasancta almost the whole next year to feel at home in the new school. It was so large, her classroom was so neat and trim! She missed the old tree that had stood outside her window; these new desks were so quiet—she missed the old banging and clatter. And the noise from the street now, cars tooting and honking all day long as they whizzed by—she had never noticed that in the old school; it was a dreadful distraction for the children.

For a long time she would not use the elevator in the new building; she preferred to shuffle up the stairs by herself, a hand on the rubber-covered railing, her rosary clicking with her slow steps, her breath coming short as she got to the top. And although the gymnasium was very fine with its high brick walls and all its gear and tackle she secretly could not believe that all this talk of physical education nowadays had very much sense in it. Children years ago had grown up strong and healthy without all this swinging on ropes. The one thing which she honestly preferred in the new school to the old was the library; it was a clean bright room with a small but exciting collection of books. But there was so much bustle and dash to the new building—even the children seemed affected by it; they had never scurried through the halls like this in the old school—that Sister Calasancta was a little bit bewildered and amazed.

Somehow, she could not feel a part of it; it was too fast and too new. She worked hard, tried eagerly to put herself into the swing of the new building. But it was months before she could get used to the soft dull tread of the composition floors, months before she could remember that the new electric clock which hung on her wall did not need winding every night after school. The novelty put a strain on her, and she worked on obstinately under the strain and in spite of it. The spring of that first year in the new school she again fell sick; this time she had a doctor; and a substitute had to teach her children for the last four weeks of the school year.

She felt this illness cruelly, much more than she had felt any of the previous attacks. The physical suffering was not so great as the mental. She confessed to herself that she was tired, and of itself the lying in bed was almost a welcome relief; but she kept regretting the way she was shamefully failing her responsibilities. She knew that she was looked upon by the parish as a sort of Baysweep institution; everyone in the parish knew her, most of them had at one time or another been taught by her; and she felt that by her stupid illness she was disappointing their affectionate expectations. She felt that she had no right to be sick. Illness was too comfortable for her. Lying in bed, she felt positively guilty.

Besides, she could not understand why she should be ill. It was no pain; only weakness—a sort of empty, lazy feeling; and the doctor said there was nothing wrong. She ate well, her digestion was good, and in spite of the days in bed she slept like a log every night straight through. There was nothing wrong with her, really; she felt as good as ever; it was only this weakness. She could not understand it. After three weeks in bed she deliberately forced herself to get up. Being on her feet strengthened her somewhat, but it took her a week of determined shuffling about the convent to gain enough strength to return to school. Once there, however, she quickly forgot about her weakness in the swift routine of those final few days of class work.

True, after this bout of illness she stooped more than ever, and her feet, after years of pacing the schoolroom, at last began to swell and to bother her. But in the few years that followed she felt on the whole very strong and able; and except for her increasing deafness she was as quick as ever in the classroom.

Her deafness worried her. The old fear that she would be moved from Baysweep had changed with the years into a new fear, even more frightening, that she would grow too old for Baysweep.

She had seen the old retired nuns at the Mound, hobbling about with no teeth in their mouths or with sightless eyes, only half living because age had deprived them of usefulness. Sister Calasancta in her old age was more deeply attached to Baysweep than ever; now she felt sure that if one must be moved it was better to go in youth into a new place to work. It was a desolate thought that one might be sent in the disgrace of years to a soft and empty retirement, where there would be nothing but memories.

Every spring before the next year's assignments were made, Baysweep burst forth in a new quiet beauty. The sun setting red over the church steeple, the tender shooting green and white grass, the familiar pink faces of children—they all seemed as fresh and clear to Sister Calasancta as they had on the day she had come; and each year in the springtime more than ever they seemed filled with a haunting elusive sweetness. She could never quite place that sweetness, never be sure of just what it was composed; but it was always present like a fragrance in the air, to be breathed in deeply. There were vines creeping up the walls of the new school now; it sometimes seemed to her that the new school had always been there. She could remember the old building and the old days, but they were far away. She sometimes talked hesitantly to the younger nuns of the marvelous changes that had taken place. She would have talked much more but she was afraid of boring them. She was very happy.

One day late in April she stood outside the school door watching three little girls playing jacks on the sidewalk. It was a quiet sunshiny afternoon, and the children cast long quickly moving shadows on the cement. Something in their intent absorption in the game made Sister Calasancta linger. As she stood there Sister Berchmans, the superior that year, came up beside her and with a mysterious smile silently beckoned her to come into the school. In the little vestibule just inside the door Sister Berchmans turned and said, "Sister, I have something to tell you."

A great throb shook Sister Calasancta's heart and she felt suddenly faint; the feeling must have shown in her face because Sister Berchmans quickly said, "No, no, it is good news!"

Then with her smile still mysterious she whispered close to Sister Calasancta's ear. "It is really a secret but I thought best to warn you. I shall not tell you much." She glanced over her shoulder. "Sister, do you know what day Sunday is?"

"Sunday?" Sister Calasancta tried to think. "No!" she cried anxiously. "No—tell me, Sister. What is it? Don't tease me!"

Sister Berchmans was smiling triumphantly. "We thought you would not remember it. How long is it since you took the veil, Sister?"

Slowly the anxious wrinkles on Sister Calasancta's face relaxed; her cheeks began to flush. With a little gasp she cried, "Sister! That is not Sunday!"

"Fifty years next Sunday," said Sister Berchmans, "is your golden anniversary. We wrote to the Mound to make sure. Now—" she began to whisper again—"they're planning a little celebration, the parent-teachers' association. It's to be a surprise on you, but I thought perhaps it might be a shock if you weren't warned. Now this is all I'm going to tell you." With a tantalizing smile of satisfaction she began to hurry away. Sister Calasancta caught her by the arm and stared at her closely.

"Fifty years! But you're sure, Sister?!"

"Jubilee!" cried Sister Berchmans. "Jubilee!" She screwed her lips up tight and her eyes smiled.

"But it doesn't seem . . ." began Sister Calasancta, sighing and playing nervously with her rosary.

Sister Berchmans broke away. "Never mind what it seems!" Smiling over her shoulder, she hurried out the door.

But with so much revealed it was easy for Sister Calasancta to find out more—easy and strangely thrilling. There were only three days left and she saw them already decorating the gymnasium with yellow and white crepe paper; she saw ladies of the parish whispering with nuns; and when she came up the conspirators began talking loudly about how we needed rain. Secrets were being whispered in every corridor of the school: plans for the program, plans for the refreshments. And Sister Calasancta, walking about with a guileless look on her old face, eagerly ferreted out the secrets with intense insatiable delight.

Fifty years a nun, and all but the first few months spent in Baysweep! The thought made her proud, though she knew that rightly it should not; and she tried to atone for the pride by telling herself over and over that there was really no cause for such a huge demonstration—a little message of congratulation was all she deserved. Yet the impressiveness of the preparations made her glow with a rich happiness; and the extra joy of discovering secrets turned the happiness into a sort of glee. To think that they would try to surprise her!

On Saturday morning she stayed in the convent, although she usually spent that time cleaning and tidying her classroom. But today she felt that her presence in the school might interrupt some important business there. She had even begun to worry about all the plans that were being kept from her; she could not help wondering if they would get everything attended to properly, the dinner and all; if she could have helped them herself she would have felt safer about those delicate arrangements.

After the noon meal on Saturday she decided that she was becoming too nervous and fidgety from thinking about the celebration; it worried her, and she made up her mind to relax. But she had just begun correcting Friday's arithmetic test when suddenly a terrible thought came to her, and her heart gave a jump and tripped over inside her. Running to Sister Berchmans, she drew her aside and whispered fearfully, "Sister, I—I will not have to make a speech?"

Sister Berchmans' face crinkled in silent laughter. "No, Sister, no," she cried. Then she put her arm around Sister Calasancta and soothingly scolded her, "You know, Sister, this is to be a surprise on you. You must not be worrying this way."

"I wouldn't know what to say if they should call on me, Sister. Truly I wouldn't. You won't let them call on me?"

"No, dear, no. Can't you trust me?"

All the same, Sister Calasancta worried all afternoon about that speech. What if they should call on her unexpectedly—Sister

Berchmans might not even know their plans. Suppose somebody from the parish called out, "Speech! Speech!" The terrifying thought upset the rest of the day for her; and that night, for the first time in many years, she was too excited to fall asleep.

She lay awake for a long time, listening to the soft breathing about her, and to the leaves rustling like whispers in the darkness outside. Now she began to dread the next day's celebration with a terror as great as her eagerness had been. She tried to fix her attention on the beats of her pulse, on the sound of the leaves, on her own breathing; but it was all no use.

She lay wide awake and nervous, staring into the clear moonlit dormitory with its white mound-like beds all about and the shadow-pattern of a tree branch waving slowly on the wall opposite the window. She felt that she could never get to sleep. She wanted to forget about that speech. She wondered how many people would be there tomorrow. It would be a hard day; she should have a good night's sleep to face it. The big clock downstairs clicked, buzzed springily for a second, and struck twelve. She had never in her life been so restless; how that clock banged! Every year on Christmas Eve she stayed up till twelve for midnight Mass; and she was always tired next day.

When the dull brassy tones of the clock had died out, in the stillness she remembered with a curious sense of peace that now it was Sunday, the day of her anniversary. Sunday, the day of rest, the day of the Lord, there was nothing to worry about. She suddenly felt very sleepy and calm. Fifty years a Sister, and all but the first few months spent in Baysweep—it had been a beautiful time. She dreamily remembered the great spreading oak tree outside her classroom window in the old school, and how the acorns had dropped thickly on the white gravel of the schoolyard. There was nothing to worry about.

They were all her friends. Strange, in all her life she had really had no single intimate friend, no one loved above others; it had always been friends, a community of friends all equally dear, her Sisters, her children, her children's children. And now if they asked her for a speech tomorrow they would do so in love; they would not expect too much. She knew them all and they knew her. They would be smiling at her as she rose to speak; she would stand there before them, smile, and in a way they would understand she would say simply, "My dear friends, thank you." There was nothing to worry about. She fell asleep softly, quietly, and almost at once her faint tired breathing was lost in the murmurous darkness.

In the morning when the nuns rose early for the first Mass they smiled among themselves. They were all very excited about the jubilee that day, and it amused them a little to see Sister Calasancta, the cause of their excitement, lying so peacefully in her bed while they were up and fluttering about to congratulate her. They left her undisturbed for a short while, knowing that she would need the strength of sleep that day. But when at last they came eagerly to rouse her they saw that quietly, peacefully, with the trace of a smile on her old face, she had left Baysweep.

Index

Suggested Readings

BIOGRAPHICAL

Karen Armstrong, *Through the Narrow Gate*, New York, St Martin's, 1981
Monica Baldwin, *The Called and the Chosen*, London, Hamish Hamilton, 1957
Frank Bianco, *Voices of Silence*, New York, Paragon, 1992
Barbara Ferraro and Patricia Hussey, with Jane O'Reilly, *No Turning Back*, New York, Poseidon Press, 1990
Herbert Kelly, *No Pious Person*, London, Faith Press, 1960
Sister Kirtsy, *The Choice*, London, Hodder & Stoughton, 1982
Julia Lieblich, *Sisters: Lives of Devotion and Defiance*, New York, Ballantine, 1992
Paul I Murphy, *La Popessa*, New York, Warner Books, 1983
Martin L Smith, *Benson of Cowley*, New York, Oxford, 1980
Thomas Jay Williams, *Priscilla Lydia Sellon: The Restorer After Three Centuries of the Religious Life in the English Church*, London, SPCK, 1950

HISTORICAL

A M Allchin, *The Silent Rebellion: Anglican Religious Communities, 1845-1900*, London, SCM Press, 1958
Peter Anson, *The Call of the Cloister*, London, SPCK, 1964
Valerie Bonham, *A Joyous Service*, Windsor, CSJB Convent, 1989
Sister Catherine Louise, *The House of My Pilgrimage*, Roxbury, Mass, Society of St Margaret, 1981
Community of St Mary the Virgin, Wantage, England, *A Hundred Years of Blessing*, London, SPCK, 1946
Sister Mary Hilary, *Ten Decades of Praise*, Milwaukee, DeKoven Foundation, 1965
Rachel Hosmer, *My Life Remembered*, Cambridge, Mass, Cowley Publications, 1991
Thomas P McCarthy, *Guide to the Catholic Sisterhoods in the United States*, Washington, DC, Catholic University of America, 1952

Sister Louis Sharum, *Write the Vision Down*, Ft Smith, Ark, St Scholastica's Monastery, 1979

NONFICTION

Sister Barbara Ann, *Beekless Bluebirds and Featherless Penguins*, Catonsville, Md, Scriptorium Publications, 1990

Marcelle Bernstein, *The Nuns*, Philadelphia, Lippincott, 1985

Suzanne Campbell-Jones, *In Habit*, New York, Pantheon Books, 1978

Alan Harrison, *Bound for Life*, London, Mowbray, 1983

Sister Maria del Rey, *Bernie Becomes a Nun*, New York, Farrar Straus Cudahy, 1956

Thomas Merton, *The Silent Life*, New York, Farrar Straus Cudahy, 1957

Henri J M Nouwen, *The Genesee Diary*, New York, Doubleday, 1966

FICTION

William E Barrett, *The Lilies of the Field*, New York, Doubleday, 1961

William Kelly, *Gimini*, New York, Doubleday, 1959

Iris Murdoch, *Nuns and Soldiers*, New York, Viking, 1980

OPERA

Gian-Carlo Menotti, *The Saint of Bleeker Street*, New York, G Schirmer, 1954

A NOTE ON THE EDITOR

James B Simpson, an Episcopal priest, lives in Washington, DC. He is currently at work on a new edition of the reference work *Simpson's Contemporary Quotations*, covering world events of the last half of the twentieth century.